...honkwiler is the fearless new voice of the American Heart-
...nd. His words burn with the clear fury of corn whiskey, and
...th Street Power & Light is more than a thrilling trip into a post-
...merican landscape—it will make you question just what keeps
...e lights on at home."
—**Taylor Brown**, author of *In the Season of Blood and Gold*
...nd *Fallen Land*

"Shonkwiler's *8th Street Power & Light* is a fast-paced literary
thriller set in a dystopian future where big business and government have merged. This insightful book reverberates with our
country's current challenges. The tightly woven plot features
protagonist Samuel, a flawed character who pursues justice even
as he's sleeping with his friend's girl. The twists and turns will
leave you breathless, but it's Shonkwiler's restraint with language and dialogue that'll keep you coming back for more."
—**Aline Ohanesian**, author of *Orhan's Inheritance*

"Shonkwiler is proving the Western isn't dead. He cross-polli-
nates noir and post-apocalyptic fiction to create a darkly human
little beast with jaws wide open."
—**Brian Evenson**, author of *Collapse of Horses, Windeye,* and
ALA-RUSA award winner *Last Days*

"In this atmospheric and entertaining tale, Eric Shonkwiler
smartly puts the Western story's need for justice, and the Noir
crime's hard-boiled means to achieve this, inside a post-apocalyptic landscape, to ask questions about community, society, and
democracy that are highly relevant for our times. How commu-

nities must care for their poorest and most vulnerable members, and at the same time deal with corruption and crime in an effective manner. This novel is also a riveting tale of love, friendship, compassion, and violence, and would make Raymond Chandler and Cormac McCarthy proud."
—**Berit Ellingsen**, author of *Not Dark Yet*

"8th Street Power & Light is a terrific science fiction noir novel featuring a protagonist as damaged as the almost-recognizable America he's enduring. A first-rate read."
—**Scott Phillips**, author of *Hop Alley, Cottonwood*, and *The Ice Harvest*

"Fans of hard-boiled noir will appreciate Shonkwiler's style, in which spare syntax and tight dialogue rule the day. A star-crossed affair, unfolded with nuance, and the descriptions of a city lit up at night beat with the rhythm of poetry."
—**Britta Coleman**, author of *Potter Springs*

"I was privileged to hear Eric Shonkwiler read from *8th Street Power & Light* recently, and hot damn, can he ever write. The world in Shonkwiler's imagination is dark, electric, gritty. Thoroughly original work."
—**Kathy Fish***, author of *Rift* and *Together We Can Bury It*

"Shonkwiler's world is made of rust. In this relentless novel, no life is safe, no story too far-fetched and no bone unbroken. There is a reckoning coming. You will need a tetanus shot."
—**Andrew F. Sullivan,** author of *WASTE* and *All We Want is Everything*

"Shonkwiler's imagination wouldn't pass any field sobriety tests. This is deranged stuff, but it's also oddly tender."
—**Joshua Mohr**, author of *All This Life, Some Things That Meant the World to Me*, and *Termite Parade*

ABOVE ALL MEN
ERIC SHONKWILER'S 1ST NOVEL

"Revelatory."
–William Wright, **Chicago Book Review**

"Shonkwiler has taken an iconic landscape and filtered it through near-collapse and fear, then through loyalty and love."
–**Susan Straight**, National Book Award finalist

"Well-written and possibly prophetic."
–Tammy McCartney, **San Franscisco Book Review**

"Shonkwiler renders the degraded deprivation...in artful, distinctively crafted language."
–Zach Kopp, **Examiner.com**

"Shonkwiler writes sparsely, but deeply—someone who knows that water, land and sky can transform a life at each encounter."
–Jean Bartlett, **San Jose Mercury News**

"Shonkwiler's words are brilliantly poetic—quiet creepers that seem stark and undecorated on the surface, but the lines hum with underlying emotion."
–Leah Angstman, **Los Angeles Review of Books**

"Painfully beautiful shots. His imagery is that arresting...We can hope Eric Shonkwiler's future is fraught with books as honed as this one."
–Ann Beman, **museum of americana**

8TH STREET POWER & LIGHT

A NOVEL

MG Press
http://midwestgothic.com/mgpress

ISBN: 978-1-944850-03-6

Cover design © 2016 Lauren Crawford

Author photo © Sabrina Renkar

8TH STREET POWER & LIGHT

A NOVEL

ERIC SHONKWILER

For my friends.

1

He saw himself projected huge and transparent on the brick of the empty store across the street, image fading as the streetlights flickered on. Violet bruised the bulbs until they warmed and candied the wet pavement orange. A Power & Light truck turned onto 8th. Samuel limbered off the frame of the window and backed a pace. It was floor to ceiling, and if it were once a door and to what he didn't know. The building had been an ironworks long ago and now was a diner called The Remedy, his apartment above it.

Is it guilt? Johanna rose through the sheets. She stretched, laced her fingers together and pushed her arms out. You get so serious after.

He turned to her, then looked back out the window. The streetlights burned yellow. I don't know. I don't think that's what it is.

You could stay here for a little while. Gil's on your route now. Maybe work through a few of those books on your shelf, show up at The Capitol in a few days. She patted the covers. I don't have anywhere to be. Aaron's out drinking.

Samuel stiffened. He reached to pull her from the bed and she brought him down and he could feel how warm she was through the sheets. Their breath mingling. She lifted up and caught his lips.

We could leave. The Light boys aren't going to be happy with you back.

He rose, hovered there, and slipped away. He picked up her underwear and handed them over. I tried that already. And I asked you to go with me.

She slid them on and got her jeans. You couldn't have expected me to. Not really.

He moved toward the window. The streetlights made a bright avenue of the intersection, and above them the checkered windows of The Inn, The Manse. 8th Street had lit up The Capitol as a beacon, and he could see the light from it, almost blue, rising to the clouds. Not far below it lay her apartment building, the porch of the abandoned house across the street, and the lamp he left there as signal, unlit. Samuel propped himself on the frame again. How is he? Aaron.

A quick shuffle of cloth and her feet padded on the floor. He's good. He brought in a whole town a month ago. They kept him drunk for three days straight.

Samuel grinned to no one, and it faded. I do have to get out there.

She put her arms around his waist, chin over his shoulder. As tall as he was. She let go and got into her coat and buttoned it. He shrugged into his jacket and slipped the knife in his belt.

We could tell him.

Is there something to tell?

Samuel faced her. Isn't there?

That first time, Sam. She smiled. It was lovely, and perfect, and then you were gone. I just thought— Her eyes ran to the ceiling, the sky. I thought maybe that's all this was. I don't know what we're doing.

Neither do I. But I don't want it hanging over me if I'm back here to stay.

Her hands faltered on the last button. So, we're done?

No. Samuel looked at her, just a few feet away, and he unable to touch her.

They went down the stairs, leaning outside to scan the street. Empty, the rain soft. He waved her on and she was slow to kiss him, and the kiss was slow, before she headed north. When she was out of sight, he started the other way.

Detch sat in the corner booth in the diner and he stood, waving, distiller's overalls baggy, and Samuel nodded and kept walking. A man in a slicker stepped out of a restaurant and lit a cigarette. Samuel crossed Q, passed the storefronts now displaying clothes, a butcher. Drains pattered water onto the sidewalk below the overpass. The streetlamps fell behind him and the way darkened, lit only from the diffusion of the clouds. There was no wind and the rain kept the smell of the distillery down until he was walking past it, the converted steelworks venting corn char and yeast. Further on was The Boneyard, and P&L Central on to the south. He cut west by the silo storage, over a choke of rail lines and across a vacant lot toward The Singles. A woman squatted on the stoop of a shotgun house, smoking in an overcoat. Candles lit the windows behind her. He went on, combing along the silent conveyors of a gravel company, the mounds of sand and rock slowly planing with time, gravity. A small tent city huddled in a copse of trees to the north, and a man in a shawl stood before a fire, arms held out, faces on the other side of the flames watching him preach.

Samuel circled back into The Singles at M. There were more lights in the houses than he'd known there to be, more light in the city as a whole. Through the dark of the bare trees and bushes he saw a shadow between the houses, and forming from the little light in the street, a woman holding a sawed-off shotgun, ready to drop. She squared with him, and Samuel touched the knife with his palm and looked to his side, where Red would have been.

She lifted her chin. You just turn right around, whoever you are.

I'm a heel, lady. This is my old route.

You think that trucks with me?

It ought to. Used to be you couldn't swing a gun without hitting tea around here.

She smiled. Well, this is my post now. O Street has The

Singles covered.

Samuel eyed her, head tilted. Noise from a house beside them. You're assigned here?

She looked over her shoulder. A sob, a choke, and then the woman he'd seen smoking minutes before rushed into the open. The O Streeter grabbed for the woman's shoulders and he thought they might embrace but she spun and pointed back at the house.

They killed Billie! Help, please!

The women ran to the house and Samuel followed, leaping over the steps and through the transom. A girl lay on the floor just inside, lit by a single lamp overturned and guttering from lack of fuel. A drying line of saliva ran down her cheek. No older than Samuel. The O Streeter stood over the body and Samuel knelt and pushed his free hand toward her for space. The other woman righted the lamp, the end table.

Samuel reached for the girl on the floor and stopped. Is anyone else here?

Someone did this to her. They did this. The woman paced in a tight circuit.

Who? One of Fish's goons? The O Streeter looked up at the other. I've been walking all night. I didn't see anyone.

You said Fish? He's still around? Samuel shook his head and turned back to the girl. Small burn on her lip. Swollen shoulder. He touched fingers to her throat and pulled back her eyelids and looked at the pupils. What's your name?

The woman was speaking to herself, running a conversation with her hands. Liza. She took a step back. She's blind. She won't see nothin' anyway.

Samuel checked the girl's arms. He checked between her fingers and toes. No trackmarks. And yours, Calamity. What's your name?

Heather. She nodded toward the girl. Aren't you gonna do something for her?

There's nothing to do. He was still a moment, then probed

at her shoulder and felt the dislocation. When he glanced toward Liza she was gone, the doorway black. Staring down at the girl's face he vaguely recalled her, ex-Power & Light.

Heather spun, hung on the door. I can rest easy nights with you around. Won't have anybody to look after in a week. She walked out.

Through the house, he found the accoutrements of a life blown up. Pictures in a worn paper sack: Girls at a lake, a dog, crumpled. None of her. Dark-eyed parents, the dead girl blue. A tick mattress and blanket for a bed in the back room. He brought the lamp from the end table into the bedroom and held it out over the bed. Wet bootprints. He lifted the blanket and found a glass pipe gummed with resin, still warm. He brought the blanket out and covered the body and left, slipping through the strip of yard between the properties to get back to the street where he'd first seen Liza. He snuck by the house and climbed over the railing and opened the front door.

Liza. He waited. He heard a breath stop short of a cough. It was dark inside. He came forward and went down a hallway by feel, footsteps muted on carpet. When he looked in the second doorway, she stood right in front of him and leapt back.

Jesus Christ. Get away from me! She fell and scrambled to a window. Samuel put his hand on the lock and she heaved at the window but didn't seem to realize. She was muttering like he wasn't there.

Liza. Tell me where you got the meth. The tea.

She quit struggling. I ain't talkin'. Not to no O Streeter, not to no one.

I'm not O Street. And I couldn't care less how high you get in your own damn house. I just want to know who sold it to you. Was it Fish?

She squirmed. Her breath was rancid and smoky. You let Billie die. You let them come right in and take her.

Look. He softened his face. I'm not gonna tell anyone what you tell me. This ain't the old world. You don't get paraded into the station or to court. You just tell me what I need to know and I go away. Okay? I'll walk right out. Billie gets avenged, you don't get bothered.

She stilled and looked at him, finally. I didn't buy it. It was give to me.

By who?

Some guy.

Where?

He was tryin' to get rid of me. I was on— She turned her head. On F. It's this old store. 10th and F. One of those neighborhoods where the lights end. You can smell the place. That's why I went in. I been off for weeks, but then.

Samuel dropped his arm. He started out of the house. She followed after him, rambling, and he ducked through the front door. He turned north, Liza falling behind. Coming over O Street, a P&L truck flashed its brights. He blocked the beams with his hand, giving a small wave. The truck went the way he'd come and soon turned east. At the crest of the overpass he stopped, breathed. There was more light everywhere. In The Singles, soft and waxy from flame through glass, hard yellow from the city's expanding territory. The corridor of O Street went past his sight, the changeless haze in a brighter sky, given further depth along with the city, further dimension.

Going back, he saw someone in the doorway of The Remedy. Smoke clung around him until he broke through it and his hair lit up in the street.

What say, ugly?

Samuel slowed and grinned. You smell me coming into town, or what?

Aaron put a finger to his nose. Like a bloodhound.

They shook hands roughly and slapped each other's back. I see the place went to shit without me.

Blame the immigrants. Aaron pitched his cigarette into the gutter. You eat? He led Samuel into the diner, holding the door. A few distillery workers sat in the booths, and Rick was coming through the kitchen doors carrying a rack of glasses.

Sam, welcome back! Here to stay?

He sat at the counter, shrugged. Appears so. Can I get the usual?

Rick dropped the rack onto another and wiped his hands dry on his apron. He took up two mugs and poured from the tap in front of him. I'll have it right out. He passed the beers over and went into the back.

So where you been? You alone? Aaron wheeled around on the stool to face Samuel.

Yeah. I was with Red for a while, in Utah. Split to see the folks, got antsy and bought a ticket back to metropolis.

Figured you'd taken enough time for things to cool off?

I just thought it was time to get back to work. Tired of feeling useless out there.

Aaron drank from his beer. At least you can be drunk and useless here. You could'a stayed, you know. No one was forcing you out.

It would've been bad. Probably still will be. He drank, the beer nearly tasteless. I guess I just wanted to be here, regardless.

You can say you missed me. I hear that a lot.

Uh huh. His eyes went off to the bar mirror and his smile got distant. You notice more tea on the street? More users?

Have you been out hunting already?

It's why I'm here. Already came up on a murder. An addict.

Those people on the fringes die all the time. This is just the first fresh one you stumbled on. Trouble of having so many people around.

It's not just some OD. One of the ladies there mentioned Fish.

Fish? That old so-and-so?

Samuel nodded. We never did track him down.

Aaron leaned in. So, what you're saying is, Fish is the one that got away?

He put a hand to his forehead. I see your humor hasn't changed. He moved to stand. I'm gonna go.

Fishin'? No. Not tonight. Tonight I'm getting you loaded. That's an order. He tapped Samuel's glass. New directive from the top of 8th Street. Finish your beer and we'll go get a bottle.

Samuel pointed to the kitchen. I got a burger comin'.

Finish your beer and I'll go get a bottle. He stood and pushed Samuel's mug into his hand before walking out.

Samuel drank his beer, looking over his shoulders. He ate the burger when it came. A few of The Still workers left, and Rick cleared their tables and came around to refill Samuel's glass and stood by.

Samuel pulled from the head. How's things been?

Rick shrugged, one-shouldered. Business is picking up steady and beef's getting cheap, so I'm happy. We had a heck of a fire about a week ago.

Where at?

Bottoms. Looked like the sun coming up early. Must have been some kind of explosion, or something. It made the lights blink. Quiet otherwise.

A P&L truck pulled up outside. Two men came through the door and sat at the bar. Rick patted the counter in front of Samuel and went to take their orders. One of the workers eyed Samuel for a second, looked away and back.

Didn't you get thrown out?

Not me. I just went on vacation.

I was you I'd have stayed gone. You don't have that butcher watching over you now.

Samuel stilled. He pushed his plate forward and stood, and as he came near, the workers sat back in their chairs.

The quiet one had his eyes on the bar. Samuel leaned toward them.

Why talk like that, then? He smacked the countertop and left. It had gotten cooler, and the rain broke into a fine mist. The streetlights wore halos. Aaron was coming down the street with a fifth of moonshine in his hand.

Get tired of waiting?

Tired of the locals. Samuel nodded to the truck.

Fuck 'em. Let's get drunk. Aaron handed the bottle up to him on the diner steps. Straight from the copper teet.

Samuel pulled the cap and drank. He kept his lips tight on the bottle, and his eyes watered. When he let go, the bottle popped and he blew out a flammable breath. Bwah. God. He wiped his eyes with the back of his hand and gave Aaron the bottle. They walked south until they reached a ratty awning and stood against the bricks. The store was vacant, but a table and chairs sat on the patio. Aaron put the bottle on the table, tipped the chair of rain, and sat. The restaurant with the smoking worker went dark. The same man opened the door and locked it, nodded at them from the stairs and took Q east. Next door was a butcher shop, new, closed. On down a glassmaker, racks of bottles in the window, closed. Nobody else was on the street, and the mist insulated against the noise from deeper in the city. The P&L workers came out of The Remedy and got in their truck. They drove past.

I'm sorry I wasn't there to help, that night. Or talk some sense into them after.

Samuel shook his head. Sense is a foreign language to someone like Bradshaw. He'd have just put you on the train with us. He looked off after the truck.

Aaron played with the bottle, then nudged Samuel.

As much as that fuck-up with Graham, I bet half of 'em hate you for bedding Maggie the way you did. The hit and run.

I'm not gonna live that down, am I? I didn't know what I

was doing.

Drunk is the excuse of the city, Sam. He tilted the bottle toward him. She's been a wreck. I think you broke her heart. Aaron drank and capped the bottle. They went to the street and headed south, took the parkway ramp up, rising over the outskirts of the lighted part of the city. Trains, dead construction yards, the roofs of warehouses, all faintly coppered by the light off the clouds. The city ended a few miles past, but in the dark it could have gone forever to the west. They turned back, toward the city's heart. The Inn windows were going out one by one. Each room similar, he knew, could imagine the people inside reaching for the switches, their beds cut by the blinds, corrugated light. A mongrel sedan drove past on 9th and he and Aaron watched it, watched the brakelights go up. Vapor in a tail behind it, rising to the clouds atop the city.

The night went on. They went to the Alley Bar and Aaron tried to introduce the bartender to Samuel. The men in the bar watched her move behind the counter as if their heads were on a track. Not long after they'd come in Samuel and Aaron were out, and found themselves walking around The Capitol building. The ground was dug up and a small trencher stood beside a wire spool. A P&L truck idled across the street, the driver asleep inside. Samuel's neck loosened and he blinked hard at a blur in his vision. They'd gone down the polished stone walk of a bank, and Aaron took a seat in front of a sculpture, now toppled. It seemed a moment later and he was standing in the street, singing. Samuel was laughing, propped against a wall. When he came-to again, they were back at The Capitol, and he felt well. He glanced around, saw them leaning against the bronze feet of Lincoln. A puddle of vomit off to one side. He blinked, sat back.

What's got people in The Singles? Are we lighting it up?

What dried you out all of a sudden? Here. He held the bottle out to Samuel, looked down the mall. We all thought it was whores, some madam setting up.

We're in prostitution now?

I wish. You got that clammy backed-up-balls-need-their-ashes-hauled look to you. But it ain't whores. It's just these women. Like the hobos but smart enough to live inside. We'll need to find you an honest woman.

Good luck with that.

I could make it happen. You think I couldn't? Half a the people here today were roped 'cuz of me. I think I can convince a woman to put a bag over your head for a night.

You sell lights and running water to people shitting in holes in the ground.

He stuck a thumb to his chest. I got a whole town to ride in while you were gone. He drank. The bottle sunk to a quarter. Aaron belched, shook it off. He took a deep breath and stood and raised the bottle as if addressing an audience. Good afternoon, all. My associate and I are here representing 8th Street Power & Light.

Here we go. Samuel rolled his eyes.

We've come to tell you that, after all that's happened to us as a people, as a nation: war, storms, famine—He pointed at Samuel. Sir, you look like you've got some stories of hardship. I bet you all do. I see trouble on everyone's face, I see those hard years. But we're here to tell you this isn't the end. There is a place that's rising, getting back up. Not fifty miles away there is a city with all the amenities you used to have. Lights, cars, clean running water. We at 8th Street are bringing a part of the world back to life, and we need your help. We've got everything in place: a full square mile of city lit up and ready for living—That's apartments, stores, even restaurants. Farmers come every week with fresh produce, and trains arrive daily with supplies. We keep our streets and our citizens clean. No drugs—That's in our charter. What we need is people. Hard workers, skilled laborers. Doctors and nurses, electricians or plumbers. But we want you no matter your experience. We can train you to work on our light crews, restoring power to the city, or you can work in our distillery. You heard me right, we have a distillery. We brew beer and whiskey, and the ethanol we don't drink fuels our automobiles. Aaron lifted the bottle high and drank from it. He set the bottle beside his feet and held his hands out to no one. We're trying to restore a city. To restore a part of America. We have the infrastructure—the houses, the apartments. The businesses and the roads. We have the cars, and the lights, and the whiskey. What we need are people to walk those streets, people to live in those houses, to turn the lights on at night. People we can live and work beside. What we need, are citizens. We have over a thousand already. He stopped, pivoting at the waist to scan the street. Samuel could see the verve drop out of him, and Aaron tilted and caught himself on the statue before he dropped onto the concrete. Will you join them? He turned to face Samuel and smiled, reaching for the bottle. Samuel beat him to it and drank off half. He smirked, sat back.

It's a decent vision.

Idn't it, though?

They both looked down the length of the mall, up at the sky. Across the pavement a neon sign hanging over an apartment entrance flickered on: Presi nt. A P&L worker stepped outside, nodded, and went back in. The sign turned off.

You know eventually we'll run this place, right? If you can manage to stick around?

Samuel laughed.

I daydream about it all the time. You and I take over for Steiner and Bradshaw. Rogan takes over the garage, starts cranking out some real cars. I marry Johanna. The city'll be full in a few more years, and we can start building new ones. Start helping other folks. He smiled. I got this picture in my head, man. Right here, right in front, you and me in a convertible, deep, dark red. Shining like the paint's still wet. He grinned. Lincoln staring down like 'damn.' Johanna, and your future gal sitting on the back. You and me wearin' suits.

Got them fancy hats.

Samuel looked away. I hope that's how it all works out.

They sat there awhile, passing the liquor until it was down to corners, and Aaron drained it. Engines rumbled from blocks away, faded. The sky darkened as the clouds rose higher and the city seemed to open. A radio tower topped the bank to the left, catching static, the sound of earth and sun. Aaron heaved the bottle end over end toward the gutter across the street. He looked at Samuel, grinning.

2

The apartment reverberated, a train shuttling into the station. It was light out. Midmorning. He swung his feet to the floor and stood and the motion began a slow, rolling pound in his head. His skull felt packed with snow, and he vised it between his forearms and fumbled toward the window, almost walking into the bookcase. He recovered and slouched against the windowframe. The streets were drying. He staggered into the bathroom and found the shower in the dark. After dressing he put the knife in his belt and stepped out.

Sheila made him eggs and toast with coffee, sliding a pepper shaker down the counter to him. Through the windows he watched the farmers come into The Haymarket and set up their stalls. He finished his coffee and thanked Sheila and left. The sidewalks were only beginning to fill with workers leaving The Inn. Clutches headed this way and that, weaving through the stalls. A farmer waved. At 9th and O a man stopped him, pointing across the street to a small park and fountain, an O Streeter trimming the row of shrubs along a decorative wall.

Would you look at that?

Samuel nodded. At what?

He's trimming hedges. Trimming hedges. The man pivoted to look at Samuel. Say, you think they mow lawns in the summer? You seen 'em do that?

They do.

The man shook his head, smiling, fat dimples appearing. Samuel ducked away, heading east. All down O Street the stores were open and people milled about. On half of the traffic signs and on the poles and placards was a small poster, handmade, advertising a movie at the theater on Saturday. Plywood blocked the tinker's store windows, 'tinker' written across each, and paint covered the inside glass of the door. Through a visor clear of the paint Samuel could see flashes of light, sparks from welding. At 11th he saw a wooden structure anchored into the sidewalk. It was a pillory, holes for the neck and wrists, a curved piece of rebar for a primitive lock. He turned south for The Capitol on 14th. There were two mongrels idling down the street, and when he neared them he saw Rogan in the mirror.

Hey brother. Rogan shifted in the bucket seat and stretched his hand out for Samuel to shake. What brought you back?

He shook, slipped loose for a quick slap. Same thing that brought me here before. The train.

Rogan smirked. Try and stick around this time.

Samuel patted the hood of Rogan's mongrel and went on to the west entrance of The Capitol. Two O Streeters passed him going out, and one dipped his hat, holding the door. Samuel took a right, heading down the main hall toward the old senate chambers. Stone floors, dull from scuffing. The ceiling was high and tiled with mosaics. Everything within arm's reach had been vandalized long before and O Streeters still scrubbed at paint, laying spackle over holes. He knocked on the chamber doors and heard an assent and opened them. Steiner sat behind a table on the left, facing the entrance. A man in his twenties stood beside him, tall and lean and when Steiner rose he dwarfed him.

Sam! Here's a surprise. You here to sign back up?

I never signed anything to begin with. You got paperwork now? A contract?

Nah. He shook his head. Though maybe we need one for you. Steiner looked over to the man beside him. Would you get someone out to find Finley, make sure he and the townfolk know the old heel is back?

The man left, brushing past Samuel.

I promoted Gil Finley to heel once you and Red left.

He's clearly been hittin' the streets hard. It took me about fifteen minutes to find sign in The Singles. I'm kinda glad I started early.

He looked off. We're gonna regret letting that place go to seed.

That ain't the worst of it. Kid overdosed there last night. Girl named Billie.

Steiner thought, then nodded. I remember her. Had some troubles on the job a while back, had to be let go. Not surprising that's where she wound up.

And Heather, throws a sawed-off around and says she's O Street?

Yeah. We let her be sort of autonomous out there. She's kept the place from falling straight to hell. Things got kinda strange in that neighborhood once you left.

Who's heading O Street now that Gil's heeling?

He pointed to the door. Fella just walked out. Vince Harrawood. He came in about as soon as you left, said he'd been on the coast. He's got a good grip on things. Good shooter. He'll be a complement to you two, gumshoeing.

He gonna actually have them out in the city, working?

Not everyone's as eager as you to tackle a methhead. Speaking of. Red ain't with you, is he?

No. He worked his jaw, looked down for a second. It's just me.

Good. Even so. This might require some smoothing over with Bradshaw.

He sighed, looked toward the door. What's the deal with the stockade?

That. We don't use it all that much, but we figure it's more humane than pitching everyone that does wrong onto a train.

You think?

Is there a problem, Sam?

I'm just wondering if I got off at the wrong stop. What happened here?

Steiner came around the desk. We put the stocks up to keep the drunks in line, and it does. You see someone dealing, you're welcome to smack 'em down. That's your job description. Running this city and giving me lip ain't. He paused. You know what. Get over here.

Samuel came forward, standing beside a chair.

You left before we could come down on you. Bradshaw and I talked it over. We were gonna put you on a kind of probation after what happened by The Bottoms. You may not have pulled the trigger, but a company man still died because of you. I can't have you stirring shit up like you and Red used to.

You mean doing our jobs.

What did I say? Steiner closed his eyes and craned his head back. You're back on. But your credit's docked. You're on a leash. Report in on your plans, tell me the results. And don't go breaking any legs you don't have to. I want names, addresses. If you don't toe the line you won't like what happens. You hear me?

He exhaled, hot. I'm going to 10th and F tonight to knock over a cook.

See, you've got the hang of it already.

He went out. Upstairs, Beth's door was closed with a placard fixed to it: BETH DOUBEK. He opened it and stopped in the doorway. She sat writing with pen and paper behind a desk. Two women and a boy stood in front of her. The boy's shoes were large and worn, holes in the toes, and he stared at Samuel, and Samuel smiled at him. Beth hadn't looked up. A young man worked a ledger at another desk, set across from them. Setting the pen down, Beth folded her hands in the middle of the table.

There's a lot to learn about the city, but you'll get the

hang of it quick. My official rundown is this: The city you're standing in was founded by Lester Bradshaw, Al Steiner, and myself. Bradshaw's the head of the electric side of the company, the P&L of 8th Street P&L, and he runs the faces, the people who go out and find folks like you. Al runs the branch of workers called O Street. They keep the peace, do maintenance work and keep our cars running. With a place like this, there's a lot to be done, so you'll see workers out all the time. I, myself, aside from being the entirety of the welcoming committee, also keep track of the logistic side of the city: The trains, the goods, the trading. Taxes, essentially. I'd complain about what century this is, but I'm actually pretty good at it. She took a deep breath. You following me?

They nodded. So far.

The city itself is set up on a grid. Numbered streets run north and south, lettered east to west. Remember that, and you'll never get lost. Your apartment is a room at an old hotel, The Inn, on 9th. She spun the paper around and slid the pen forward. Signing here means you agree to everything we've said. The rent, the laws. You're going to stay clean. You'll obey posted signs, won't trespass on company property, et cetera.

Is there somewhere to trespass? I haven't seen anything like that.

That refers mostly to The Bottoms. There was a gas leak, and we don't have the equipment to determine if it's safe or not, so it's been fenced off. We also don't necessarily want you walking right into P&L Central HQ without an appointment, so there's that, too. She paused, watched their expressions. You'll be briefed at The Inn on specific emergency procedures. It's not fun to talk about it, but it's the world we live in.

Like what kind of emergency?

The cartels found us, once. Just a small gang, and we handled it fine, but nevertheless. There's no telling what might happen, and that's why we've got the procedures in place, and people like Sam, there, to protect us. She pointed at him.

The women glanced back, and the child stared again. One of them signed the paper, and Beth scanned it. After a moment she looked up, stood, and shook hands with them.

Best of luck to you here. She smiled at the boy, and the three of them filed out. Beth stretched in her chair and looked askew at Samuel. You're hardly a sight for sore eyes, but I'm glad you're above ground. She straightened the papers and slid them into a folder. Stop by for dinner.

Tonight? He almost laughed. Okay.

Coming back into The Haymarket he found Johanna sitting on one of the raised patios along 8th Street, two blocks of restaurants and coffee shops empty when he'd left, slowly filling. The farmers were arrayed below the patios, nearly a dozen in all. Preserves, jars of corn, tomatoes. Bound sheaves of tobacco and marijuana. At Johanna's feet was a stall full of chicory, ground and unground, and Ostry was talking at her and passed her up a mug of coffee heated from a small camp-stove on his cart. When she saw Samuel coming she gestured to Ostry, and he bent again at the stove. By the time Samuel was beside him, Ostry had poured another mug.

Missed seein' you around here, Sam. Got any word on you all sellin' your engines yet?

Samuel took the mug. There might be. I'm fresh in. He walked up onto the patio and stood by the table. A couple crossed the street toward Ostry's cart. I'll ask for you. He turned to Johanna, setting his mug down. A breeze stole its wick of steam. It felt like early autumn, or seeing her pulled him there.

I heard you were back in town. She smiled, eyes darting to Ostry and the new customers.

Just last night. You on break?

She nodded. Have to get back to the depot pretty soon.

His lips were tight. He looked over her shoulder for a moment, at the street, the vendors, people looking through jars and the few fresh goods.

She bent over the table. What's wrong?

Did you and Aaron get serious while I was gone? He was talking about marrying you. Has this whole plan.

To the south two farmers unloaded their cart. A crate of jars fell and smashed on the pavement. Johanna winced. It's not like we've talked about it. She turned her mug. You were gone a long time. I couldn't expect, had no idea that— She flattened her hands on the table. Don't hold it against me. I had to keep living here. This is the first place that's made me feel safe in years. If I had known.

He clenched his hand around the mug, felt it burn. I would have kept you safe.

Now's your chance to prove that, I guess. She smiled, finished her coffee and stood. I should go. One of the Union Pacifics was robbed out west. The whole station is having a fit. She took her mug and handed it to Ostry and thanked him. Samuel watched her walk to the street, and she went down the sidewalk to the depot. Ostry turned, resting an arm on the patio cement and squinting up at Samuel.

Lookin' to be a dry summer, I hear.

Like all the rest.

3

By evening the clouds had thinned, and it was cold. Going north on 8th he watched a train leave the station and round off into the coming night. He followed the creek as the trracks did, skirting the city. A football stadium on his right, university dorms and halls, courtyards and greens, all dark. He was well into unlit territory when the streetlamps went up, and the night beyond them came darker, scraps of cloud carried off and the rest of the sky black. Across the river, a granary station. The side of a silo was lit up by a barrelfire, and he went to the creek edge to get a better look. A square of light that didn't waver or dim. Nothing else. He moved on. Past the university, neighborhoods grew into spotty woods. He caught Vine and followed it to Whittier, walking beside the crumbling sidewalk, and he cut across a yard and stopped at a red house. He knocked on the door. He knocked again and heard footsteps and Beth opened it.

You're early. It's gonna be a while.

What're you making?

Hell if I know. She opened the door wide and he came in, shutting it behind him. It was dark except for candlelight. She headed to the kitchen, and he followed.

I thought you said it'd be a while.

Since I don't know what I'm making yet.

She browsed her cupboards, and he rested against a countertop. A pot smacked on the island in the middle of the room. Small sheets of plywood hung over the windows. She put chicken breasts from the icebox into a glass dish and a pot of green beans on the stove.

I've got potatoes, but you'll have to mash them or whatever. I barely eat at home as it is.

This is fine.

You're in my way. She reached past him and opened a cupboard, taking down a few jars of spices. Samuel slipped to another counter, and she poured some seasoning into her hand and dropped it over the chicken. She set the chicken inside the stove and the room flooded with heat. So what have you been doing?

Wandering. I've had some free time recently. He smirked.

She closed the stove and narrowed her eyes. I didn't make him leave. Or you.

I don't think that's how he saw it.

Beth pushed him to the front of the house. I've got furniture. Go sit. She pointed to a chair in the dim living room. Blankets hung from the curtain rods over the picture windows. She lit a small lamp and sat opposite him in a chair across the room and stared. Vent if you want to.

There's nothing to say. You know what I'm mad about.

We didn't have a choice. She bent forward. Only half of my job here is the comings and goings. The rest of it is keeping people in check. There are a lot of big egos in this town.

But it was you that pushed Red to leave. You convinced him. That night he was all for fighting it. Even Al was on the fence. Then he went and saw you, and he folded.

I had to. If he hadn't left, Bradshaw would have gone off. Then Al would go off on him.

Bradshaw's an ass anyway. We don't need him.

You don't know what we need. She cracked her neck to one side. The fact that you're back proves that. At least Red had the sense to keep away.

He thumbed toward the kitchen. Your pot's boiling over.

Dammit. She rushed from the room. There was a clatter. You don't win the argument because I can't cook, Samuel Parrish.

Wouldn't dream it.

She was gone awhile, and the kitchen noise stopped. He sat looking over the room. Dark wood mantel over the fireplace, nicks blackened with age. When he smelled smoke he rose and found her standing with her back to the counter, a cigarette in hand.

It's probably ready.

They served their own plates and returned to their chairs. Samuel watched his plate or the covered windows, and Beth watched him. When they finished they went into the kitchen and put their plates in the sink. Samuel stopped his hand on the faucet, looking over to Beth.

It works. It's the one utility I've got.

He ran the sink full of water and washed the dishes while she moved about the kitchen putting things away. Eventually she stood beside him, drying. He took a dishrag from her and dried his hands, then wrung it in his fists. I gotta go bust up a tea shop. Thank you for dinner.

Any time.

Really?

Shit no. Leave me be. Beth walked him to the door. It was black out, clear, dim stars. She hung just within the door. Be careful.

He went to the street. He palmed the hilt of the knife and headed south, passing squat subdivisions and complexes, replica houses. On campus he cut through the green to Q Street. A Light worker hunched under the gutterless eave of a laundry, his face going yellow with flame as he lit a pipe. Samuel called to him, and the worker straightened, rapped the pipe on the wall beside him, and started west, fading into the nearest alley. Samuel lingered in his steps, then went on south, air blowing warm from restaurants, diners parting around him. New faces. A corner pub had a short line of smokers in front of its window. Tobacco, marijuana. Samuel nodded past them. Two P&L trucks and a mongrel sedan were parked a few yards down the street, and he could feel the workers watching him.

The border of lights fell behind him, and he moved onto the sidewalk, covered over with trees. Slabs of pavement lifted by roots. Small houses and garages boarded up. A commotion between plots, like something thrown through the mounded leaves, and he heard claws on bark. He stopped, breathed, let his muscles ease from their roach. He went a block further than the store to circle around and come at it from the front. The property was an old converted house, the gutter hanging down across the porch steps. Plastic bottles were piled in the alley on the far side, and he could smell the solvents and the cut-green scent of the Mormon tea. He stepped up onto the porch and opened the storm door. A ring of rust where a coffeecan had held it wide. He pushed open the door and peered into the dark. The front of the store was lit by an electric lantern on the empty counter, showing empty shelves, posters for beer. Glass crunched under his boots. He stepped further into the store and saw a row of freezer cases along the sidewall. The top half of the cases were fogged, and below that he saw a table crowded with a pot and flasks, hands moving.

Samuel walked toward the doors and crouched in front of them. The cook was going back and forth from the table to one behind him and it took two circles before he froze. Samuel drew the knife. A moment passed and the cook dove toward the back of the store and Samuel leapt with him, racing and finding the door and bracing against it until he felt the cook slam into the other side. He heard him scramble back and Samuel met him again as he opened the glass door and Samuel kicked it closed, the glass cracking around the cook's forehead before the door wobbled open again. He swept the knife up for play but the cook stuck his hand out to ward it off, and his thumb docked at the knuckle. It swung by a string of sinew, and the cook fell back into the cooler and lay there clutching his hand to his soiled apron. Samuel stopped the door with his foot. He stepped into the cooler, shaking his head.

Shit. Sorry about that. He considered the knife in his hand, the streak of blood, and sighed. You want to take a guess why I'm here?

The cook sobbed. There was blood on his forehead and on his chest. He gummed at an answer, and Samuel nudged his leg. Beat me up, I guess. Rob me. He was holding his breath, and he leaned onto his elbow to sit up, scooting away from Samuel.

I'm here to shut you down. Tell me who you're working with.

The cook clutched his hand and stared at it. My goddamn thumb.

You've got another. Listen, I'll get right to the point. I'm looking for Fish.

I'm just tryin' to make a way for myself. I'm just doin' what they tell me to. He lolled his head, eyes cast down.

Samuel crouched. You need to start talking. I'll start taking my pick of fingers. You'll never play piano again.

The cook rocked, looking at Samuel. What?

Samuel raised his eyebrows, breathed deep, and took a fistful of the cook's hair and heaved him up by it. He passed the knife just under his knuckles and dropped the hank of hair into the man's lap. The cook flopped and rolled away. He went limp.

God. All I know is he gives me the plants, and I give him the stuff, and he pays me.

Where do I find him?

I don't know. He finds me. The cook dropped his head. His apron was wet with blood.

Samuel noticed the fumes. Hey. He kicked the cook in the thigh. Get up. Get out of here. He kicked him again. The cook rolled to his feet. He almost hit the glass case and Samuel pushed the broken door open and followed him into the store.

He shoved him toward the front, and the man let go of his hand long enough to open the screen door. Samuel watched him hobble to the street, and he turned back and started knocking the plywood from the windows, the boards swinging and dropping off. He paused by the cooler and thought a moment before kicking the glass out of the broken door and turning over the table, shattering decanters and vials before running out. He headed uptown, imagined vapors rising off him, an explosion. On O Street he turned west. A bearded man, white-haired, waved from the pillory as he passed, hand lifted.

Where you been, boy?

Raj? What are you stuck in here for?

O Street likes to say it's drunk and disorderly, usually.

Here. Hold on. Samuel looked around himself before pushing at the lock, knocking it past the eyelet with the butt of his knife. He lifted the top half of the pillory over, and Raj grabbed his hips and stretched, twisting his back. A funk of jake sweat and dirt rolled off him.

I'm a bit surprised to see you. He rubbed his wrists. Happy, though.

Apparently someone needs to stick around and look after you.

I don't need looking after. He patted his belly. I am a self-regulating machine.

That right?

Regulating myself straight into the grave.

He shook his head. Try to stay out of that thing. Eventually they'll get a proper lock for it. He ducked away before Raj could say more. At the intersection of 8th and Q he saw Steiner standing in the window of The Remedy with a beer in his hand, and Samuel stopped in front of the sidewalk. Steiner pushed out and set his mug on the steps.

Need your help with something.

Samuel shrugged, halfhearted. They crossed the street

and started up the ramp for O. Painted in one of the gird-
ers beside them was a name or word: safari. Steiner walked
in the middle of the road, along the divide. Hands stuffed in
coat pockets. Samuel looked over.

I rolled that cook like I said.

And? Steiner was looking straight ahead.

I'm after Fish. He was second dick in charge over tea
when Red and I ran the dealers out of The Singles.

Steiner barely nodded. Just don't hurt anyone that signed
the charter.

Samuel kept his eyes forward. They went on until the
overpass rejoined solid ground, and they turned toward The
Singles. Past the plant. There were several people out, lingering in doorways. Heather saw the two of them and spun away.
Steiner went on out of the neighborhood, following 2nd until
he made a turn on a small sidestreet without a sign. He gained
the porch of a house with an attached garage, a sheet of siding
gone. Samuel raised an eyebrow and Steiner opened the front
door. Heat washed out into the night behind them. The living
room was dark, low-hanging lamps on chains in two corners
and a man and Maggie Bradshaw sitting on a sunken couch
backed against a wall. Another man stepped into a doorway
beside them, tall and shirtless. Powder on an end table, a copper pipe hammered and soldered to a bowl. Steiner locked
eyes with Maggie, and tilted his head to the door.

Get up.

She stood, hand on the arm of the couch for balance. The
man beside her was staring, cut lean and pale. He made to
reach for her arm and missed. Maggie crossed the room to
Steiner, and he took off his jacket and slipped it on her.

I wish you'd stop finding me. She gathered the jacket
around her neck and went outside.

Steiner pointed at the man on the couch. This is the last
time I'm gonna warn you, Tover. You touch her again and I'll
fucking kill you.

She came to me. It's a free country.

Not anymore it ain't.

Man, fuck you. Tover rose to his feet. Get outta my house. He threw a hand toward the door, and Samuel brushed his jacket aside and rested his hand on the knife. Tover's eyes widened. And just who the hell are you?

Steiner put an arm out between them. He's the guy that doesn't give warnings.

Tover ran his tongue across his lips. The man in the doorway was examining the chips of paint on the frame in front of him, picking with his nails. Steiner fumed from his nose and turned out the door, Samuel behind him. Maggie crouched on the porch steps and Samuel moved to stand by her while Steiner paused, fists tightening.

Fuck it.

He turned back, reaching in through the open doorway and ripping one of the lamps from its chain in the ceiling and hurling it against the wall. The oil caught and Steiner stomped past the two of them into the yard. The shirtless man rushed from the house and Steiner hung him out with a fist. He flopped to the ground, lay still. Samuel touched Maggie's shoulder and took her out to stand on the sidewalk. Tover didn't appear, and the man rolled to his stomach and crawled off. Maggie glanced to the street.

Where's my dad?

Lester's not coming for you anymore. Steiner's mouth tightened, and he caught Samuel's eye. He put his arm around her and they headed back toward the city. Samuel stood on an islet of sidewalk, watching the fire dim and die, the two of them shrink into the northward dark. One house down someone stuck their head out of a window. Samuel headed up on 2nd, and closing on O Street he saw Detch coming the other way and stopped in the road. Detch raised a hand, quickened his pace.

Hey, Sam, it's good to see you back.

Samuel caught wind of him, stale weed. He nodded, then pivoted to point behind himself, toward The Singles. What happened here? What's going on?

Detch shrugged. It turned into this kind of haven. Just a couple women at first, a few months back. These tough older ladies from up north. Then they took in a girl fell out of the city, and it's just grew from there. Girls come in from out-side, or they have trouble at home. O Street don't care about a Light boy wants to speedbag his girlfriend, you know? So they come out here. They take care of each other. They keep the tea and jake out, too, mostly. And now we got our own O Streeter.

We?

The girls and I get along. They like me. No rent if you don't mind readin' by candle.

Samuel grimaced. It doesn't seem so quiet. I just pulled what looks like a deputy shitheel from a house on the south side. And apparently a low-class dealer has graduated to run-ning the whole tea operation around here.

Yeah. Detch nodded. Fish took over after you blew every-thing down. He's still getting to know the line, I guess.

You know where he works?

Not around here. Detch shook his head. I don't bother with that kind of thing. We're easy targets, if someone gets a mind to really hurt us. Billie proved it.

Samuel walked past him. That's true of everyone.

4

In the morning he cleaned his knife with a rag and sharpened it with stone and oil, leaning against the front window, greasing the blade between finger and thumb. He set it on the table and took out a book from the shelf as a mongrel rolled to a stop in front of the diner. Someone came up the stairs. He slid the box below his bed and the book back into place. Who is it?

It's Gil. Bradshaw wants you to come out with me to The Bottoms. One of the Light boys saw a couple Mexicans wander in.

Mexicans? The cartel?

No. At least probably not. Do you need a minute?

He got his knife and followed Gil downstairs. Outside the sky was clear and dry. Rogan sat behind the wheel of the mongrel, and he nodded to Samuel in the mirror before they took off. The sun shone through a gap in the buildings. Gil rolled down a window and Samuel smelled bread.

What am I coming along for? Expecting they're gonna fight?

Bradshaw wants to get a feel for them. Find out what they've seen and all. You're the only one knows Spanish well enough. None of the faces do. Charlie's still learning.

Samuel was quiet. How'd a Light boy find them and not O Street?

Travis and Hurst were fishing copper out of a house, saw a kid pissing out a window.

Rogan took them down 9th Street, and the main of the city went by in less than a minute. It emptied them amid strip malls and developments, yards overgrown, and whole buildings open to the air like dollhouses, blackened from old fires. A long-dead tree rested against the eave of a split-level. Weeds grew over the pinched gutters. Samuel saw the paths plying the tall grasses, a part in the blond field beside an on-ramp, and above them a trio of deer walking the overpass. Their heads bobbed, bent, came up with forage.

The car stopped a few minutes later, and they got out, shutting the doors quietly. Rogan lit a cigarette, and Gil led them a few blocks south until they were within sight of the last row of houses in the city. When they were near, Gil point-ed out a ranch house with trampled grass in the backyard. They circled around it and stopped on the sidewalk before go-ing in. There were indentations in the carpet for chairs, a TV stand in the front room. Gil had gone into an open doorway to the side, and Samuel went ahead. There were waterstains on the ceiling and the offwhite paint throughout the rooms was blistered. A pocket full of water in a corner of the kitchen. He tested the paint and it dented, pinched it and the blister ruptured and a brown digestion poured down the wall. The cabinets were all bare. No signs, no smells but mold. He met Gil at the door, and at the sight of them Rogan turned and they started for the car.

Can you drive us around some? I know he saw the kid around here.

Sure. I got a bit. Rogan tossed his cigarette. He started the mongrel, and they piled in and rolled off. They coasted around the neighborhood, making circuits of the outer blocks and going inward. In sight of the gas leak and the fence sur-rounding, the houses inside loomed mostly untouched. Warning signs were posted every hundred feet, handwritten or spraypainted. When they had covered nearly half of The Bottoms, Rogan headed north. Gil flipped down his visor, picked his teeth in the mirror and tilted it to see Samuel.

Did you see anything while you were out in the world,

Sam?

No. It was quiet, mostly. I wasn't too far south. Have you?

He tapped on his door. No. I only ever saw the caravan we smoked before you and Red rolled into town. The faces bring back their stories and all. People talking about raiding parties or whatever you want to call them. But I don't think anyone's seen anything firsthand for months.

Probably just haven't found us yet.

That's the kind of optimism 8th Street's been missing. Gil stretched, reached for the visor, and let go. Maybe they got wiped out by some flu.

Maybe they adopted a bunch of puppies. Saw the error of their ways. Rogan dropped his hand from the top of the wheel, kept them steady with a knee while he lit a cigarette.

They were soon past the south end, and Samuel looked out, let his eyes laze. The lines of siding on the houses blurred together, colors flickered door to door. Samuel sat up. Either of you know a guy named Fish?

There was no answer. Rogan met his eye in the mirror again. Coming into The Haymarket they perked at the sight of two people fighting on the corner of 8th and P. Samuel opened his door and stepped out before Rogan had the car stopped and Samuel strode toward the pair, Raj and another hobo. A truck swerved around him, and Samuel flipped the driver off as it went on north, turning away. The hobo reached for Raj's hair, pulling, and Samuel grabbed him by a backpack and swung him off his feet. As he rolled, a cardboard sign flew from a string on his neck and lay flat on the ground. The back was blank but for 'DEUT 23:15' in charcoal, and on the front, white paint had been drizzled: In this Country the United States God has Abandoned and we Live in Sin There is No Place and no Mountain to hide from The Sun. Samuel shot a look at Raj and then to the hobo, beginning to stand. He was blind or nearly, holding his head at an odd angle. Samuel picked up the sign and pushed it into his hand.

What are you two fighting about?

This place is the harlot. The hobo pointed toward Raj. He needs brought back! The hobo got to his feet and tried restringing the sign, but his fingers had no dexterity. Behind them Rogan honked the car horn and drove away. The hobo lifted his head to watch the car leave, then backed down the street, shuffling, his shoes untied, tongues drooping out to reveal pale and dirty ankles. The sign lay on the ground.

Samuel smiled thinly. What'd you say to him?

Nothin'. He's crazier'n a shithouse mouse. Hadn't seen him for a while, near a year.

Samuel glanced around. A P&L worker lurked behind the diner window, watching. The hobo was turning under O Street.

What do you think about God? What's a man like you think of God speaking to us?

I figure if I don't expect anything I'll be less likely to get disappointed.

God loves you, Sam.

He raised an eyebrow and Raj grinned.

He might, you don't know. Got a buck for a beer?

Samuel followed his glance to The Remedy. Come on. Samuel went up the steps and opened the door. He ordered beers, and they sat at a booth. You ever deal with Fish?

Raj wiped foam from his lips. I've heard of him. He's one of the guys you look for if you want whusk or tea.

Where do you look for him?

He shrugged. I've never had to. I go out to The Jungle. There's always someone comin' through there, trying to sell. Keep an eye out there long enough and you'll see him bringing in jake.

The door opened, and Aaron stepped in. He pointed at Samuel. We're havin' an early drunk at Norton's. Need you to report in.

Samuel sighed. You got anything else you can tell me,

Raj?

I don't think I told you much just now.

Very true. Enjoy the beer. He followed Aaron out. They cut down Q, and Aaron looked over at him.

Tried finding you last night. You were working?

He nodded. Took out a tea cook, cut off his thumb.

You what now?

He shrugged. Didn't mean to.

Aaron looked sidelong at him. Gross.

They cut across 9th on P and passed The Manse apartments. They kept on, greeting civilians out for the evening. The door to a restaurant opened, and Samuel's eyes rolled at the rich garlic pouring out into the air, a couple exiting and shaking Aaron's hand. At the corner a busker strummed a bleached guitar, a battered case at his feet. A small crowd lingered nearby, listening. Aaron threw change into the case, a pile of coins there already. They went through the high traffic until they came out past the brunt of the lighted district. A bowl of tinfoil in the gutter caught Samuel's eye, and he toed it, saw the burn. Detch was crouched on the curb at 13th and P, elbow resting on a knee and the other crooked to hold a cigarette. He nodded when he saw them coming. They cut into the alley and down a ramp to the bar. It had been the back of a theater long before, now Norton's. They came to an anteroom, decorative stage controls on their left, an ATM that someone had cut open years ago, husk never moved. Norton stood behind the bar and waved them on. There were Light men settled into chairs, on stools, smoking and drinking. When Samuel rounded the corner, Norton swept his hand at him.

Ain't you too young to be in here?

Samuel smirked, and they came up to the bar. When's the last time you saw your pecker without a mirror, Norton?

He grinned wide. What am I gettin' you?

Aaron elbowed Samuel. Sammy here cut off a man's

thumb for 8th Street. I believe the deal is bourbon for blood, right?

Norton raised his eyebrows. That's the tradition. He reached down under the bar and came up with a bottle of amber liquor. You boys had this before?

Guess I never turned in the blood.

Well it ain't quite bourbon, but it's close as I can come without some real time to age it. He poured two glasses full and watched them knock the liquor back. What's the verdict?

Samuel opened his mouth. It's all right.

Norton frowned. I like to think it's a sight better than all right.

I'm just not much for drinking. He set the glass on the bar. There was a moment before Norton and Aaron broke smiles and laughed.

One more to grow on, and I'll switch you to shine. Norton poured their glasses again and one for himself.

We'll take it to go, thanks. Aaron turned and pointed at Johanna, sitting in the corner booth, looking away. He glanced at Samuel and muttered loudly, hand to his mouth. See that blonde over there? Legs for days? I'm gonna take her home tonight.

She smiled at them and shook her head, sliding across the bench for Aaron to take a seat. How was your meeting?

Aaron shrugged. Fine. Faces split the action as always. Charlie goes west, I go east. Head off in a few days. He puffed his chest. Locate resources, sell the city, grow rich off taxes like olden-day politicians.

Samuel perched his fingers on his glass. Who're you after this time?

The usual. Bradshaw said we've gotta get some plumbers or something. Pipe busted in the north, and Norton spent two hours getting the water shut off.

Who's up there to see that in the first place? Even I don't bother going past the creek.

Aaron shrugged. Guess someone went for a joyride.

They reached for their drinks. Samuel turned at the sound of the door, and a group of P&L boys came in, Maggie Bradshaw with them. She saw them in the corner and looked away.

There you go, Sam. Aaron reached across and smacked his arm. Get back in the graces.

They gathered at the bar. Maggie leaned against it, near the end.

Samuel got up. You know what. He smirked at Aaron, gave Johanna a brief look and circled around the tables to stand beside Maggie. She faced forward, watching him in the bar mirror. One of the workers glared but said nothing. Samuel pushed his glass forward. What was it I was getting you out of last night?

Why do you ask? She set her own glass down. Do you suddenly care?

I just want to know if I should be watching out for you. Or anyone else.

No, Sam. You don't have to worry. She smiled, and turned away.

Samuel asked for another shot. Everyone at the counter was quiet while he waited. I'd lean off you all if someone would tell me where Fish is brewing tea.

No one but Maggie flinched. Her eyes snapped to his in the mirror. Norton handed him his drink and Samuel turned with it and came back to the table.

What happened? Aaron nodded toward Maggie.

He shrugged. Just this. He held up his glass.

You're a dick. Aaron threw his arm over the booth and scanned the bar to the pool tables. Two games were on, Charlie and a few Light workers. He spun back. Wanna play?

Samuel lifted his hand. No, very much no.

I'll reserve us a table. Be right back. He rose and wandered off, stopped by a Still worker at the bar.

Samuel took up his glass, smile lingering, and saw Johanna looking at him from over the rim. He exhaled and downed his shot and set it back. Soon the bar was full and loud. Aaron returned and pulled Johanna away to play a game and after a minute Samuel got up to watch. They played without the eight ball, lost or stolen. Everything began to go on swimmingly. The busker had come in and was playing in a corner, guitar case at his feet. Samuel joined them on the next game and then Maggie was sitting in the booth with them and he on a chair at the end of the table and he could only vaguely recollect how they got there. She was laughing and Aaron gesturing wide. Johanna was looking above Samuel and then he tipped back in his chair and crashed and the breath caught in his lungs. The floor gluey, bits of glass, paper, pennies deviating the topography. Someone hoisted him up, two Light workers held his arms and dragged him toward the back. He relaxed and let them carry him until they threw him into the alley and he caught his feet. When he turned around three men came toward him, and then Aaron appeared under the bare bulb overhead and he hauled against the middle man's neck. Samuel leapt forward and jabbed one in the nose and kicked at the other, the man latching onto his foot and stepping back.

You ain't such hot shit.

Samuel pulled himself in by the knee and cracked the man across the jaw. He lost his balance and fell to the ground and someone booted him in the ribs. The one he'd jabbed twisted his heel into Samuel's side and he caught the leg. He managed to kick up and the first man went to his knees. A chain of flares lit in Samuel's left eye as he rose, and he stumbled back. Cool blood ran down his cheek. The second man charged, and Samuel led his punch by and lifted his knee and felt the man's teeth clack. Aaron was on the ground with the other worker but Johanna had her thumbs covering his eyes and his hands were held out and still.

Okay, okay. I'm done.

Johanna stood away, and he rose without any sudden movement and started to pick up one of the other workers when Norton pushed them back, a shotgun in hand.

Did we reach an understanding? He jerked the gun to get the workers moving, and Samuel let them shoulder by. What the hell, boys?

They started it. Aaron glared after the workers, leaving the mouth of the alley. He pointed at Samuel's face. You're bleedin' pretty good.

Samuel touched his temple, hand running with blood, and slung it toward the ground. Johanna looked Aaron over in the light from the door.

I've got the shine and bandages ready.

Norton held the door, and Johanna sat them on a bench in a long alcove off the entryway. Aaron leaned himself into a corner and closed his eyes. His cheek red and swelling, and his lip busted.

Johanna lifted the shine and a clean rag. Who's first?

Aaron pointed. Him. I don't like pain.

She turned. Samuel looked down at himself. Bootprints all across his chest and stomach. Johanna took his head in her hand and pushed it to the side. She brought the rag to his face and started wiping through the blood. Samuel led her hand up to the cut and she dabbed at it, redoused the rag and pressed. She took the rag away and it was bright red where she'd bunched it. She tilted his head, mouth pinched, looking him over.

I'm gonna see if they've got something to sew you up with.

He nodded, watching her go. The cut at his temple felt cold and open.

I saw you checkin' out her ass. Aaron reached a hand out and slapped Samuel's arm, and Samuel stiffened. It's okay. I snuck a peek, too. He closed his eyes again, and Samuel watched him, swallowed. A minute passed and she returned, hands empty.

All they had was tape. I can sew you up at home if you'll help me drag him.

Sure. He stood, stretching against his ribs. Come on, bud. Let's hobble out of here. Samuel guided Aaron forward, and Johanna led them out the door. A wind had picked up from the west, and it hummed along the rope of a flag pole hanging over a building. They went south, past the unused bars and restaurants, the lower streets filled with houses and small complexes. Two men huddled together under an awning, passing something from hand to hand. Samuel glanced over at Johanna and Aaron, and they all kept going. Off H and 11th Aaron opened the door to an apartment building and led them up the stairs to Johanna's door. He unlocked it and went in, disappearing into the bathroom. Johanna flicked the lights on and took off her shoes with Samuel still in the doorway. She went down the hall to her room and returned with a needle and thread and set them on the kitchen table, just a few feet from the door. After a minute the toilet flushed, and Aaron came out, his head lolling.

I just woke up holdin' my dong. I'm going to bed. Aaron crossed the hall and kissed Johanna.

Thanks for your help.

My pleasure. Now sleep. He patted Samuel on the back and went to the bedroom.

Johanna pressed her lips together. Come sit down. She waved him into the kitchen. It was small, little space after the appliances. Aaron was muttering. Samuel put his hand on the tabletop, studying the swell of his knuckles. Johanna took two glasses from the cupboard and a bottle of shine from the top of the refrigerator.

He's already passed out, I'm sure. She poured the glasses two fingers deep and set them on the table before getting a rag. She bent toward him and tipped the bottle of shine over into the rag and swabbed at his temple. She'd put up her hair.

Neck and collar smooth, blouse dipping at the breastbone. Down at the back of her neck. She took the rag away. How in the world did you get cut so bad?

Weak skin, I guess.

She pursed her lips. Mhm. Here. She handed one of the glasses to him. Drink. I'm pretty good at this, but it'll still make you sweat.

He winced the moonshine down. Johanna threaded the needle and took hold of his face. She pinched the cut together, and he felt her test the angle of the needle on his skin and then she pushed it through and drew the thread. Faint trace of flowers from her wrist. The needle went in again. The cut pulling closed. After four more rounds she knotted the thread and set the needle down and examined her work. She held him still and dabbed the cloth over the wound. Her hand holding his jaw slid and she cupped his chin. It took her a moment to let go.

I think you're set.

Thank you. He shut his eyes, worked the side of his face.

You should go.

Samuel opened them. He got up, and she followed him to the door and opened it for him. It was cold in the hall. He turned and she put her hand on the frame. He followed it along her arm to her shoulder and neck. He wanted to take her hair down.

Come back around the end of the week, and we'll cut those out.

A pang at the length of time, at seeing her again. They both seemed to hang there in the doorway until he opened his mouth to speak, and she cut him off, reading what he would say.

I don't want to get in the way of you and Maggie.

Samuel twisted like he'd taken a blow. Steiner and I pulled her out of a tea den last night. I asked her what was going on.

She sank against the wall, looking down. I thought you were getting back at me.

For what?

I don't know. For Aaron. Saying no. She hesitated. We shouldn't be talking about this right now.

Samuel lingered and turned away, heading downstairs. Heartsick and alert out in the open. The wind had shifted to the south, and the breeze was at his back all the way home. The cut felt like a burn in the cold, and at his window the lights looked like gears, wheeling with each blink.

5

His brow stuck to the pillow when he woke. The sky showed white through the windows and as he sat up he remembered everything of the night before and laid back. Eventually he showered and dressed, midsection stiff, tender. On Samuel's way downstairs, Aaron opened the door at the bottom, carrying two glasses and a bottle under his arm.

Hey, sunshine. G'won back up. I got your breakfast.

Samuel turned and held the door for him. That doesn't look like bacon.

Aaron set the glasses down on the table. They held raw eggs and hot sauce and he poured several fingers of moonshine in both glasses. In the light his cheek showed flecks of purple, and his lip dragged. He offered one of the glasses, and Samuel held it almost at arm's length.

If you can keep it down, you'll mend quick. Hair of the dog, li'l pep.

I'm not that hungover. Don't think I've ever been that hungover.

Well. He looked down for a moment. Egg's broke. He knocked glasses with Samuel and reached to touch the glass to the table before slurping the drink into his mouth. He swallowed hugely, his Adam's apple dipping to the bottom of his throat. When he brought his head up he was smiling.

If this makes me puke, I'm aiming for you. Samuel breathed deep and threw it back. The yolk hit his teeth and split cold, the hot sauce and shine burning, and he sputtered and reached for the table. Oh. You're awful. He coughed and swung his arm to grab onto Aaron, missing.

Breathe.

He smacked the table. He wiped at his eyes and held in another cough and straightened. You made that up, didn't you? You just wanted to see if I'd drink it.

Huh uh. He wiped a knuckle over the corner of his mouth. It's a real thing. My pop used to drink them. Prairie oysters.

Are you finished for the day, or did you want to torture me more?

I thought we'd go out and wander some. Patrol.

Samuel raised an eyebrow, skin taut at the cut. Really.

Nah. Do some day-drinking. Maybe get on that bartender from The Alley for you or track down Maggie. She'd warmed up to you, by night's end.

He sighed, motioned to the door, and they went out. Sheila poured them beers and shook her head as she pushed the glasses forward. Samuel was already a little lightheaded, and he could feel the egg drifting in the beer. Wandering down 9th they passed the seamstress' shop, a few closed storefronts with their windows and walls blank, other shops with old signs still hung. An art gallery, a bookstore, a pawn shop. Aaron thumbed at a garage on the corner with its bays open.

That'd make a decent bar. Wouldn't that make a decent bar? You know, for good weather. Open the doors, maybe throw counters around the holes they got there. Be a good day bar. Do your serious drinking elsewhere. Your broody drinking.

Did you have something before your prairie oyster?

Maybe.

Samuel laughed. I don't think we need another bar.

Someday. There's enough room here for a couple hundred thousand. Did you know that?

That's a lot of bars.

People, jackass. Three hundred thousand people used to live here.

They went on. More empty buildings, the courthouse. Two blocks further south, the boundary of light was marked off by P&L trucks, workers at poles. One waved at Aaron, stopped when he recognized Samuel. To the west the buildings spread apart, room for yards of steel, mills, and parking lots. They stopped at The Alley Bar where someone had scratched into the rust of the door: NO BUMS. An older woman looked up from shelving bottles of fruit brandy when they entered. The room was half full of Still workers, and the air was thick with yeast and murky daylight. They took seats at the counter, and Aaron flagged the bartender over.

Two shots of pure apiece, ma'am. Just so you don't have to come right back.

She smiled and set their glasses in a row, pouring back and forth along them. Getting an early start?

Aaron held his first shot. Rumor is you get drunk early enough in the day they don't let you do anything else. He met his glass with Samuel's, and they knocked them against the counter and drank. Near silence in the bar. Aaron eyed him and then the door and they raised their second shots.

They wandered, Samuel drunk. A P&L truck sped by on F, honked twice, and Aaron waved after them. Several blocks down the street they walked through unlit territory. They heard an engine from the south, and the truck came into sight on 17th, the left headlight busted and grill warped. The driver stopped when he saw them. Pale enough to show through the glass of the windshield. Aaron went a few paces ahead.

He wreck his truck?

Samuel started over. He looks like one of the partiers Red and I found.

The driver threw it into park. The window was down and he was staring at the wheel, his hands in his lap but still clutched. There was a coil of copper wiring and two empty bottles in the bed.

You all right?

The driver nodded slightly. He fished in his shirt pocket for a cigarette and put it on his lip. He reached again and came out with a lighter and cupped it to his mouth. Striking the wheel, the flame cutting out. The driver looked into the mirror, still scratching at the lighter, and he straightened as though he'd seen something in the reflection. He dropped his hands for a moment, and when he raised the lighter back to his mouth Samuel took it. He lit it and held it out and the driver leaned and sucked in the flame until the tobacco crackled and he said a quiet 'mm.' A thin waft of tea in the smoke.

I just ran over my best friend.

He what? Aaron looked the way the driver had come.

Samuel reached past the wheel and turned the truck off. He pulled the keys. The driver didn't move but to ash the cigarette into the well of the gear shift.

Come on out here, bud. Samuel opened the door. He handed the keys over to Aaron and took the driver by the arm. What's your name?

Travis. He got out of the truck, and Samuel led him a few feet away. He's dead. I think he's dead.

Where?

Hospital parking lot. He pulled on the cigarette. That's kinda funny.

Samuel looked at Aaron. Go back, see if he's there?

Sure. Aaron got in the truck, looking from Samuel to Travis before he spun it south. Samuel watched him go but Travis hadn't moved, as if he were still pointed ahead by the bench seat. Samuel walked him to the curb and they went up 17th. The Capitol reared over the apartments and houses. He could think of nothing to say.

I meant to hit him. It wasn't an accident.

Just take it easy. You seem a little out of it right now.

I'm not. I was, but I'm not anymore. I know what's coming. I know what I did.

All right. We're gonna figure this out. Aaron'll come back and let us know what happened.

He jerked his arm down. I'm not in denial, okay? I'm not in shock. I ran him over and I heard him bust. Just take me in.

His eyes were red. Samuel took a step away. Why'd you do it?

Who knows. We were both sky high. I thought I was driving a hundred miles an hour until I saw you two sittin' still. He flicked his cigarette away.

Aaron was coming back in the truck, and he slowed and stopped, shaking his head. Samuel rounded them to the passenger door and shoved Travis inside. Aaron drove them to the west entrance of The Capitol. It was quiet behind the doors, and their footsteps echoed down the halls. Samuel knocked on the chamber doors, and Steiner opened them.

What's going on? I was just going for lunch.

Samuel pulled Travis forward a step. He ran over a guy. Another Light boy down on Highway 2. What am I supposed to do with him?

Steiner peered at Travis, and Travis wouldn't meet his eyes. There's a holding tank at the courthouse. I was headed that way, but I need to consider firing you first.

Samuel blanched. What for? That fight?

I like you, Sam. It's Bradshaw you rub the wrong way. You go around beating the piss out of his people like this and he's liable to firebomb your apartment.

Aaron stepped in. They started it, Al. I mean, Sam had his back to them, and they threw his chair over. He didn't do anything.

It doesn't matter. Steiner pinched the bridge of his nose. It's this very type of shit that's gonna make me throw you out.

I was out drinking. As a civilian.

You're a heel 24/7. He sighed. Aaron, hold onto this for me. He took Travis from Samuel and pushed him to Aaron, then ducked inside the chamber. Samuel followed him in, and Steiner closed the door.

Look. What's going to happen is he's going to come to me saying he's got people saw you kill Graham that day, and Red was the one holding back. I'm not saying it was, and I'm not asking. You're the heel I got, and I want to keep you. But that's what I heard the P&L is gonna level at you, and I don't have the power to stop it. If Bradshaw gets it in his head, he'll see you out of here or worse, just so he's got a better grip on the place.

You can't fight him on it? He already got rid of Red on this.

I'll kick and scream, but he's the one that lets people read books after the sun sets. To the civilians he's the miracle worker. I'm just the scary one doesn't dress as good. He opened the door. That's what I'm trying to keep from hanging over your head, got it? It skates this time, but there ain't no next time. If it happens again I'll just feed you to him, before I get rode out myself.

All right. I'll be raising dust in The Jungle for Fish and his boys.

Sure. Steiner waved him off and they stepped out. Steiner grabbed Travis by his elbow. Come on, dipshit. He took him down the hall, Travis sullen, shuffling. They went out the west entrance and Aaron pivoted on his heel, rocking. So you're in some trouble, huh?

Like you didn't already hear about it.

He put an arm around Samuel. Come on then, my place. Can't bother anyone there. I got some apple brandy stashed away. He spun and shoved Samuel one-handed. You haven't seen my new apartment. Oh, man. Bradshaw moved me out of The Manse and into a penthouse.

Yeah?

Oh yeah. He opened the doors, and they went through. It was bright enough that they winced, Samuel covering his eyes.

Forgot I was drunk.

Aaron grinned. Steiner was just ducking into a mongrel with Travis in the backseat. The engine turned over, and Steiner headed to K, turned west and drove out of sight. On the way north a couple with a child between them stopped Aaron and asked how he was. Stopped by another citizen a block later. Samuel went a few paces ahead and leaned against a wall. Wind scooped down from the north, and the clouds parted long enough for a beam of light to cross the street. Aaron turned away from the civilian and Samuel saw his grin drop, and they continued north to 13th and P. Aaron unlocked a door to one of the newer buildings in the city. The lights were bright and the floor polished limestone. They climbed the stairs to the penthouse, and he opened the door, waving Samuel in.

It's all right if you're jealous. I understand. He flourished to the open room. The ceilings were high, the walls bare, slight antishadows where pictures had hung. White tile, a fireplace. A granite countertop in the kitchen was covered in bottles of shine, half-gone. Past the kitchen a set of French doors led out to a balcony and a view of the street. They could see The Inn, the university grounds to the north. He put his face to the glass of the doors. The city sprawled, block after block, a palette of gray and brick.

I've never been up this high.

Aaron laughed. We gotta get you to the top of The Capitol, then.

Samuel made to turn his head, but did not. Below, on 12th, two Light workers had stopped their trucks and leaned out of their windows to talk. They were twinned, opposite, opposite and exact plumes of exhaust fogging behind them. He left the glass, scanned the bare room. You don't have any furniture.

Aaron shrugged and smiled. None of it seemed to fit. He

waved Samuel into the kitchen and got two glasses from a shelf. He set out a bottle of apple brandy and raised another bottle. Fella in one of the last towns gave this to me. Sorghum whiskey, he said. I traded him some high proof for it. Had to ask what sorghum was. I figured it was candy.

I'll drink whatever.

He poured two glasses half full of the whiskey and handed Samuel his, turning to the room. When they started renovating this building, they found a big drum right there— He pointed. Apparently someone'd burned all the old furniture to keep warm.

Do you have a bed, at least?

At Johanna's. By the time I feel like sleeping I don't wanna climb all these stairs.

Samuel rolled his eyes, turned away before his jaw hardened. He took a drink and set the glass on the counter before putting his back to it and looking out at the skyline. All this for batting your eyelashes.

Jealous don't become you. Aaron raised his glass and drank deep. They were quiet for a minute, and Aaron tipped his head south. That's the first time I ever saw somethin' like that. It was his buddy, Hurst. He held up intertwined fingers. Those two used to be like this.

I didn't mean to make you see it.

He waved a hand in front of him. No, it's okay. It just made me think. He turned back from the doors and drained the glass to a quarter. Hard to believe I didn't see much death where I'm from, but I didn't. Not much. Not like that. Sickness, mostly. And that ain't the same.

No.

Hit him real hard. Hard enough to make him bleed. Little puddle running to the gutter, like anything, like rain. You don't think about that, do you? People walking around out there. You don't think about what it takes to keep 'em moving, alive.

I do, sometimes.

He looked at the glass in his hand, then at Samuel. It doesn't take much to turn you inside out. He moved to the counter to refill it, poured it full, and halted, holding the bottle. You think we're special things, special beings. But you take something away, and we're just. He gestured again. He drank.

Samuel reached for his own glass. Outside the clouds grew thicker. I think you oughta at least bring your chairs in here.

Aaron ignored him. He was staring at the floor. Did you feel anything when you killed that deputy? What was it like?

He was slow to speak. No. You mean like when he died? Did I know?

I don't know. I guess. I guess I can't wrap my head around how simple it is—he held out a hand—and how huge it is. I don't know how it can be that way. Do you know, did you feel when it happened? It seems like you ought to feel it.

You do. The heart stops.

Aaron swallowed nothing.

Samuel drank his whiskey down by half. When I first found Red, out there in the desert, I couldn't sleep. For two weeks after. Maybe a nod here and there. Then one day Red asked me what I'd done. He made me show him where I'd stuck the knife—Samuel put two fingers to his ribs, mid-chest—and he told me what had happened. That I probably'd nicked the heart or the descending aorta, and his lung, and he bled out. Knowing what I'd done, exactly, it took the weight off. I could sleep.

Aaron rubbed his nose, eyes shut. So I was thinking I'd go raid that store, the big one past The Bottoms. Get some barstools here for the counter. Some real fancy couch in front of the fireplace.

6

Toward evening the clouds descended, and when the lights came on there was no change in the brightness of the city, only the hue. Readying to go out, he stopped by the window at the sight of Aaron and Gil coming down Q. They spotted him and waved, both drunk. He met them on the sidewalk, Aaron grinning. The smell of a bar preceded them, weed and beer.

We're your backup this evening. Gonna help you stamp out all this tea floating around.

Did you ever stop drinking? Samuel glanced away, a mongrel coming.

I'm no quitter. Aaron spun north, overspun, and corrected. Lead the way.

Samuel stared at them both. The mongrel parked across the street and Rogan rolled down the window and waved Samuel over.

We found those Mexicans. Want you to talk to them.

Samuel turned back to Aaron and Gil. Sorry boys. He opened the door. Maybe next time.

Hey, I speak español. Aaron spread his arms. Yo, tequila más, por favor.

Samuel got in the car, and Rogan turned around in the street, Aaron and Gil already going inside The Remedy.

I interrupt a date?

You saved my liver.

Rogan smiled. Gotta watch that Aaron. Boy has a hollow leg. They drove toward The Capitol, waited at O for pedestrians. Good kid, though. Lush or not.

Samuel nodded, turned to the window. Rogan stopped the mongrel at the west entrance, and Samuel got out. He glanced back at Rogan, got a nod, and went in. A guard pointed him toward the basement stairwell, and Samuel followed his direction. At the foot of the steps he heard a shout, and Samuel saw Steiner ducking into a room from a narrow hallway. Bare pipes ran overhead, popping with heat. The door was shut when Samuel came to it, and opening it he saw two teenagers sitting together in the back of the room, chairs and a table with a plate of crackers and water on it in front of them. The boy had a shaved head and three blue, sunblown tattoos on his arms. The girl stood and she reached her hand out in front of the boy, staring Samuel down. Samuel looked to Steiner, and stepped forward.

Cálmate. Cómo estás?

The girl mugged at him. Muy bien.

Samuel waited. The boy looked at his arms and crossed them as though he would hide the tattoos. Samuel pointed. Puedo ver tus brazos?

The girl curled her lips. Fuck you.

I want to help you, but you need to talk. He cocked his head. Estás en el cartel o viniste a causa de el?

No. No sé por qué.

The boy had yet to make eye contact. Samuel sidestepped and stooped to his height. Y tú? He said nothing. Descuida, no somos malos.

The girl's stare went fiery. Oh? Entonces por qué andan sus trocas tirando para nosotros? You think I don't know?

No hay drogas. Yo acabo con ellas.

She laughed. The boy rocked slightly. Samuel held his arms out toward him.

Sus brazos. He turned them palms-up. The boy watched from the corner of his eye, and when Samuel reached for his wrists he whirled at him and Samuel ducked.

Aléjate de mí!

Steiner crossed the room with a step and pinned the boy against the wall. Don't fuck with my man. He stared at him and the girl and took a step back, the boy dropping to his feet. Samuel took his wrists and turned them upward. Partly hidden in the blue ink of his tattoos were trackmarks pitted in the soft underside of his arms. He grimaced and let go, then pointed toward the girl.

Methamphetamina o heroin?

Los dos. Meth, principalmente.

Quién les vendió?

No se. Un hombre.

Describen.

She looked at the ceiling. Era alto, con pelo castaño. Un poco gordo. She waved her hand by her face to dismiss the description.

Okay. Samuel sighed. La troca, cuando la viste?

Cuatro, hace cinco días?

Y la troca, tenían un símbolo de—he held up a fist—puño y rayo?

She nodded. Samuel stood up and put a hand through his hair. He turned to Steiner. They aren't from the cartel. They're just kids on the run.

Is that all they said?

She said we sold them drugs, in another town. From a P&L truck.

Steiner glanced at the girl. We lost a truck a couple months ago. Someone got a hold of it while one of the boys was raiding a store for Light supplies. He glanced back and forth across the room, sighed, and swept a hand to the door. All right. Send 'em off.

Samuel looked at the pair. Vayanse.

The girl hesitated a moment and touched the boy's back. He seemed to come to life, and they filed past Steiner and out into the corridor. Samuel was watching Steiner, reading him.

It's no wonder we've got so many addicts these days.

We're making them.

You know better than that, Sam. It don't take much to turn moonshine to gas.

He looked at the door, some noise coming down the hall. Someone in the city is awful good at keeping them supplied. Sounds about like another recruitment program. Whoever the faces don't get, the tea will.

Now you're just talking out your ass.

He shrugged. The door opened and Bradshaw stood in its place, scanned the room.

Where are they?

Let 'em go. Sam interrogated them. They're on the run from the cartel themselves.

Bradshaw rolled his neck. Is that all you thought to ask?

Samuel turned to square with him. They said someone in a Light truck was selling drugs. The boy was in withdrawals.

Hell, less the grand theft, I call that entrepreneurship. How about where the cartel is? You ask them that? How many there are?

I didn't need to ask. The answer is 'nearly everywhere' and 'so many it doesn't matter.' You aren't going to fight the whole cartel if they get a mind to come at us.

Bradshaw breathed, looked at Steiner. Speaking of fighting—

Steiner stopped him. Look. That was a fight your boys started. Everyone was drinking, everyone was off the clock. He's been reporting in regularly, just like I asked him.

I don't care about what line he's toeing now. Bradshaw pushed a hand toward Samuel. I know it was you. Who you plan on killing next?

I plan on going to bed, after this. If there are some Light boys in my way, though, I won't make any guarantees.

You hear that, Al?

I'm standing right here. Quit being such a queen.

Bradshaw stuck a finger into Samuel's chest. I've got two

witnesses from that night say you're the one that pulled the trigger. We may not have a court of law yet, but I figure letting Beth and Norton hear all the evidence against you ought to be good enough.

I would have taken the rap for Red. I told him as much. Samuel looked across to Steiner. But he did it. He was protecting me.

We've heard this before. Am I supposed to believe your account, or two unbiased witnesses?

Unbiased? Samuel laughed.

Shut up. Steiner cut in. Sam, get. Lester and me will talk this out.

Samuel shifted from the wall, watching Bradshaw and passing slowly, waiting for a move. He went through the corridor to the stairs and left the building. There were a few people still about. Doors here and there shutting behind drunks, a man asleep on the stoop of a church. He passed under a low skywalk coming onto O Street and saw through a restaurant window, mopping.

Aaron was asleep in Samuel's apartment stairwell. He rose up, blinked. Hey. Evenin'.

You all right?

Ah. Johanna kicked me out.

You know you got an apartment of your own. I just saw it. Samuel glanced over his shoulder, into the night.

All them steps, though. Aaron shrugged.

Come on. Up.

No, hold on. He slid up the wall and shook himself out. I wanted to talk to you. Let's go for a drink. Just one round.

The bolt struck Samuel and let off, his hackles sitting. It's late, bud.

One drink. Aaron scooped his arm around Samuel and spun him out onto the sidewalk. They headed east, for Norton's. Leavin' the day after tomorrow, and she tosses me out.

You'll be back in a few days.

Still. It's not like it's a vacation. It's a job, and the world ain't so kind.

Samuel carried his weight, off the curb and onto it, past 8th, on to 9th.

I'm worried about Travis, Sam. He swung his head, loose. What makes you do that? His best friend.

Drugs.

Aaron shook his head. Nothin' gets you that high.

The rest of the walk was quiet, and Aaron let off Samuel's shoulder. They ducked down the alley to Norton's and found it desolate. The bartender was gone, and Maggie and Detch sat elbow to elbow, Detch nodding. He leaned closer at their entrance.

We'll take care of you. You don't need to worry about them coming 'round.

You don't know. Maggie scooted in on her stool, chin over her glass. She was pale, and her eyes seemed weighted and dark. Aaron steered Samuel to the bar, and Samuel tried to pull them away to a booth, and Aaron broke off and sat on Maggie's left.

Hey, folks. Where's the barkeep?

We've been helping ourselves. Detch stretched over the counter and lifted a bottle of shine and slid it down the bartop. Aaron twisted off the spigot and drank, handed the bottle to Samuel. Detch leaned back past Maggie. You all see that jukebox, there? He pointed.

What? Aaron took the bottle back and moved away from the counter. I'll be damned. Does it work?

Maggie fixed it. It's got records and everything.

She looked into her drink.

Samuel watched her. Why aren't you playing it?

Detch shrugged. We were talking, let it run down.

Aaron went over to the machine, puzzling. Okay, what do you—

Quarter in the coin return. Maggie framed her brow with

a hand, sunk lower. Samuel was a seat down and he spun forward in the stool. He drank from the bottle. The jukebox clanked and Aaron held his hands up. A song began.

Oh, that is something. Oh, listen to that. He beamed. He came back to them and put an arm around Maggie and hugged her close. Samuel saw her smile in the mirror. The jukebox produced a guitar, a ratcheting sound he couldn't place, a croon. Aaron let her go and turned to the bottle, slugged, slapped Samuel's back, and climbed the stairs for the bathroom.

He's got the right idea. Detch stood and followed after him. Samuel and Maggie were quiet. The song kept on, a woman joining the man singing.

I'm clean.

She hadn't moved. Samuel looked at her to be sure she'd spoken.

This is 48 hours. About 48 hours. Not even a whiff.

That's good. That's really good.

Thank you. She drank from her glass. She lifted her chin to swallow, with difficulty. I'm sorry you got roiled up with the boys.

It's part of living here, I feel like. They'll just never leave me be.

It was my fault. Well, really it's my dad's fault. But you could blame most things on him, if you wanted to. You wouldn't be far from wrong.

Samuel smiled. I do not like your dad. I hope that's all right.

It is. She smiled back, the corners of her mouth flattened. They could see Aaron coming, Detch right behind him. They both arranged themselves straight, perpendicular to the counter. Aaron clapped him on the back again.

Pick you a song, Sam. That is some kind of glorious. Heard it up in the bathroom when she really started to wail. Chills. He grinned, glanced into the mirror. Samuel smiled back and pushed the bottle for him to take. The door opened and one of the regular bartenders walked in with a man in P&L overalls. Detch was beside Aaron at the corner of the bar and he turned to face them. They came on, the bartender slipping behind the counter and the P&L man turning his head, watching Detch from the corner of his eye. He stood beside Maggie.

You doing okay? Lester was worried about you. Hadn't seen you in a bit.

I'm fine. He doesn't need to worry about me.

Maggie? Detch put his arm on the bar. Let's go. I made up a room for you.

She's got her own room, in her own house. The P&L man stared Detch down.

I can figure out where I want to go. She got up, broke through them both, pedaling away from them like she was seeing something else. She turned and began to trot to the exit, slowed, and walked out the door.

Jesus. The P&L cocked his head. You can take her dress shopping tomorrow, buddy. I had orders. He advanced on Detch, and Detch sidestepped but squared with him.

She told me what you're up to. I'm looking out for her.

Listen here, you nigger son of a bitch. He pushed Detch, throwing him back, and Samuel grabbed the man's nearest wrist and curled it in his fist and brought it to the bar top.

Detch, I'll give you a couple hits for that.

Fuck him, Sam. Fuck you, pal. Detch pointed, threw his arm in the air and turned away. I'm gonna try to catch up with her. He went out, the door slamming closed.

Aaron put his hand on Samuel's shoulder. Maybe let go of the guy's arm, Sam.

Samuel locked eyes with the P&L man. Watch your mouth.

The man jerked his wrist out of Samuel's lock and pushed away from him, nearly tripping over a stool. You know, I heard all the talk about you and that other heel. But I hadn't decided you were an asshole until just now.

You're breaking my heart. Samuel turned from him, reaching for the bottle already in Aaron's hand. Aaron drank, set the bottle down.

Did you want to go after them?

I doubt that would de-escalate the situation.

He shrugged, looked past Samuel at the bartender, the P&L man now at the end of the bar. Another day in the life, huh?

They left shortly after. Samuel led them up his stairs, unlocked the door, and moved aside for Aaron to come in. All I've really got is the chairs, unless you wanna sleep in the tub.

Did that once. Wrenched my back and knocked a bar of soap on my head in the middle of the night. Hurt.

Well. Samuel pulled the chairs from the table and set them across from each other. Aaron stood looking at them, his eyes drooping.

Should've had more to drink.

Should have punched that Light boy. Samuel threw Aaron a thin sleeping bag from under the bed, a pillow right after.

I can feel it lurking. Aaron set the pillow up against a chairback. This'd be one of those blubbering drunk nights if I'd had a few more sips.

Lucky for me.

Lucky for you. Some of us are human. I need to vent, every so often.

Samuel dropped onto the bed, kicked off his boots. The lights were still on, and he shaded his eyes with his forearm, let out a low sigh. Aaron was shifting in the chair, adjusting the sleeping bag. Samuel rolled over, rolled back. We're doing a good thing, building this city, right?

What? Yeah, man. Just look around you. Who do you see other than us that has electricity? Cars? Women walking around like they aren't afraid to take you home at night?

But there's a lot of people getting hurt along the way. Maggie's a perfect example. The girl who OD'd, and you know she's not the only one. Travis and Hurst.

Look. Aaron rocked his head from side to side. It's not the simplest way of living, but people are happy here. Living better than they have been in years. If you want to weigh that against dead drug addicts, be my guest. But we didn't invent the habit, man. It just followed us here.

It's a sickness, not a habit.

I never got a cold by choice.

He sighed. Is that it, though? We're doing all this so people can have booze again?

What are you looking for? Hope? God?

I don't know. I don't believe in him. I guess I just don't believe that we can let ten people get crushed at the fringes so that a thousand can live happily. I don't like that math. Pain is heavier than comfort.

It must be a lovely world inside your head. Aaron smirked.

It's very clean.

He laughed. Samuel stood, groaning, went over to the lightswitch and put them in the dark. Streetlight framed Samuel and boxed across the ceiling.

You see that, bud? Everywhere else, you don't get to know what's outside your wall.

Samuel sighed. Back when I had to leave home, when I killed that deputy, you know, it haunted me, like I said. But it wasn't because I thought I'd done something wrong. It was just because I'd taken a life—the gravity of that, right? But it was what I had to do. That's my problem. None of this is something we had to do. You can argue Travis was gonna get hooked on tea and kill someone with or without 8th Street's help, but we're involved in it. It's our mess. There's a book over your shoulder, there, on physics. Half physics, anyway. I hardly understand it. Read it backward and forward. Samuel went back to his bed and slumped, elbows on his knees. It talks about how you never really made a choice in your life, because when you break it down, we're all just atoms. The stuff happening in our brains, me talking to you, is just chemistry, physics. If you examined us under a microscope, nothing about what I'm saying would have a message or meaning. It would just be sound waves moving the air, the cells in your ear. And your brain listening to me is just emitting the electricity it should when it hears those waves. And it talks about this thing called entanglement.

Do what, now?

It just means all our atoms are related, whether they seem like it or not. They're tangled up with each other, affecting each other. I don't know. I'm tired. It bothers me. I think about not having a choice, and it bothers me, and having a choice bothers me. Those hobos live out in the cold by choice, because of their crazy-ass religion. But we come along and get them hooked, let them stay hooked. Get drunk, jaked, killed. I let them. Nobody's holding a gun to our neck saying we've got to have streetlights on, and we've got to let people fall to hell. Restart the whole cycle. Melt the glaciers again.

Oh— Aaron put his hands to his face, moaning. My atoms cry out for libation.

Quit it.

We're all here by choice, Sammy. We all came here because we wanted to. If we got here and we decided getting high all day was what we wanted to do with our time, well, god bless us, we can. Stupidity ain't your fault.

Stupid doesn't have to be this easy.

What made you so saintly? Jesus appear in your beer foam?

No. Samuel shook his head in the dark. It was my dad. He was always trying to help people. To a fault. My mom was a little more practical, but it never quite rubbed off on me.

Listen to your momma. Aaron sighed. This would have been way more fun with some high proof. I'm just sayin'. I could'a waxed philosophical, too.

Some time went by before the door below opened. Footsteps, hard heels, coming up the stairs. A cold wash of adrenaline swept through Samuel and he couldn't move fast enough to get through his apartment door, to get up. She was already there, knocking, by chance.

Aaron's chair skidded. Someone's here. You want me to answer it?

What? He sat up, speaking a little loud. Aaron's hand lit on the doorknob and then the skipping of Johanna running downstairs and the door slamming shut.

The hell? Aaron went over to the window. Did I scare off your girlfriend?

Samuel rose from the bed and pretended at sluggishness. His hands were shaking. Didn't know I had one.

The room bright come morning. Aaron slept turned in on himself, head in his elbow. Samuel got up and showered. After a few minutes, Aaron knocked on the bathroom door and said goodbye through it. For a while the water just ran.

He ate breakfast downstairs, and Gil passed outside the window, looked in, and opened the door. Samuel finished his eggs as Gil leaned on the counter beside him. His eyes were dark. He lifted his chin for Sheila and pointed at the coffee pot. When she brought him a mug he took it and drank and twisted on the stool to look at Samuel. A long sigh.

Al told me to go with you, on patrol. He thought I could learn a thing or two from you.

That sounds bad. Am I off probation or getting fired?

Gil raised an eyebrow. I don't know anything about it.

Well. Samuel looked at him. Just do whatever you didn't do running O Street.

Please hold your grudge a little quieter, whatever it's about.

Samuel smiled. I would have thought you'd be better at playing ignorant, with all the practice you get.

When Red killed Graham? How could we have done anything?

Samuel turned back to his plate. He folded a piece of bacon in half. Possibilities are endless. You could have helped cover, could have told us there were P&L boys in the house. That they were all packing, for god knows what reason.

I didn't know about them having guns. All I knew was that they throw parties north of The Bottoms sometimes. If you want to be a fool about it, that's your business. But you're back and Steiner wants me to step up. So help me out.

Samuel stuffed the piece of bacon in his mouth and finished his coffee. He thanked Sheila, and Gil followed him. They started south on 8th.

What happened to your face?

Nobody told you?

I thought it'd be politer to ask.

They crossed under O Street and kept on until Samuel cut west through the lot to walk the edge of The Singles. A wind blew heavy across their backs, unbroken by buildings or trees.

Where're we headed?

Hobo jungle. They drink a lot of jake. If we find a lead on jake, we might find a lead on all this tea coming in. They might even know the guy I'm looking for.

Who's that?

Ex-P&L shit called Fish. I asked you and Rogan about him yesterday.

They were coming up on the gravel company. Someone had climbed one of the flattened mounds of sand and the steps were small and the stride short. A child playing. They passed alongside the fence and then picked up the trail north, woodsmoke in the wind. Through the trees Samuel could make out the light of the fire. They neared the camp and he led them around the fence, stepping over a flattened section. The preacher was at the fire and he had seen them. He turned and spoke and two others came out from their tents while another retreated into one. At the circle Samuel raised his hand and whispered aside to Gil.

Try to keep your mouth shut.

The preacher pointed at them with a blackened stick. Since when do you work for O Street?

Gil works for me. Got promoted.

The two others came close to the fire. The wind snapped it to the ground, smoke billowing and dissolving across the field.

I wanted to ask if you had any visits from a guy named Fish, or anyone new selling jake.

One of the other hobos looked to another and whispered. The preacher jutted his chin forward. Nope.

No, you haven't seen him, or no, nobody new?

No nothing. Don't like the looks of you. And I don't like the looks of him.

I'm friends with Raj. He'll vouch for me.

He's a whore. He'll befriend anyone that buys him a drink.

Samuel narrowed his eyes, pointing at a shopping cart piled with empty shine bottles. And you won't? That's not why you're out here? Living off us?

The preacher shook his head slowly. We pick what we can, from time to time. Don't mean we owe you anything.

I'm not saying you do.

Don't matter. We're out here livin' how we can because it's sinful livin' in there. He pointed toward the city. You settin' foot can't be anything good.

We're gonna be out here more often if you don't help us now. Pestering you. Maybe put up a couple houses, ruin your view.

Well. I like a audience.

Samuel eyed the preacher for a moment, the others at the fire, then turned and headed for the fence. Gil wound around a tree and caught up to him after they crossed over the wire.

That's it?

I don't exactly have a lot of leverage over them.

So what now?

You want to help me out? He turned and pointed back to The Jungle. Post up here, and wait for someone to walk by. If he's not a bum, shake him down. See if he's got jake or tea and see where he got it. Two to one he's a dealer.

They were coming near O Street, and Samuel turned. To the west the street went on for over a mile, lined with abandoned gas stations and garages, restaurants with broken signs, signs fallen like trees. A P&L truck honked twice and drove around them and gunned over the bridge.

What are you gonna do?

They started up the bridge, taking the sidewalk. Go for a stroll. He pointed below them, at The Singles.

Can I put an O Streeter on it and come along with you?

You could. I'd prefer going solo.

It's just I want to get it right. You got Steiner in a twist, with whatever you said. He thought I was slacking off somewhere instead of doing my job.

Samuel turned to him. Weren't you?

No. I mean, maybe I wasn't out as much as I should have been, but you also got a less liberal view of things than me.

He hooked his thumb on his beltloop. There's nothing to this, Gil. You wear out your shoes, you find people. That's it. If you don't do the first part, you don't get the second. I can tell nobody's been out walking the streets because there's sign everywhere. They just smoke and sell out in the open. The P&L boys that use are more open about it, too. It wouldn't be in the charter if 8th Street thought it was harmless.

Gil said nothing. He was looking away. There should be some boys at the garage, if we can stop off, put them on The Jungle.

They cut back below the bridge to 8th. Passing the old

power substation and The Still, the gate wide at The Bone-yard. The dump truck squatted out front of the main garage. They worked their way through the wrecks and scraps of old cars. A young man pried the headlights from a coupe beside them. The bay doors hung half-open as they rounded the corner of the garage, two men contemplating the exposed engine of a truck. Rogan held off to the side with one arm greased in oil up to his elbow.

Hey fellas. You need something?

Gil pointed to the men. One of them lazy bastards, there. Do some recon for me.

Samuel looked off into the depths of the yard. Gil and the others were laughing. The fence at the back was lined with fiberglass sheeting, two crows on the top line of barbwire, heads quirked. He walked off, away from the O Streeters. He could see their blinking, the blanking of the gray light from their eyes. From near the corner of the yard, metal scraped on metal. He skimmed the path between dismantled wagons and saw three men drop a radiator to the ground.

Sam, you ready? I got hilljack and dipshit on the case, over there.

He turned. Gil was thumbing at the garage, the men cleaning off with rags.

You know we could take one of these heaps out, if you like.

Samuel passed him, nodding to Rogan on the way. You gotta get used to walking at some point. You don't see as much from a car.

They went west out of The Boneyard, taking the first street they came to and passing the remains of the plant. The chain-link fence warped and bowed like wood, dried weeds woven through like a basket. Engines revved to the east.

I guess you knocked Reese's jaw loose. Has to drink his meals.

Sorry to hear that.

You learned all this just wandering around? How'd you end up with Red in the first place?

Samuel scratched at his jaw. Killed a couple guys. Ran so I wouldn't get thrown in jail or hung. Found Red.

You serious?

Yeah. He pointed to the first row of homes on 3rd. They crossed an empty lot toward them.

That's some shit. Gil blew. I just came here because my town was falling apart.

Samuel raised his hand to cut him off. He stepped over the wires of a sagging fence and waited on Gil at the curb that formed the border of the neighborhood, rounding off into the northeast to meet the gravel company. Signs of life he was unused to, paths between homes wearing into the grass, leaves swept off porches. Lamps alight in the day. No one was about, and they wandered, crossing the lettered streets back and forth, until Samuel stopped them, pointing at a spot of withered grass beside a back door.

Watch for dead patches like that. That's where someone's been pissing jake. He started ahead, but before they reached the end of the block, the door to the jake house opened, and Heather stumbled out, gathering her coat about herself and swinging her shotgun.

I thought I said not to come around here?

Samuel gave a look to Gil. Listen, Calamity. If I thought you were doing your job right, I wouldn't come out to your beat.

She strode down the steps of the house and out of the yard. She bore down on Samuel, gripping the barrel of the shotgun in her left hand. Gil stepped between them, arms out.

I apologize for him, Heather. He insults me all the time, too.

She hovered a few paces away. Her eyes were red, and shine wafted from her clothing. I know your type, Parrish. You were born important and you think that lasts forever.

That's surprisingly lucid coming from someone that would explode if you shook 'em.

Heather narrowed her eyes.

Gil hung his head, cracking a smile. You guys want to keep flirting or should we get back to work?

We do fine by ourselves. We don't need anyone stirring up trouble.

Samuel feigned with his hands. All right. You just come to me when you need a mess cleaned up. He walked past her. Gil said something to her, and then he was beside Samuel. Through the branches and dead wires overhead the sky was getting darker. They went on silently, out of The Singles and back onto 8th.

We'll head north, have a look in around the park.

Sure. Gil nodded.

In The Haymarket they worked through the passing civilians, a fair bustle in the few stores. They ducked inside The Inn, wandered a few floors. Outside they patrolled north to the pedestrian bridge, and Samuel looked out over the trickle of water. Below them the rails gathered, then parted to the northeast. A dull boom echoed from past the highway, the bend of the creek. Nearly half a mile down the bank was the granary station. He watched, set his hand on the butt of the knife. Gil was silent and stepped up to the railing. A mongrel pulled into the lot at the mouth of the bridge, and a door slammed. Vince Harrawood approached, climbed the incline, and stood beside them.

Never thought I'd see you out in the cold, Gil. He ribbed him with an elbow and looked to Samuel. How much you make him walk?

Some. Samuel sized him up, the angle of his hip, hand resting on his belt.

Hold him to it. I think half the reason Steiner promoted him was 'cause he was worried about the man's health.

Boy, leadership's turned you into an ass, huh? Gil feigned

to slap at Harrawood's face, and Harrawood caught his hand and twisted it, spun Gil around. Jesus, man.

Samuel backed up a step. He peered at the granary, pointed. You know if we're lighting up over the creek?

Harrawood shook his head, still holding Gil in a lock. Actually, yeah. I think we might be stringing lights for a warehouse. Diversify our shine storage. He let go of Gil and pushed him away. Go on about your business. I just can't walk by Finley here without giving him shit.

Samuel raised his chin. Sure. He gave a low wave and looked at Gil. Harrawood got back in the mongrel and drove off.

Gil flung his arm forward, worked his shoulder. He is one son of a bitch.

More like two stuffed into one asshole.

Gil smiled. They went quiet, the wind humming through the beams of the bridge. He turned to Samuel. So, where'd you guys usually find folks on the east side? That's what Steiner's giving me. Said east is a bit lighter. He squinted into the breeze. Split the territory at 13th. It's got a lot more people now.

You find dealers the places you'd expect. Low traffic areas, mainly, cover to run to. He stopped. How'd you end up in charge of O Street if you didn't know this sort of thing?

First on the scene, I guess. I'm one of the early citizens. Wandered through with a family of pickers and never left.

Well. Let's quit for now. I'm gonna eat dinner and have a beer or two. If you want we can meet back up, look in on Heckle and Jeckle, or you can call it for the day.

I'll come along. For dinner, too, if you don't mind.

Inside they slipped off their coats and ordered burgers and beer. Johanna sat at a window, looking out. Gil drank one quickly and got another, waving to an O Streeter and two Still workers as they came in. Detch followed soon after and took his seat in the corner. The diner filled with a muttering.

You like this work?

Samuel nodded. As much as I like anything.

Gil took a sip of his new beer. If you hadn't killed those two guys, what would you be doing?

His eyes narrowed, then let off. He opened a hand on the counter, away from his mug. That kinda determined everything after. He glanced off and back, took a drink. Everything would be different. Guess I'd farm. It's what my dad did.

You couldn't just start over? There's other places to be than here.

He groaned, head cocked back. Did the only thing I thought I could. And I like it here. He looked out the window. It was almost dark, the lights about to flicker on. Their glasses refilled. They ate and stacked their plates, had another round. Johanna got up and left, passing quickly across the window toward the stairwell door. Samuel drained his beer and patted the countertop beside the glass. I had a surprisingly decent time with you, Gil.

Yeah, me too. You ain't such a prick after all.

He smiled. You aren't such a dumbass. Still lazy, though.

Hey, we can go for a patrol. I'm up for it.

Samuel rose. I'm not. He went out. He thought he could smell her on the wind, in the cold from the north. She met him at the door of the apartment, still in her coat.

I think we should tell him now.

What?

He'll leave in the morning, and he'll have the trip to occupy him, let him cool down.

The beer drained from his head. He stepped in and shut the door. That seems like cheating.

This is cheating. This is us, cheating. We have feelings for each other and we sleep together, and we miss each other when we're not around, right? Johanna breathed deep and turned to the window. It's getting so that I can't deal with him. It makes my stomach turn. I want to be with you.

What changed? What changed from that night?

It was one night. One night when you were scared and you needed me. You can't blame me for not leaving the city with that to go on. She turned to him. I thought all we had was that night, and that I was comforting you, and that would have been enough. I could think about it, sometimes, and life here would go on. But then you came back. They stood a few feet apart. He's probably gonna come by to see you, too. I shouldn't be anywhere near here. I just had to see you. I had to talk to you.

You'll leave him, then? What will we do?

Be together. She smiled, tense. He could see the idea unfurling in her eyes. This could be our city, our home.

He shook his head slightly. He sighed. I don't want to tell him. Not now. He'll be out there on the road with nothing to think about but us. He'll stew in it. It doesn't seem fair, to leave him without any say.

She frowned. Maybe.

He'll be back in four days. We'll wait, and we'll tell him then.

She came toward him, kissed his cheek and passed him for the stairs. He felt out of time, his hands reaching to hold her too late, moving to the window too late to see her go up the block. Now the room was dark and cold. Glyphs of streetlight coming in through the glass. He went to his bookshelf and drew out a book, but a horn bleated before he turned a page. Aaron standing in the open sunroof of a recovered limousine, waving him down. Samuel went out, and Aaron was still sticking up through the roof of the car.

C'mon, we gotta party it up before I go.

I'm not done healing from the last time.

No Light boys. In fact, we're trying something new. Roving bar. He ran his hand over the limo roof. Rogan and Steiner fixed it up for special occasions. You, me, and Jo. Just picked her up.

Samuel glanced sidelong at him and smiled, climbing in. You still cashing in on your town?

Aaron ducked back to the interior and closed the sunroof. Johanna was seated in the front beside him. That's my big score. Bradshaw gets on his knees every time he sees me. Makin' Johanna jealous.

Hawkins was in the driver seat, and he passed a bottle back through the front panel to them. Where next?

Iowa, for all I care. We can roll out to my assignments in this rig. That'll turn heads.

I'm not sitting through your speech again. Samuel took the bottle from him and tilted it back. The limo ground into motion and they pulled out onto the street, turning wide. Old upholstery covered the interior, and there was a rough wooden rack for bottles of shine mounted on one side. Hawkins took them on O Street, and they headed east. Sleet dotted the windshield, dried out before they passed 13th.

I had Finley in tow all day today.

Aaron lifted an eyebrow. Oh, so you'll take him on patrol, but not me?

Never took me, either. Johanna reached for the bottle. I don't get to have any fun.

Samuel handed it over. You want me to ask Steiner if I can start a junior heel brigade? Get you some sashes and pocketknives?

Aaron laughed, rubbed Johanna's knee. Samuel closed his eyes, turned to look away.

She smiled. Could be fun, yeah.

They passed the bottle back and forth, up to Hawkins, and the limo kept on. He circled them around the lit parts of town, and they watched the people on the sidewalks slow and stare after them.

Who'd have thought we'd end up here, you know? Aaron leaned forward, holding the bottle. If you told me I'd be a thousand miles from where I was born and riding in a limo, hell, two years ago, I'd call you a crazy man. I don't know that I thought I'd see anything like this when I got on that train. Not again. Aaron sat back, stretched. Something's been bothering me, though. For a little while.

Samuel met Johanna's eye.

Music. Hearing Maggie's jukebox. We need us some music in this town. Get a radio station going. Wouldn't that be great? Radios in everyone's rooms.

Johanna smiled at him, a little tight. Cruise with the stereo on, top down in the summer?

Aaron leaned over and kissed her. Her eyes pinched shut. That's right. My dad loved music. Had a computer with just thousands of songs. Big speakers. Losing all that music to the aurora just about killed him. He put his head to the window, staring through the tinted glass, up between the buildings. When we're in charge, man. We'll start bringing things back. Maybe our kids'll get to fly planes. See rockets go up.

Samuel gave a soft chuckle. He took another drink and gave the bottle back.

Hawkins brought the limo past The Capitol and onto O Street. They drove east, into the dark. Aaron had him pull over so they could take turns pissing in an alley. They were drunk, and settling into the limo again, Samuel's head spun. The bottle of shine went from foot to foot, rolling. The last of the buildings shrank away, and the trees clustered and then opened up to the country. Johanna leaned against Aaron and she set the bottle between them, running low. He was whispering in her ear. Samuel faced away but watched them, watched her mouth, the turn of her lips, and then he looked out, their headlights skating over an empty highway. Aaron finished the bottle of shine and dropped it over to Hawkins' side of the car.

Can we get the lights off back here?

Hawkins reached for a switch, and the lights went out. The stark outline of a glass house, black timber and hollow walls on a rise, the sky through it gray, perhaps moonlit. They took an exit and Hawkins swung the car down and they turned back. Against the dashboard lights Samuel saw Aaron put his arms around her. He could feel the air growing warmer. He closed his eyes.

7

It was late afternoon when he woke. He peeled the pillow from his temple and a shape there the color of a waterstain. The cut hurt faintly and more when he sat up and the blood pumped through it again. At the window he found leaves, dust blowing. The remains of a hangover thrummed in his head. He wasn't standing more than a minute before Gil came up 8th from the south, and Samuel went into the bathroom. He stripped and showered, turning his face away from the jet of water. The bruising on his stomach was dark, purple and yellow, a nebula of capillaries. When he cut the water he heard Gil knocking, and he wrapped a towel around his waist and opened the door.

Y'know, I'd like to be the guy that gets to sit around and wait to be called on, rather than the one doing all the calling.

Samuel rested a hand, clutching the towel at his stomach. Maybe you should be a face.

Gil gave a dull smirk, then sidestepped. I got a lead on that guy, Fish. You wanna come check it out with me?

Samuel studied him. Let me get dressed.

The sky was slate, clouds thinning. It felt like early morning but the clock down the street read 4:00. Gil took him south until K Street, and they went east.

What's this lead? Your boys find someone at The Jungle?

Ran into Rogan this morning. He said Vince has the boys out driving around. Found a place seems likely for a hideout. High traffic in the grass, fresh trash. Out in my territory, if you can believe it. You know where the cemetery is? For the longest time I didn't think this town even had one.

I know it. You couldn't get us a ride for that trip?

Gil glanced at him. You were the one said I needed to start walking.

They crossed 9th, and the city dump truck rolled by, headed toward The Bottoms, the tailgate up and suspension low. The neighborhood dropped to small, abandoned businesses. Lawyers offices with the paint still etched onto the glass, an unused bar. A barbershop, its pole stopped and color faded on the southern exposure.

You hear Bradshaw's been working at the theater? He fixed up one of the projectors, got everything wired. They're screening a movie tomorrow.

I saw the signs. What's playing?

No idea. But they brought everything from the university library, so they've got a lot to choose from. Gonna make it a big to-do.

They passed The Capitol. A mongrel waited at the west entrance, a driver Samuel couldn't quite see. The street wound southward, and they picked up J and continued east, past the school. Trees walled in the houses, numerous and same. Small yards. Pinned below the branches of a shrub lay a deflated ball, blue marbled. Dead traffic lights still hung over an intersection, and the pavement turned to brick. The empty houses grew. An engine sounded behind them, and the same mongrel from The Capitol passed on their left, honked twice, and turned north shortly after.

Was that Harrawood?

I didn't see. Gil shook his head.

Samuel stopped, listening. Gil went a few more paces before turning.

Something wrong?

The mongrel headed the way it had come. Samuel panned to follow the sound. Shit. It's the granary.

Do what? Sam, we're halfway there.

We've been had. They wanted to keep us out of the way.

What are you talking about? They who?

Samuel turned back. Gil called after him, and Samuel kept going, breaking into a run. He turned north at the next street. Hollow houses, narrow strips of pavement, blurs. The sun was setting and the clouds broke. He was on O Street at the eastern end of the lights before he heard another engine. A P&L truck idled in front of a diner, and he passed it quickly, head averted. He took the 180 overpass up near The Haymarket. Wide mud wheeltracks, several sets, dried under his feet. He followed them over and went east. The road dipped ahead, and in the depression a pool of water had formed and clouded. Across the creek the lights began to go up in the city. Half a mile on was the granary, the barrelfire and light he'd seen when going to Beth's. Samuel crossed wide of the pool and, closing on the granary, dropped into the creekbed for cover. The sky darkened, and over the bank he could barely see the tops of the nearest silos. He checked the knife and climbed up, sneaking to the back of the warehouse. The whole area was paved, and chunks of concrete had broken up and drifted like plates of earth. Grass grew and died in the gaps. At the corner of the warehouse, he saw the barrel and a trailer on blocks, its door boarded over. He went up the side of the building and listened. Voices, dragging metal on concrete. Heartbeat throbbing twice in his throat before he checked it, took the knife out, and rounded the last corner to the front. Orange light seeped from a crack under the door. He knocked. The door slid open on a track.

Didn't hear you roll up. You ready for the next load? The man in the entrance squinted, and Samuel saw it was Tover. Two small lamps shone in the middle of the warehouse and a halogen worklamp in a corner threw light across the room. Oh, shit.

He backpedaled, began to turn. Samuel decked him, and Tover fell back. Behind him were tables and boxes of glassware, decanters and flasks, hotplates. Crates of Mormon tea.

The thumbless cook dropped a box to put his hands in the air, the box crashing, spilling glass. A third man, Fish, stood in the open near the worklamp. Samuel stepped forward and raised the knife.

You're Fish, right? He reached back and found the door and ran it closed. Tover lurched and Samuel pushed him down with his boot. Samuel jabbed the knife toward the cook. Tell him I'll take his thumbs.

What? The cook jerked.

Tell him I'll do to him what I did to you. Probably worse.

The cook stammered. I wadn't makin' anything, I swear. Just— He cut his eyes to Fish. I'm just buying some jake. I ain't cooking anymore.

Fish stepped backward. He neared a table with a pair of heavy tongs, and he snatched it up. He lifted his free hand, palm forward. Look. Can't we settle this up? I'll cut you in on the vig if you forget about this.

You killed a girl. I won't forget.

What? I never killed no one.

Samuel kicked the nearest table over, glass sliding across the concrete floor like water. Before he brought his foot back, Fish flung the tongs at Samuel, skimming his beltbuckle, and then he felt the impact at his hips as Tover checked him from behind. He saw the cook and Fish squeeze through the door before Tover threw a wide punch and rose, and Samuel wrenched at his leg and Tover fell, his head rapping against the floor. Samuel got to his feet and rushed out the door, the pair off the concrete already and heading for the creek before Samuel could start after them. They split off, and Samuel chased Fish eastward, backlit by the city. He could hear the man's footsteps thudding across the dirt. Samuel gained quick, and Fish looked back and leapt, rolling down the bank to the creek. His first steps mired him in the sand, and Samuel flew a punch across his temple and dragged him to the ground by his jacket. He knelt on his chest. Fish's eyes watered, his face a mass of wrinkles, fighting the pain.

Listen, man. You're the heel, right? I know where all the dealers are. Everyone.

Samuel hit him again and leaned closer. That right?

All of 'em. I can show you the whole operation. He drew his hands in to shove Samuel back, but Samuel pushed his head down into the sand, weighing on it. He brought the knife to Fish's eye and he froze, staring wide. You don't know what's going on here. Please let me up. I'll talk. I want to talk.

He adjusted, bringing his elbow down on Fish's collar. Samuel's wrist was curled around and the knife hovered an inch above the man's face. Fish stared at the blade and away and to the sky.

So talk.

I'm up on the ladder, but you won't care about me once I tell you everything. It ain't me that's in charge. I ain't calling any shots.

Headlights swept the bank. Samuel reared back and struck Fish's chest. He brought the knife to Fish's eye again and a truck door slammed. The sand inches from their head blew, and a rifle reported from across the creek. Fish started, and the blade sank and Samuel rolled off him, whirling to see the far bank. Fish was struggling to his feet, his hands cupping his eye and he was grinning, nearly laughing, turning about.

It's still there! I can see!

Another gunshot, and Fish dropped to the ground. Samuel bolted for a bend in the water, stumbled and clawed himself upright, climbed the bank. Nothing on the far side now, just the shadows of tall weeds, the city behind. He climbed up to the bridge, his boots layered with silt, and clung to a girder, listening, watching. The body of Fish around the bend, lit by the glow off the clouds.

When he'd caught his breath, he trotted across the bridge into The Haymarket, keeping close to the buildings, shadows.

A P&L truck sat in front of The Remedy. He took R to 7th, and crossed the parking lot below the overpass, going west and south. Descending into The Singles there were only a few houses lit, a figure walking down M. On 3rd he passed the plant's guard shack, windows broken. An addict stuck his head through the blank pane, yelled at Samuel.

You holdin' down there?

Samuel swept his jacket aside to show him the knife and the man faded back. He went on a few paces and turned to find the addict from the window gripping half a brick and running at him. Samuel drew the knife and held it out like a saber. I know you got problems. Don't make me one of them.

The addict lowered his arm, dropped the brick. You don't have anything? He folded onto the pavement. Samuel went on. The man sobbed.

On H he crossed the old tracks and rose out of the warehouses into the dark residences. He went into Johanna's apartment building and found her door, knocked. She answered, her cheeks flushed and coat hanging off an arm.

I thought we might be avoiding each other for a while.

He frowned. I would have, but someone just tried to kill me. I need a place to get my bearings.

What? What happened? She pulled him inside and shut the door.

Were you going out?

I just got in. I had to have a drink.

He nodded and leaned up against the kitchen wall. I found a tea outfit north of The Haymarket, and the guy I've been hunting. I had him, but someone in a truck pulled up and shot at us. Killed him.

Do you know who it was?

I've got suspicions.

She moved past him, reaching above the refrigerator for the bottle of moonshine. She poured two glasses and gestured for him to sit at the table. What do you want to do?

He took up the glass, holding it, eyes closed.

Sam?

He looked at her and drank. I'm thinking. He pulled the shine down to half and then shot it back. I'm gonna go to The Boneyard, see if anyone's there.

Shouldn't you tell Steiner about this? You need backup.

There may not be any to be had. He set the glass down. The way Fish was talking, it could go all the way to the top. If it does, and I go to Steiner with it, that could be the end of the project. We'd go to war with Bradshaw and half on either side'd be dead in the streets. Samuel took the bottle and poured his glass full again. Odds are if I go without the whole story he'll fire me. I went off probation and a guy got killed. They've taken a pretty hard line about that.

You think it was one of Bradshaw's men that shot at you?

Yeah, I do.

Because you're shutting down the tea? She sat, leaning over the table and as quickly sitting back in the chair. And they're in charge of it. Why?

Money, I imagine. Why else?

Can that be all? In a city like this?

He shook his head. I don't know. It's greed. It's got to be.

This doesn't sit right with me. She grimaced.

It sure doesn't with me, either.

Something's off. Stay tonight. She reached for her glass. Stay with me. It'd be a shame if you went and died just as we were about to get together.

We shouldn't. Not while you're still with him.

Shouldn't already sailed. I'll be chaste if you want, but you're not going out there. She started rummaging through the cabinets. He watched her move, and he felt the first fingers of moonshine hit. The world seemed to narrow around her, to bend. She sang. After she had everything together, she turned the lights down and set a few candles on the table. Pulling out the plates to serve dinner she dropped one and it shattered on the floor. She turned to him and smiled slightly. She stopped singing. He joined her on the floor picking it up, and she got down another plate and they sat together. He thought of a small town in the east, some gentle valley, a house with blue flowerboxes under the open windows and he was never a killer. A flash of his father, of himself as his father, in a field. In the wake of the premonition he only saw the two of them, together, in a small cocoon of candlelight, and they hung suspended in the dark, the apartment past the light black, and the city black, far away and all its people shuttling through it silently. Then he kissed her.

In the night he woke naked and uncovered and only now a little cold. He slipped off the bed, watching to see if Johanna would wake, and began to dress. The knife slapped his thigh as he pulled up his jeans, and she stirred, opened her eyes as though she'd never gone to sleep.

I dream about that night. Usually people dream about weird things, like someone's chasing them through a field or something, right? But I dream about that night, sometimes. I just know it's that night, in the way you do in dreams, the way you know a thing. Once I actually saw you, waiting by the lamp, blood on you. But you couldn't hear me.

He finished dressing, adjusted the knife on his belt.

Nobody's gonna be there this late.

He leaned over and kissed her. The air around her was thick. Aren't you offended someone tried to kill me? I am. He felt the room shiver with her laugh. I'm just gonna swing by the yard and my place, maybe P&L Central, see what there is to see.

The plants have to be getting here somehow, right? The Mormon tea? Isn't that how they make it?

He nodded. Most of the time. None of it is anything that's just lying around.

I've got shipping manifests, logs. I can check them to see if there've been any discrepancies. We never get a carload of anything that's unaccounted for. They'd have to doctor the books, make it seem like someone shipped in lettuce, something. The train bosses get their pay. If you want proof, it'll be there.

Well, shit.

She grinned. Come by the depot. I'll do some digging.

Samuel shook his head for a second, smiling. Do me one more favor, then. He bent to kiss her. Clear your schedule for tonight.

The movie?

He kissed her again and left. Her lips and the bed and everything else held to him like a loose shroud as he walked down the hall, the stairs. It was the dead hour before the notion of dawn, bitter cold outside and bright. They had been shut in with the curtains drawn, and in that time the sky had fallen close to the light, and it snowed heavily. He moved along the uneven sidewalk with his arms crossed and his collar pulled to his neck. Marblings of snow laced the pavement, shifting in the wind and settling back, drifting in the gutters. The Boneyard sat dark. He climbed the fence and dropped behind a smashed caravan, gathered himself. His hand rested on the knife, and he walked quietly among the wrecks, still enough he could hear the snowflakes break on the roofs of the cars. The garage doors were closed. He rapped on a side door and waited, blowing on his hands. After a minute the door opened, and Rogan stuck his head out.

Who you lookin' for, Sam?

Samuel's face puzzled. Do you ever sleep?

No. What do you need?

I'm looking for some O Streeters.

Specific ones, or will I do?

Samuel glanced aside, an old calendar on the wall, a woman wearing a checkered flag. Someone took a shot at me last night. Killed my suspect and nearly got me.

No one's here for backup, if that's what you need.

No. I was hoping the one that tried to kill me was here.

Why would someone try to kill you?

Because I found something out.

Rogan leaned forward, hushed. And what's that, exactly?

The company is in on the tea being sold here. At least a part of it is. And there's one man behind it all, getting his profits cut whenever I bloody a nose.

Rogan straightened and looked into the air above Samuel's head. Why don't you come inside? It don't sound safe for you in the open.

They can't kill me. It's the same as telling Steiner.

Don't be so sure. Your line of work? It doesn't even have to look like an accident. Just like you finally met your match.

Samuel gave a half-smile and walked away. The gate opened ahead of him, and he turned back to see Rogan out front of the garage, at the console. He lifted his chin, and Samuel went out. There were two trucks at The Still, the doors open and crates going on. The breath of the men hanging still in the air. He went on north to his apartment. Inside he put a chair under the doorknob and set it tight and lay down on the bed. He never slept. He could hear the burdening of snow on the streets and rooftops, the city being crushed.

8

Day came on like the beginning of another night, the color drawing from the sky. Steam covered the window, and he wiped it with a sleeve. The streets were bedded with snow, some of the sidewalks cleared by shopkeepers. Tiretracks on Q led down 8th. Stepping out he was somewhere else entirely, some other city, an earlier one. It was midmorning, and he set off for Beth's house on the north end. Outside the corridors of the city the wind felt less concentrated but it blew constantly and he stopped in the suburbs to put his back to a tree and to cup feeling into his face. Beth stepped off her porch as it came into view. He waved.

You got a minute? I need your help.

I'm running late. You can follow me if it's important.

He fell in with her. Did you know Bradshaw was behind the tea on the street?

A blink. Yes. Was that all you came to ask me?

He faltered. They tried to kill me last night. Someone shot at me, nicked a guy I was questioning.

I doubt they meant to kill you.

Is everyone in on this but me? Do none of you give a damn?

She turned on him. It's not about giving a damn. We all give a damn. You just care about the wrong thing, stumbled on something you oughtn't have. This is the way the world spins.

I'm not talking about the world. People act like we're not responsible for this place just because everywhere else is worse. We're responsible for these people, Beth. You more than most. We're ruining lives here, ending them. They wound with a curve, the street splitting two ways. Ahead he could see through the trees and roofs, for a moment, a banking highrise, The Capitol. He could think of nothing else to say, and she hadn't heard him.

You should quit. If you're troubled by what we do. It's not going to change. I could get you work on the railroad. Take Johanna and move out to the edge.

What do you mean, take Johanna? He reeled, overacted his stare.

Please. I could see it on both of you. Beth stuck her hand out. I mean it. Get away from all this, for your sake and the city's.

He watched her walk on, now on the north side of town and engines near, people. He started for the train depot. Along the way citizens were bundled and smiling, shrugging up their coats. He climbed the platform and walked through the door of the ticket booth. It was barely warmer inside. The counter clerk was shapeless with blankets, and he tried to stand, fell back into his chair. His eyes were sunken and he had a fresh sore by his ear.

You're not supposed to be back here.

Samuel strode on and opened the door. There was a narrow compartment hallway like a traincar itself. The doors all along the hall hung open, tiny vacant rooms, and he stopped at the sight of Johanna's back in one. She heard him and wheeled around on her chair, a manifest in her hand. Samuel came in and shut the door behind him.

Beth knows. I went to talk to her, and she knows all about it. And about us.

Johanna pushed back in her seat. They were silent for a stretch, and she scanned the papers in her hand, raised them and flipped the manifest around. This is coming in about fifteen minutes.

Samuel took the manifest. The underlined items read

'supplies, qty. x.' All others were named and weighed. Where from?

Arizona, near Utah. Comes in on the BNSF. She turned back to her desk, opened a drawer, and pulled another sheet. Her hand shook slightly. The same thing shows up every week. Sometimes more often. She pulled a cigarette from another drawer and lit it. What did she say?

She wants us to leave the city.

To hell with that. She drew, turned her head aside. Her lips formed a lopsided kiss, blew smoke. Why?

For the city's sake and ours, she said.

We're not gonna fall apart without tea. And an affair won't make the place tumble, either.

I don't know. Maybe you were on to something, with the greed. Maybe it isn't the whole picture. I don't see why Beth would tolerate it, just to let Bradshaw line his pockets.

A train horn, from the south. She stood, and they went down the empty hall and out the door, Samuel smiling at the clerk. Johanna kept smoking, and he stepped to the railing. The sky was thinning out to a flat white. The wind hadn't let up. When he came back over he left enough space between them that they could have been strangers, passengers waiting. A truck was coming down Q Street and he nodded to it.

I think this is for me.

Be careful.

He smiled and she went in. The truck slowed and broke over a drift near the station, and came to a stop. Harrawood was in the passenger seat. Both the driver and he stared at Samuel as they parked and neither got out. Through the windshield he could see the men talk. The train sounded its horn from the edge of town, the brakes as it got close. The clerk came out of the office and jumped off the platform, waving. There was a bristling in the air, a shudder at its parting, and the dark bulk of the engine swept along the track. Steam, smoke, then the first car and second, on, and the train stopped. Samuel turned back to the truck and watched Harrawood get out, flipping a hood over his head. He trudged through the snow around the platform and walked to the engine, lifting himself up to the window and knocking. Samuel took the platform stairs and slipped to the truck, watching the driver and pointing at his window. The man rolled it down. Samuel leaned his elbow on the door.

Be funny as hell if you just backed out of here. Left him hangin'.

Why would I do that?

Because there's a fifty-fifty chance that I bloody you. Samuel pointed to Harrawood, still on the train. Odds slide toward him if you leave.

The driver glared at him. You gonna cut off my thumbs or something?

Samuel mused. Might. Now, I do have a question for you, and then you can roll your window back up. I know it's cold out.

He thinned his eyes. Shoot.

You give a damn that you're killing people with this business? I get the feeling Vince doesn't have a soul. But I see some light in your eyes.

I'll tell you what I got told. You're bad for business. Keep this shit up, and either you pack your bags or you get put in one.

Samuel stared. The driver rolled the window up. Harrawood was coming back to the truck, and Samuel met him on the sidewalk. Neither of them said anything. Harrawood ducked the jab, but Samuel landed his right and Harrawood bent double, his breath caught. Samuel stooped to speak in his ear.

Bit different when I'm not a hundred yards away, ain't it?

Little bit. Harrawood growled through the spasms of his chest.

He patted Harrawood's shoulder and went back to the

station. Johanna was just inside the front booth, watching. The clerk was still gone, and they were alone.

Was that?

The guy that shot at me. You wanna get sick in a bit, go home?

She smiled. Let me get you my key.

Outside he heard a dull roar. He left the station and started walking toward the city center. The sound solidified, resolved into a metal dragging. When he reached 9th the dump truck turned the corner with a plow fixed to it, sparks bouncing to the undercarriage. P&L men and O Streeters cleared the sidewalk with shovels, more the other way. He walked to the nearest group, just down 9th from O Street. At his approach one of the men straightened, forearm on his shovel. Samuel smiled, opened his mouth to speak and he saw the man's jaw, swollen, and his eyes narrow. It was Reese. Samuel kept walking. The work halted and began again.

He fell asleep on Johanna's couch. Drifting off he was thinking of the trail of the case toward Bradshaw, but he dreamt about Aaron knowing. They went through the city, and Aaron was training to be a heel. He had a knife, and they patrolled an altered Singles, bigger, bred with The Haymarket. He never looked at Samuel askance nor said a word but he knew, and the dread that flowed with every moment created such a hollow in Samuel that he thought he might come apart like a brick of ash in a breeze. Then she was beside him, and he stirred up into the room, and his body split with panic, recognizing her shape too late, the weight and shadow of anyone else, and what that meant. She put her hand on his thigh, soft.

It's all right. It's me.

He breathed. I miss anything?

Nope. The train left, no problem. Not before I snuck this

off, though. She held up a withered stalk of Mormon tea. He took it and stared off, holding the stalk between his hands, and they were quiet for a long while. Did you see the boys shoveling the sidewalks?

I saw the truck. She shifted on the couch to see him better, considering him. He said nothing, looked away and back to smile at her and he bowed his head to the floor. She pulled him to her lap. He still wore the dream like a heavy coat.

Come on. She took his hand and pulled him to his feet. They stripped on their way to the shower, and she turned the water on and let it warm and before they were underneath it he was inside her, pushed up against the glass of the stall. They made it into the water but he never let his face past hers, never opened his eyes.

When he was dressed, he wiped the mirror with his palm and looked himself over. Pink tissue bordering the cut on his face. He told her he'd be back and left her drying her hair. His was still wet, and it froze before he crossed the street. People were out walking on the cleared pavement, coming out of buildings, some already heading for the theater. A bell rang when he swung the seamstress' door open, and the woman looked up from the register. Jackets hung on rails between cabinets, and there were mirrors along the walls, racks of shirts. Her hand was under the counter, reaching, and he smiled.

Reflex?

She grimaced. It's hard to get rid of.

I'm a heel. He tapped the knife with a finger. I've got a permit, as it were.

Are you going to the premiere?

Yeah. I was hoping you'd class me up.

Get over here, then. We'll get you sized. She waved him to the back, and she brought out a measuring tape. There was an alcove with a battery of mirrors, and she pushed him toward it. She wrapped the tape around his neck, lifted his arms and tugged at them. Go limp. Like this. She molded him and swatted his hand back when it settled on the butt of his knife. Just like that.

Sorry. Looking toward the register he saw the handle of a revolver on the shelf below it, covered with papers. She smiled and rolled the tape. She started looking around the racks.

You look like crap, but if you throw a jacket on, you'll be all right. There isn't time for anything else. She went over to one of the racks and took down a dark blazer. This'll work fine. You can take it for the night if you promise not to go arresting anyone in it, or whatever it is you do.

He smiled. Thanks. He walked with her to the register, and she started writing on a ledger.

I just give this to the company, right? They reimburse me?

That's right. Or you're credited.

The seamstress handed the blazer over to him. Try it on. It'll be a bit loose, I think.

He shucked off his jacket and slid on the blazer. He pulled at the front, wriggling his neck, and started buttoning up his shirt.

It works. Now I've got to close, so if you'll get out of here.

Thank you. He backed up with his jacket in hand and ducked out. The blazer was thin, and his back began to clench up in the cold. At Johanna's he knocked and waited a minute in the hall before the door opened. She was wearing a dress and sweater. Her eyes lit up at him.

Do I have enough time to get you out of those clothes?

9

He left first. The sky clear and black, and through the cracks between buildings, he made the wink of the moon. It was several blocks before he came to streetlights and people, some ahead and collecting behind him as he went north. On P Street trucks parked along one side, their headlights on and washing the sidewalk and windows yellow. Closing on the theater he saw other streets done the same, directing the city. He thought of seeing it from the sky, what pattern it might make, a square, a pinwheel. The streetlights as globes and the trucks as beams.

The snow had mounded in the gutters and it narrowed the sidewalks. Some citizens were walking in the middle of the pavement. A crowd gathered in front of the theater and all the neon lights and the marquee were done up, and standing away from everyone a woman with tears in her eyes, smiling. The hobo busker had been cleaned, dressed, and brought to play while people filed inside. Through the glass Samuel saw Bradshaw, Beth, and Steiner standing together in front of the ticket booth. Bradshaw was grinning and welcoming people inside. He was near the doors and in the thick of the crowd when Johanna hooked her arm through his, took his hand and dropped it as quickly.

Fancy meeting you here.

He smiled, ducked his head and fought the blush. Johanna filed behind him at the doors, putting an older man between them, and they went through. Samuel made eye contact with Steiner and nodded. Closing in, he watched

Bradshaw for any sign, any twitch or tell. His face was plastic, grinning, and then Samuel was shaking his hand.

Sam. I hope you know it's all business. I don't have any hard feelings toward you.

Well, give it time.

Bradshaw's eyes narrowed, and he let go of Samuel's hand. He greeted the next man, and Samuel stopped in front of Beth.

I'd figure this is too many people at once for you.

I've always liked the movies. And Lester thought I should get out in front of the public more. She read his face and cut him off. Let's not ruin the evening. I see you're on a date.

He inhaled sharply.

I won't tell. She thumbed left. Move along.

He filed down to Steiner, glancing back as Johanna shook hands with Bradshaw, saw him mouth 'Miss Larsen, pleased to see you,' and his eyes were vacant. Steiner grabbed his hand.

Yadda yadda, so great you could make it.

Samuel raised an eyebrow at him, pulled his hand back. You and Lester sitting together for the movie? Got some opera box made up?

I'm leaving as soon as the lights are down. This gladhanding ain't my scene.

And Bradshaw?

He's got to stay on to keep the projectors running. Why?

The line pressed, and Samuel went ahead, frowning an apology. A P&L worker split the line in two, handing off little bags of popcorn and directing couples and families, single people left and right. Johanna was split to his line, and he felt her near at the doors. The lights were low, and the theater almost full already. The line slowed, and she bumped into him, hand brushing his. His face warmed. Several rows down, he saw a few empty seats, and they were still open when he got to them, and he slid in, on his toes past the seated viewers in the row. Johanna sat beside him, and when he looked over he saw Beth, and she pushed by and sat on his left.

What? It's my favorite movie. She tossed a piece of popcorn into her mouth. She winked, and leaned forward to see Johanna. You ever see it?

I don't think so.

They couldn't have picked a better picture. And by 'they,' I mean me.

Johanna laughed. People were talking quietly all through the theater, and over them Samuel heard the doors to the other screen shut, and then the light closed in their room and the screen ahead flickered, lit blue. Johanna took his hand in the dark. Beth's eyes shifted, and he saw she saw the movement. His hand started sweating, and he pulled lightly, but Johanna held him firm. The projector clicked, and shapes crossed the screen before a shield appeared in black and white, and the music started. The picture tracked, shadows of fingers on the screen and the beam of light from the booth overhead shifted. A map of Africa and the credits, a globe. Johanna smiled in the seat next to him. He watched the movie with his mind off, trying to listen for the door. When it was around halfway through, he saw from the corner of his eye someone stand and walk out. Samuel put his hand over Johanna's and shuffled by the moviegoers. It was cooler in the lobby and the front of the theater was cavernous. He felt odd in the quiet and color, a shift greater than just opening a door. A truck rolled down the street outside. A girl passed Samuel, smiling. He found a stairwell the way she'd come and halfway up Bradshaw came out of the projector room.

You have a complaint? I'm new at this whole projectionist thing.

The movie's fine. I just came to make it clear that I'm not letting up on this tea business. I don't care what threats you sling at me, probation, whatever. I'm not stopping. I'm not running. And I know it's you.

I'd love to know what you're talking about.

Samuel gave a little smirk. You can play ignorant. You can be ignorant, for all I care. Tell your boys that either they stop, or I start a war.

Bradshaw took a step down. Just who's gonna fight this war, Sam?

Steiner. I tell Steiner.

Did it ever occur to you that he knows?

His eyes narrowed. That doesn't change anything.

You know it does. If I didn't already have O Street behind me, and I do, they would follow Al. At best you bring this fight on and bloody my nose.

Or I could end this here. Samuel pushed his jacket back for the knife. People have died over this already. I'm sure you wouldn't be the last.

You might be. A voice behind him. Samuel closed his eyes for a breath and turned to see Harrawood, pistol out.

Now. Bradshaw lifted a finger. Here's the other option. The other option is I keep you alive, and on the payroll, and you do what Al and I brought you in for in the first place.

Which is what?

Get the city ready for the real fight. He crooked his finger south. Mexico's rushing straight for us, Sam. You think we needed you and Red for police? O Street can keep in check what we need in check. All you've been doing is maiming bums.

Then why have me do it at all?

Because now everyone knows your name. You and Red were heroes in the making. Figures the city could get behind when things got tough, and they'd trust you to take care of them. And frankly, keeping someone as adept as you at violence is a good idea. If ever there was a situation we couldn't control, we call you in. You lead the charge. Help unite the city.

Red would never have gone for this. Samuel looked back at Harrawood. The gun was still raised, and Samuel hadn't moved his hand from the knife.

It was a bit of luck, him killing Graham. If that had gone a different way he might have put two and two together already, and succeeded in doing just what you want to do. But let me tell you, it's worth more to keep people fed and happy than to keep their conscience clean. He started going down the stairs, and Samuel could barely move to let him through. Bradshaw slowed at the bottom. I've seen other cities. The faces, other people tell me about places, where they've tried. They don't make it, for one reason or another. Or they never really start.

Because they don't have you?

In part. Yeah. They don't have me. The kinds of things I had to do to keep the lights on in this place? I'm not proud of everything in my life, but I am proud of this. He opened his arms to their surroundings.

I'm not sure you should be proud.

Bradshaw shook his head. I didn't think you would agree. Just sort of hoped. If you change your mind, all you have to do is man your station. Don't overreach. Put your knife away. Shouldn't be too hard a thing for you to do.

I wouldn't bet on it.

Bradshaw cut a glare at Harrawood. Go sit down. He nodded at the theater and Harrawood left. Bradshaw looked back to Samuel. The truth is there are no fresh starts. Not anywhere. We left innocence behind in the garden. You build on the bones of others because there isn't an alternative. It's nature. If you get caught up trying to hold everyone accountable who ever made a mistake, you'd never get anywhere. You'd be too busy looking in a mirror. He paused, gestured to the room upstairs. You know you're missing a heck of a movie. Right about now Rick's tipping the Swedish lady's chin back, and he's gonna make a speech. You probably ought to hear it, actually. It's apropos.

Samuel didn't move.

Well. I'm not gonna miss it. He shook his head and went inside.

Samuel breathed deep. It took him a minute to come down the stairs and go in for the last act. Johanna leaned over when he took his seat, their arms pressed. A car pulled into the airport, the runway glossy from rain and the fog thick. The hero shot a German. Samuel rubbed at the side of his head, and the credits rolled and the lights went up. The screen was still lit with a menu: Play movie, subtitles, special features, long face of the protagonist. Beth was smiling, firm, thin. Samuel rose.

I'd have thought that was too sentimental for your taste.

I'm free to indulge in an illusion, same as you.

Johanna led them out of the row and they followed the crowd out into the night. Most kept nearby, spilling to the street and turning back, eyes distant. Gil was among them, on the sidewalk. Samuel saw Beth had already gone, and while there was still cover he put his hand on the small of Johanna's back.

I'll find you, okay? I'm gonna have a talk with Steiner.

Do you want me to come along? I could help present the evidence.

That's one too many times he's seen us together. Better if I do it solo, get a square answer from him.

Johanna nodded. All right. Find me. She moved along with the rest of the crowd, then headed west, away. Samuel stayed by Gil and watched the stragglers filter through the doors.

How'd that lead turn out?

Nothing to it. Gil crossed his arms. Got there, and Rogan took off just as soon as he saw me. Didn't even give me a ride back.

The theater was nearly empty, the audience wandering off. Someone had Bradshaw cornered, waving about, and Bradshaw smiled with his teeth, and Harrawood led the fan to the doors. He had hold of her elbow, and opening the door he saw Samuel. He kept his eyes locked with Samuel's until the woman was clear and he shut and locked the doors. Gil looked at him. Samuel turned his back and started for The Capitol, leaving Gil below the marquee. People meandered through the neighborhood, searching for an end to the night. Inside The Capitol he found Steiner at the west stairwell, hand on the banister. He turned at the sound of the door.

You looking for me?

Samuel nodded. I've got news.

He paused below the final step. Let's go up to my room.

On the third floor, Steiner led him to an office and shut the door after them. The room was large, full of furniture, and in the back was a bare mattress. Steiner went over to a table and poured a glass of shine. He drank it as easily as water and set the glass back.

What's this all about?

You won't like it. First off, I haven't reported the latest mess. I haven't had time. Everything happened at once, and there were things I needed to dig at before coming to you.

You're not my prom date, Sam. Just come out with it.

Samuel sucked on his eyetooth. Bradshaw's behind all the tea here.

He turned his head as if he hadn't heard. What?

It isn't just filtering into the city. It's being made, start to finish, in the city. Along with jake. And Bradshaw's behind it all.

You got proof?

I nearly got shot by someone driving a P&L truck. I was questioning Fish, and someone pulls up and starts shooting. Kills him before I get anything.

What's that prove?

That someone's trying to keep a secret. He took the withered stalk of Mormon tea from his pocket and held it out. This came in on a weekly from Arizona. Vince Harrawood and a lackey came to pick up the shipment personally. There's that and Fish and a pretty constant misdirection from the P&L. They honk whenever they see me so people can go to ground. I brought this up with Bradshaw at the movie, and he went from ignorant to all-knowing, suggested I'm not willing to pull the trigger on telling you, trying to get this out in the open. He said you knew.

His eyes rolled to fix Samuel, and he dropped to the couch. You think I'd let this happen? I knew he and his boys weren't clean, but you're always gonna have a little corruption in a city. That's why I got you.

It's not just his men. It's yours. Harrawood is all the way in his pocket, Finley probably partway. Which means O Street is compromised.

Steiner was quiet. You should have come to me with this first.

I wasn't sure how far it all went until now. I was worried you might throw me out or bring down the city.

Steiner was silent, staring off. Oh, it'll bring Bradshaw down, all right. He thinks movies and lights make this place run? We'll eat beans in the dark before I let him get away with this.

What do we do, then?

Steiner finished his glass, holding it to his lips. I'll call him in tomorrow. Confront him.

You don't want to track him down now?

He can't be found at night. He disappears. He keeps a

house off Leighton, but it's a decoy. Steiner refilled his glass and drank. Consider yourself off probation. I'll see you bright and early. If everything goes well, we can nip this in the bud and be done with it. Promote Maggie and keep on without missing a beat.

Samuel opened the door. And if it doesn't go well?

I've got men I know I can trust. They'll be in the wings. If Bradshaw smells something, we'll be ready.

10

Johanna had papers strewn across the table when he got in, and she hovered over the pages, hands on a chair. He lingered in the doorway, body draining of adrenaline and all the courses of possibility leaving him. A P&L finding her instead, or waiting for him. Both. He shut and locked the door, went across from her and took the other chair and pushed it fast under the doorknob.

Can you even see those?

Just barely. It's all the records I've got for BNSFs with points of origin in the desert. It's not a lot, but it's more than you think. Sometimes they roll through here coming and going just to have a decent drink. She glanced up. Did you talk to Steiner?

Yeah. He's convinced. We're gonna try to get Bradshaw tomorrow.

She frowned to one side, ran her teeth over her lip. High beams from a mongrel panned across the room as if from a lighthouse, whirled on past. I don't like this.

It's far from ideal.

No. Something's not right. We're missing something.

We'll get it out of Bradshaw tomorrow.

What did he tell you, when you talked to him at the theater?

What you'd expect.

She sighed. Why did this have to happen now?

This is how it was always gonna wash out, I suppose. Not that I saw it coming.

No. She smiled, head tilted. I meant now, like, now that

you and I—

He nodded, stepped closer. I get it.

What if we missed our chance? What if I should have gone with you, back then?

What if you didn't so we could uproot Bradshaw, clean the city?

What if Jesus came tomorrow?

He laughed. She was smiling but facing away, and he took her hand, then both of them, and she gripped his fingers.

First light. He got up and showered while she was still in bed and dressed in the old jacket. The morning was a little warmer than the night before, and the sky was covering over with clouds. He tried the door to the seamstress' shop and found it locked, hung the blazer on the doorknob and went east. It was brighter now but sourceless, the sun still hidden. From the north a mule nodded through its traces, leading Ostry to the farmer's market. Plumes of gray breath from its nose, the crack of ice under its hooves.

The west hall of The Capitol was empty except for two O Streeters, one of them pointing Samuel to the senate chamber. He went down the hall and opened the door. Steiner sat at the far end of the table, hands perched.

Sam. Glad you got here early. Take a seat.

Place is pretty dead. He sat facing the door. How do you think this is gonna play out?

With any luck he just cops to it, and we put him in a blind to Alaska.

You don't want to lock him in the stocks? Beat him around some?

We need to play this right. If we put his head on a stick, all his boys are like as not to rebel. But if we come at it reasonable. He opened his hands. No fight to put down.

What happened to all that vinegar you had last night?

I thought it over. I haven't changed my mind. We don't need him to keep the trains on time, but if we act like tyrants now, well. There's the civilians to think about, and the people loyal to him. And then there's the example we're setting. We're gonna be the world's new old-timers. People are gonna look back at the way we treated our scum and they're gonna act accordingly.

Samuel pushed back in his chair. They'll see we let him off with an exile. People are dead, out of their minds, and he's profiting from it. There is no good history lesson to find here. You're not founding fathers.

There is a lesson. Steiner looked at him, rocked back. I'm gonna tell you a story. I think only Beth knows this one. Lester and I are from the same town. He was a year behind me in school. I had a girl, together since junior high, same year as him. I got called up with the last round of draftees, war winding down. She panicked, so I married her, left for basic. Mechanic MOS. Fought for a hot minute in Libya before that all finished, then the suck in Costa Rica. Steiner broke off, continued.

When the war ended, I came back home to find Lester with my wife, and her with a baby girl. You can guess what the girl's name is. Steiner cut a knowing glance at Samuel. Wife came back to me, took the kid. Lester harassed her, threatened her when I wasn't around. After about a year of that, she left. Packed all her things. I can hardly blame her—You don't know how good Lester is at getting in your head. So of course he took Maggie, and for years I had to live in the same town as the piece of shit knocked up my wife, watch a little girl grow up should'a been mine. And he comes to me one day in my garage, about two years after the aurora. He says 'Al, I got an idea.' And he shows me a flashlight he's fixed, all the insides laid out on a piece of wood. He asked me if I could teach myself to make an engine run on corn. We hatched this city over my kitchen table. Steiner went distant, hesitating. I looked around our town, and I saw how bad everything was, and I thought, if there's something we can do, we have to do it. For kids like Maggie, at least. Give her some kind of world to live in. And I'm telling you now that if I can put my hate aside, treat Lester like a human being when really he ain't. It'll mean his work still stands. Instead of tearing it all down because he's evil, he leaves some good behind him.

So we let him go. The one person I really ought to cut up.

You ever read a Western? Ever watch those movies where the train baron sits in his car on the plains, watching China-men dig, and then the cowboy shows up and blows the man's brains out 'cause he killed his brother or something? You know how that never, ever happened in real life? It's because that train baron made this country. People like Bradshaw made it. Will hopefully remake it. They're shitty people, but they're necessary. That's just how it works. It takes that kind of mind to do this. He swept an arm across the room, out-ward. We gotta be rough fighting crime here because there's not much authority outside force, not right now. People see lights and cars, and they believe in money again. But we haven't found the badges yet to make them believe in law. It's a run-in with you or the stocks, or they won't care. The train won't solve all our problems.

There was a knock at the door, and Norton stepped in. Am I early or late?

You're right on time, brother. Steiner sat up and spread his arms. Have a seat. I was just preaching about what it takes to make a city.

Beer and long-legged women? Norton looked at Samuel. We having a crisis of faith?

Samuel dropped his hands. Something like that.

Steiner drummed the table with his fingers. I never really told you how glad I am you came back. Wish we could have kept Red around along with you, to be honest. You two make the best sort of policemen. And that's the thing—it takes all kinds. You keep Lester in check. You make sure his manifest destiny shit doesn't go out of control. That's how the world functions. The fact that I gotta balance Lester, too, doesn't mean I don't appreciate you.

That's pretty democratic.

It's the truth.

They waited. Minutes passed. Norton made smalltalk with them and checked his watch. I always get a kick out of this. He smiled, pointing at his wrist. Checking clocks these days. Who knows what time it really is? We just made it up.

Samuel looked at him. It was made up to begin with.

Half an hour later, Samuel was standing against the wall and half an hour after that, they walked out. The O Streeters hadn't seen anyone. Samuel opened the outside doors and went to the concrete dais where the statue stood. A young couple walked past, heading downtown. He turned back. The O Streeters were holding the doors and Steiner stopped between them. Samuel tilted his head.

I don't hear any trucks. It was quiet this morning, but I've never not heard any engines.

Steiner scanned the street and the mall. What do you think?

The floor's about to drop out. Where's Finley? Did you tell him to show today? Samuel waited for Steiner to answer, and in the quiet he felt his back tense. We should leave. Get to The Still.

Steiner looked back to Norton and to Samuel again. He dug in his pocket and came out with two keys and handed one to Samuel. You lead. He pointed with the remaining key to 14th, and the mongrels waiting.

Samuel unlocked the door and opened it. Sit in the back.

Steiner's face puzzled.

Let Norton drive. Samuel got in and started the engine. He grabbed the wheel and felt around at everything. He put it in drive and started down 14th, shuddering to a stop past the intersection. Turning onto K, Norton waiting behind him. He pulled ahead, driving slow, checking all the streets. In the courthouse parking lot sat a band of P&L trucks, two men apiece in each cab. Their headlights came on at once, and Samuel jerked the mongrel right, speeding up as they started to follow. The streetsigns were all facing the other way, and he lost track of where he was before peeling onto O, sliding on the packed snow. Three trucks followed behind him. A bullet cracked his driver side mirror and it swung from a wire. Sliding left onto 13th, the mongrel went wide and jolted over a curb and back onto the street. He watched the remaining mirrors and turned into a parking garage, took the first ramp he saw, below ground, and parked.

Hell.

He reached in the glovebox for a gun and found nothing. He cursed again and got out. The trucks were running overhead. He trotted around to the ramp wall and put his back to it. A truck slowed, a door opened and shut. Footsteps coming down the ramp past his head, around the mongrel, a hissing from the car. He straightened and could see the roof of the car, then rounded the ramp. A P&L worker poised and watchful, pistol in hand. He was young and when he saw Samuel, he grinned toothily. The tires were slashed.

Samuel had his hands at his sides, the knife at his right. Before he could draw, the P&L worker dropped the gun, and ran up the ramp and out into the street. Samuel recovered the gun, put it in the back of his jeans, and followed the boy out. An engine thrummed from a few blocks away. Samuel turned on O, headed for The Haymarket. There were a few people in the windows of apartments and restaurants watching. Raj was sitting on a stoop across the street, and he lifted his arm.

What's the ruckus?

Someone's tryin' to kill me. No big deal.

You need a place to hide? I got a good spot under the bridge. Blocked up the back, nobody even knows I'm there.

Samuel shook his head and went on, taking the walkway ramp down to 8th. Mongrels were clustered around The Still, and on approach he saw the flat tires and the bullet holes pocking the cars and the building. He knocked at the door and stood square with the speakeasy window. It slid open, and one of the guards looked through. The plate slid back, and the doors swung wide. Nearly all of the old works had been scrapped, rails left in the floor now mounting kettle after kettle. It was hot inside and humid, and the distillers milled about, checking temperatures and containers. Far at the back he saw the pure ethanol tanks in columns. Daylight showed through vents near the roof. O Streeters wandered or leaned against walls.

Steiner's in the AC. The guard pointed to a closed office to the side, an air conditioning unit plugged into the wall.

Samuel went in. It wasn't much cooler, but the air was less damp and the smell halved. Steiner sat at a desk with Norton and two O Streeters along the wall.

Was getting worried about you, Sam.

I tried to lead them off. Guess that didn't work.

There were some polite enough to wait for us. Steiner leaned forward. We've got folks posted at the warehouse and a couple at The Boneyard. Cover what we can of our asses.

Samuel put his hands on a chairback. How many at the warehouse?

Four? He glanced at Norton and got a nod.

How many are MIA?

Around ten. Which gives Bradshaw about forty men, assuming O Street is actually for him and not sitting it out. He pressed the side of his hand against the desk and swept across it idly.

Norton shrugged. Without The Still, they'll run out of fuel pretty quick.

Samuel gazed off at the wall, thinking. They're playing us, is my guess. They won't take The Still, but they've got us cornered at the edge of town. Bradshaw wouldn't want to gun anybody down on O, undo all that morale boosting the movie got him.

Steiner tapped his fingers on the desk. Well, what do you want to do?

I'm thinking. Samuel closed his eyes.

I got some burly friends in a few hours' reach, if we want to call for some backup.

Samuel raised an eyebrow. Bradshaw won't wait that long. He pointed to 8th. Make sure the streets are clear here, and get everyone out. Lock everything up, and get our guns into the tool-and-die across the street. They'll come here in force and shoot the doors down, and when they come back out, we'll hit them.

How about we split up, let Norton take half right next door so we can pinch 'em from either direction?

Samuel nodded. Steiner rose and waved the O Streeters outside. Norton looked at Samuel and rubbed at the side of his face.

You're working my nerves today, Sam.

Bradshaw's people can't make shine worth a damn. They need it.

Norton grimaced. Steiner followed him out and Samuel after him. The air had begun to warm under the clouds. Steiner put everyone into two files at the door and started sending them to the buildings. Norton gave a weak salute and headed off with half the men. Samuel filed in with the others, and saw Johanna coming down 8th. He trotted to meet her, motioning for Steiner to go on.

What are you doing here?

I wanted to make sure you were all right.

You need to get back to your apartment. We're probably half an hour from an attack.

Her face hardened. I'm staying with you. I can lend a hand.

Johanna. He breathed in, softened the panic in his chest. I can't make you leave?

Not for anything. She shook her head once, to one side, and he saw the doubt in her. He watched her, then started for the tool-and-die. The front entrance of the tool-and-die was locked with chains but a side door stood halfway down the alley, and they went in. The shop was cramped, many of the machines intact. The mix of O Streeters and Still workers grouped near the door between lathes. Heather paced, head down, gun on her shoulder. The shop was two stories tall with no second floor, only wide vents with heavy louvers at the front and back. Detch was already climbing one of the machines to look out. Samuel turned, pulling out the gun he'd taken from the boy in the garage and handing it to Steiner.

I'm gonna get them rustling up some tools.

A metal ringing before he could move. Detch was drumming on the machinetop, and he pulled himself in and hissed at them. Guys, I hear something.

Dammit. Samuel raised his hand. Everyone grab whatever you can for a weapon. I want whoever has a gun in behind me, first out. Got it?

He saw nods, O Streeters coming forward. He passed through the crowd and backed to the door, watching them all scramble.

Johanna came up beside him. What do you want me to do? She had a wrench in her hand, and she switched it to wipe her palm on her jeans, switched it back.

Keep your head down.

Detch's drumming returned, and Samuel heard engines. He moved to the fans at the back and listened there. Through the louvers the sun was setting, the lights kicking on along 9th just as their own went out. He swept to the door and through the murmuring crowd. Lighters came out, matches, little flames held to chests. Samuel pressed his back to the door.

Everyone hush. Lights don't mean anything once we get outside. Just make sure you get through this door in one piece, and we're gold. He waited, listened. No sound, just the shuffle and breath inside the shop. Matches winked out. The engines started onto 8th and drew closer, passed by and quieted, idling, then five measured crashes as someone shot The Still door. Samuel looked over his shoulder at everyone. Safeties? Safeties on. We don't want to ruin their surprise.

A click behind him. Samuel shoved the door open and ran ahead, halting at the mouth of the alley. Four trucks sat in front of The Still, behind the mongrels, drivers waiting inside. He put his back to the wall and pushed a hand at the group tumbling out. Heather was in the lead, and he motioned for her and two others to come closer.

Stay low. Take the drivers. He pointed to the rest. Once we open the trucks, rush 'em.

He spun and trotted, crouching, crossing behind the first and second trucks and, by the third, saw the drivers lurch in their seats to look behind themselves. At the fourth, he hung below the truck frame and pulled open the driver door. The driver spun to him, bewildered and in a haze of smoke, and before he could lift the pistol in his lap, Samuel had him on the ground. He held the driver's collar and jabbed him squarely in the nose. Shots fired from past the truck, Norton's side, then both. A window exploded above him. He took the gun from the pavement and got to his feet. The trucks were empty and his people still rushing from the tool-and-die, Johanna with them. He swung his arm for Norton's men to follow him and line up. There were P&L workers moving to the open Still door, and as Samuel dashed to the side, they faded back into The Still. One of the men he'd led with stood opposite him, and the others slid into position.

I want three to watch the perimeter. He circled a finger in the air, and a few O Streeters broke off. He inched closer to the door for those inside to hear. We got your drivers. Got you surrounded. I'd like to not—

Someone fired a few rounds out the door. A bullet hit the grill of a mongrel.

As I was saying. I'd like to not have to kill any of you. Honestly don't care if I have to. So if you all will slide your guns out the door here— A round thumped above his head. He winced. All we gotta do is shoot one of those kettles, and you all go up in flames.

He heard no reply at first, then someone walk across the concrete toward the door. Is that Sam? Maybe I get to shoot you after all.

Samuel shifted to the wall. The steel by his head was dimpled. Maybe you do. More likely I cut something off you, though. Send it home in your pocket.

Samuel grabbed the arm of the man next to him. Get me Norton, and tell Steiner to find his best shot. When he sees me give the okay, he puts two, low, into the farthest kettle he can hit.

The man nodded and scrambled around the wall. Samuel scanned the guns nearby, the trucks. On the left flank, he saw someone run to Steiner. Johanna was beside him, looking at Samuel.

Norton came around the wall and crouched down. What can I do, Sammy?

We're gonna flush 'em out by shooting a kettle.

You know the tanks are filled with rocket fuel, right?

That's the point. It's either scare them out or a couple dozen people die here, bloody.

Norton gritted his teeth. He glanced over to Steiner and Steiner gave a slow nod. A man climbed into the bed of the second truck and made his way behind the cab, laying an arm along the rail. Before Samuel could signal him The Still clattered with gunshots and he saw the man fire back. Moments later there were curses, and a clutch of P&L workers came bolting through the door. A couple O Streeters took shots, but the rest were slow to fire, some of them moving forward to tackle or clock the P&L running through. A man shouted inside, and a long scrape preceded the slide of a gun along the ground by Samuel's feet.

Throw 'em all out!

More slid past the threshold, pistols and longarms. Samuel kicked them out of the way, and the rest of the workers burst through. In the middle of them ran Harrawood, and when the others were shoved up against the trucks he sprinted through a gap and on, toward the substation. Samuel pushed off the door and chased after him, swerving around the cars and O Streeters. Harrawood ran across the street and Samuel shot wide of him, then Heather stepped out from the trucks and peppered Harrawood's leg with her shotgun, toppling him into the gravel just past the sidewalk. Samuel was on him before he could roll over to shoot back. He stepped on Harrawood's arm and brought the knife down, cutting his trigger finger off at the palm. Blood spurted over the gun, and Harrawood's eyes pinched shut. Samuel picked the gun from his hand, ejected the round in the chamber, and pulled the slide, pocketing it.

This would be where I'd kill you. But someone has to tell Bradshaw he lost.

It's gonna be such a good day for me, when you realize. The contortions of his face softened, and he stared at Samuel. I think I'll break your arms first. Then I'll take a bat—

Samuel hit him with the heel of his boot. He straightened. That's the spirit. He turned back to The Still, and Harrawood called after him. They'd started tying the Light men up and marching them into the tool-and-die. He found Steiner to one side of the shop door, watching the O Streeters drag their prisoners inside.

You get him?

Let him go. To set an example.

Steiner dulled his eyes. True, sarcastic or not.

Anybody get hurt?

One of the Light boys is pretty bad off. The rest'll probably be okay. He gestured to the men still trickling along the alley. Probably a good thing they were all a tad gun-shy. Nobody wants to kill their friends. Good for us, too.

What do we do now?

Keep them, grill them. This is a pretty big blow. We got almost a third of his men the first day of the fight. We got their guns and their trucks.

Now might be the time to hit back. Roll down the street to Central and knock it over, get our power turned on?

No. Steiner glanced in the door. No, I don't want to risk that. We could wind up hurt as bad as they were. And I ain't too concerned about being without power. Light or dark, a room with you in it is still deadly.

Well. Samuel cocked his head. Maybe I'll go get Lester's attention. He saw Johanna appear at the mouth of the alley, walking one of the last prisoners, face set. Detch left the shop as she went in, and he elbowed Samuel.

What'd you do to Vince? I saw you over by the power station. Looked like a shot in a movie: the lone detective gets his man.

Took off his trigger finger.

Is that a thing for you?

Two's just a coincidence.

Steiner sighed, waving Samuel off. Go home, both of you. Sleep. I'm gonna need you out front tomorrow. Riding a horse and calling charge.

Sure. He walked away slowly, throwing a hand up. Johanna caught up to him at the mouth of the alley and he stiffened. Will you go home now?

Sure. I got my action in.

He smiled, rueful, and led her down the street, careful to put distance between them. Detch watched them go, and Samuel felt eyes on him, prickling his neck. Samuel saw a little pat of hair at her temple flattened with sweat. They turned for H, and he breathed. The street narrowed and they kept to the sidewalk, Samuel pulling them out of the streetlights. At her building he turned around and held the door open for her and stood by. She quirked her head at him.

Are you not coming in?

Detch looked at us funny while we were leaving. I'm gonna go back to The Still, do a little work, wipe any suspicion.

We've only got one more day to ourselves.

One day until we come clean. Then. He pushed the door wider and she stepped through the threshold. She leaned out to kiss him and he closed his eyes to meet her. He let the door shut.

11

The night was warming. Samuel jogged part of the way back to The Still, slowing on 8th. The trucks and mongrels had already been pushed back, and he found The Still doors open wide. Norton supervised a few workers pushbrooming the remainder of the spilled ethanol outside. Near the back of the building, the tinker patched the shot kettle with off-color tin, sparks dropping to his feet. Samuel stood beside Norton, watching. The sparks cut, the light, and the tinker raked off his helmet, got his gear together in a bucket and walked out. Norton pivoted on his heels to watch him go.

I'd appreciate it if next time you didn't wreck my stuff.

Samuel glanced up at him. Couldn't avoid it. You got a couple bottles of that jet fuel to spare?

Norton gestured to the floor. If you got a sponge, you're welcome to it. What do you need gas for?

You'll hear about it tomorrow.

Norton pinched the scruff at the side of his jaw and glanced around The Still. Stephens. Get Sam some ethanol.

One of the nearby workers straightened from a coil and went to the rear of the building. He came back cradling a large jug in his arm and handed it over.

You got a light? Samuel hefted the jar.

Stephens pulled a book of bar matches from a shirtpocket. Here.

Thanks. Samuel took them and he nodded to Norton and went out to the street to the tool-and-die. The door was shut and locked, and when he knocked, an O Streeter opened it with a rifle in his hands. Steiner in there?

One second.

He let Samuel in and went toward the back of the shop. There was a generator from The Still squatting in the middle of the room and they'd hooked up one of the machines and had it running, the shop filled with the din. Steiner came from around the corner, wiping his hands on a bloody rag.

I figured you'd be shacking up with Johanna. Maybe you're lookin' for Detch? I don't judge.

You know, I never considered him until just now. Are you—you cutting the captives up or what?

Nah, we're just fucking with 'em. One of the men had the bright idea to turn on a planer, set up one of the prisoners like a plank of wood.

They tell you anything?

There idn't much for them to tell. Bradshaw didn't plan anything past attacking The Still, apparently. Figured we'd just topple, and they could sweep up. They're hunkering in the football stadium. He glanced at the ethanol. Take one of their trucks. Good cover.

Planned on it. Samuel started away, and an O Streeter trotted up to Steiner, whispered to him. Steiner nodded, looked at Samuel and whispered back, covering his mouth.

What was that?

We had him at the warehouse. Said he saw a Lightman snooping, sent him packin'. Guess he thought he had to be clandestine. He reached out and tapped the jug of ethanol. Boy, I'd like to see you light that.

It wasn't long past midnight, but the city lay quiet. The plow had quit at 18th, and he was careful to follow a set of tracks to 27th, where he turned north. Everything a dark bulk: trees, houses, and strips of grocery stores brightened by the blue drifts of snow. He parked the truck several blocks from Leighton. The gun tucked in his jeans and the ethanol under his arm. There was no moon, only the dim, cracked stroke of the Milky Way. He was nearly in reach of the streetsign before he could read it, heard the truck idling down the street before that. At a crouch he saw the cab, empty, and he walked as quietly as he could on the pressed snow in the tracks. The driver lay asleep across the bench seat. Three houses sat wide in the cul-de-sac, the largest in the middle. Samuel's boots punched through the crust of untouched snow in the yard, and the sound was loud but dead in his pause. He unscrewed the jug and skimmed the lid away into the backyard. A large deck surrounded the back of the house, and he padded up the steps to the screen door. He unzipped the screen with his knife and found the latch and opened it, the backdoor unlocked. Dark inside. He slipped off his boots and set them beside the door and stepped onto kitchen tile in his socks. A smell he wasn't used to, a newness. He found the living room by touch, and the windows showed enough light to pour the fuel over the couch and the curtains behind it. He set the jug by and got out the matches, catching the whole book afire and dropping it onto the couch. A blue flame crossed the fabric before the fumes went up in yellow. He found his boots and tugged them on before rounding to the front of the house. He left the yard and glanced back, the glow rising in the windows. Standing on the porch next door to Bradshaw's house was Maggie, dark against the siding, watching him. She leaned over the railing.

You looking for my dad? A thick joint lay beside her on the porch railing, and she lit it. I'll tell you where he really lives. Where he goes every night.

Samuel stepped forward. Why would you do that?

She inhaled, blew a long string of smoke out into the night. She glanced at the house beside them. The flames were bright now, large, and in the yard oblong keys of light flickered on the snow from the windows. Come inside. The guard'll wake up soon.

He lingered for a second, watching the fire, before going up the porch steps and following her into the house, passing through a cloud of smoke.

Are you high, Maggie?

Well, obviously. She struck her lighter. They were in a living room, bare except for a dead, dry Christmas tree in the corner. She blew a mouth of smoke from the joint, and went on toward an open doorway.

That's not what I mean.

Maggie stopped at the door, where a staircase descended to the basement. Please don't ask me. She went down, and Samuel saw a blue glow from the bottom of the stairs. He followed her and saw the source: a television, screen on but blank. A wall of blinking stereos.

Did you do all this?

Yeah. She faced him. I fixed my first computer a few weeks ago. Took me months. There's this game on it you'd love. You just hunt and travel around.

He scanned the room. Maggie was staring at him, and he settled back a few paces from her. We shouldn't stay down here. The fire could spread.

The guard will come. He'll knock. She picked up a music player. I don't know how to open these, or I'd try to fix it. The music might still be on it. I remember listening to them as a kid. There must be some special tool they used. She held it eye-level.

Maggie.

Phones are easier, but all the towers are dead.

Maggie. Where does your dad live?

You know, I've never shown anyone the basement. Tover, I guess, but he doesn't count. I thought since we're the same age, you might appreciate it. My dad can't work any of this stuff, the complicated stuff. He smashed the first TV I ever rebuilt. Threw it out the window.

You did the theater, then?

She smiled. He helped. But I let him take the credit. Who'd believe that Lester's junkie daughter could do anything anyway, right?

Samuel glanced over his shoulder, toward the stairs. He heard steps, pounding on the front door.

That's for me. Maggie started around him and he took her arm.

Wait. Listen. He got in front of her to see her eyes. Find Detch, all right? Get out to The Singles. They'll take care of you.

Sure. She smiled, a little broad, and they went up the stairs. She went for the door, and he lingered in the dark of the stairwell a moment. The guard held his arm up to his face, awash in the light of the fire. Samuel ducked away.

Did you see who it was?

The guard shook his head. He must have got past me. We should get you out of here. Are you good?

Samuel saw a door through the kitchen to the backyard. He slipped to it and stepped outside onto a small back porch. The front of Bradshaw's house was roaring, but the back was still blued with starlight. On the rail facing Bradshaw's was a thin glass pipe, blackened bowl, and in passing he reached and flung it into the night.

He got the truck and went northwest. It warmed, and the vibrations lulled him. If the drive had been much longer, he might have dozed off at the wheel, found the truck in a yard in the morning. He parked in front of Beth's and got out. The door was unlocked. He called out to no reply and took down one of the blankets covering the windows. He sat in a chair in the living room and slept with the knife and gun beside him.

A glare from the sun shot through the uncovered window, glowed off a front of clouds. He woke hungry and stiff, the stitches in his face tight, and searched the kitchen for food. A train clamored behind the house. Beth had left some jars of vegetables in the cupboard and a half gallon of milk in the icebox. He picked at a jar of stewed tomatoes and drank some of the milk, thin puck of ice on top, before checking upstairs. Nothing of hers there, if there had ever been. Smell of old paper coming from the walls. Passing a window, he saw the smoke rising in the southeast. He went downstairs and out the door and drove off. A bearded and filthy face looked out a window at him in a neighboring house, one eye rolled to the sky. The clouds had dragged halfway over the city. When he reached O Street he saw people out, businesses opening. Three people at a corner talking, hushing as he went by. He turned onto H and let the truck coast past Johanna's apartment, then turned north on 8th and parked beside The Still. The doors were closed, and the tool-and-die across the street was quiet. He pounded twice below the speakeasy, and a guard slid the plate open and let him in. Samuel glanced around the floor, lit by electric lanterns and half-dark. The guard closed the door behind him.

He's here. Norton's out.

Samuel gave a low wave and went to the office. Steiner slept curled in a chair, a jacket laid over his chest. Samuel spoke his name twice before pulling a chair out for himself. He slipped the knife from its sheath and spat on the blade, passing it back and forth along his jeans. He started stropping it on his belt, and Steiner muttered, lifted an eyelid.

You get him?

No. House had one guard, asleep.

Shame. Not surprised, though. He passed his fingers over the bridge of his nose. Wish I knew where to find you after. You know this tubby guy, beard, glasses, lives on the couch at The Inn?

Raj? Yeah. He helped point me to Fish.

Some P&L boys pretty near broke his skull.

Samuel gripped the knife, ran it harder down the belt. He gonna make it?

Think so. We put him up, went ahead and got him a place.

He paused. Least we could do.

Have they left the stadium yet?

Not that anyone's seen.

Samuel smacked the flat of the blade on his thigh. The tip was blunted from striking Harrawood's gun. Beth cleared out of her house. He scratched the point, catching his nail on it. This thing, whatever it is. It feels like it's been in the making for a while.

Maybe it has been. Steiner pursed his lips. Who knows with someone like Bradshaw. Wouldn't put it past him to try and seize power. Knew his options once I called him in.

Harrawood flips. Finley disappears. Aaron, one of Bradshaw's men who'd flip on him, is gone. Beth's gone.

You don't know that. She's a recluse.

He slid the knife in its sheath. Sure. It's a coincidence. But the fact that they turned out to be bad at it doesn't mean that they haven't been plotting this. He rocked his chair back. You want collections run?

No. No, that's a hundred doors you open might have a gun behind 'em. We're gonna sit tight for now. Go rest.

He went out onto the floor, and the guard pushed the door wide for him. Samuel left the truck and walked north. The city quiet, no cars on the overpass and a train cold at the station. At his apartment he took the box out and got the whetstone and oil and worked the tip of the knife back to a true point. When he finished, he left everything out and picked a book from the shelf and sat with it, looking out at the clouds in the east, curling from white to gray. The book was about cosmology. Distant stars, phenomena. Things that may never again have names. He stopped reading to open the rear window to the fire escape and climbed onto the roof. The sun settling onto the tops of buildings and the air felt almost warm, and still. He stood at the corner, facing the street where Raj was found. Snowmelt running in the gutters. A strange kinship to the architecture, to the brick and concrete and even the absence of it, the spacing of the streets and the air and the people, hidden, the ones who turned on the lights.

Three engines started up at The Still, headed east. The sound cut after a minute. He waited on the roof, the sun behind the city now, and for several minutes The Haymarket became sunk in dusk, then the streetlights went up and the sky thawed. Johanna walked north on 8th. She wore a long, dark coat and her hair down, swaying. He stepped back and went into the room. Her footsteps sounded through the door. The book was out, and the box and knife and he stood there just inside the window until she knocked. He shut the window and opened the door. She stood over him, in tall boots, and she held up a bottle of high proof.

It's time to take those stitches out.

You're being a little brash.

She came in and shut the door with her heel, locked it. You're in danger. Did you think that would give me pause, keep me away?

I thought it might, considering.

The opposite. She took in the room and set the bottle on the table, flipping the book to read the spine. Where'd you get this?

The university library. He got two glasses from the sink. She smiled and took off her coat. Black dress underneath. She draped the coat over the back of the chair and poured their glasses while Samuel put away the oil and pushed the knife to the side.

So this is what you do up here when you're all by yourself? You read physics books, sharpen your knife?

I read other things, too.

She watched him. After a moment she went over to the sink and washed her hands and came back to the table, fishing in her coat pocket for a pair of scissors. Samuel tilted his glass and looked up at her, and she took his face in her hands with the scissors against his temple. She cut a stitch and pulled it. Samuel closed his eye.

The P&L busted Raj's head open. Steiner said he's alive, but.

God. Why? She cut another stitch.

To get at me, I imagine. They must have seen me talk to Raj. Maybe heard he tried to point me to Fish.

You think they've seen us?

Someone would have leaned on me, if they'd put it together.

It won't matter, soon. We'll come clean. Deal with the fallout. She sighed. Poor Raj.

Samuel reached for his glass but didn't lift it. I thought we'd be better than this. I thought we all knew the alternative to acting like a civilization.

She cut another stitch, pulled. Her mouth pinched and she cast about for something, then took the handkerchief from underneath Samuel and dabbed at the cut. She set it on the table and peered in, close. Where I'm from? We lost lights before the aurora. Things were going to hell there. Everyone in town was sick, or on drugs. Dad was an alcoholic. He learned how to make this terrible pruno wine, so he took all the fruit and vegetables we had and bottled it. Mom and I kicked him out one day, and it wasn't a week later a neighbor found him cut up in a ditch. She moved as if she'd clear her throat. I don't blame these people we've got hiding in The Singles, all the hobos. I can't blame them for being nervous about the city. But out there you've got sickness and death and starvation, and there's no system preventing it. Whether we're remaking a society or just holding up what's left of it, this is better than everywhere else. That's what kept me here. I want the kind of life this city lets me have.

Samuel grimaced. You never told me.

Neither of us are much for biographies, I don't think. She clipped the last stitch, set the scissors down, and dipped a small cloth in her glass of shine before wiping at his temple.

Cold. She turned his head to one side and let him go. He picked up his glass and she did the same and stood by for a while before she sat down. The clouds passing the window grew heavy. It took me about four days to walk here. I was tired and starving. It was raining. I was maybe three miles away when the lights went on. I came in from the south. Had to walk past The Bottoms, all those boarded-up houses. And then I made it to O Street. She shook her head, smiled.

Red told me something once. We were out in the desert, not long after I'd found him. He and my dad are vets. Dad went home after the war, had me, farmed. Red kept fighting. It drove my dad crazy that he wasn't helping people like he thought he should, and Red went crazy fighting. Samuel opened his hands to the table. Either you care enough to try to change the world, or you live with the guilt of standing by. Both tear you apart. And if you don't care, it wouldn't bother you anyway.

Johanna said nothing, then she leaned her head to the side. Which one are you?

I don't know. Neither, I hope. I hope I'm working toward something, here.

You are. You're helping.

Which are you?

I don't go in for dichotomies. She smiled. I guess if you had asked me a week ago, I'd have said I'm the guilty one. And happy to be.

You're not. I doubt you ever were.

She leaned forward, held her glass. You didn't know me before I got here. I wasn't too concerned with my fellow man. I left my mom, after all. I didn't fight her on it.

What happened?

She wanted to stay put. Didn't trust Charlie's look. Aaron was still going tandem back then. I saw him, saw their car. Johanna shook her head. You couldn't have guilted me into staying. She barely kept me from sneaking into their trunk.

I know it's better. For most people. But does it really take so much ugliness to do it? Does it really take that kind of greed? His hand left the glass, reached to the city through the wall, to The Capitol. When I was younger, things changed so much. But I had this idea that what came before was good. That we were trying to keep something, return to it. But if this city is any indication of it, there's a reason it went away. It's intrinsic to it, to tolerating people like Bradshaw. Maybe just intrinsic to people in general.

Sam. Are you happy? Are you ever happy?

Sometimes. He smiled. But what does that say about me? That I can be happy, with things the way they are?

She put her hand to her face. I think you have to try to be. I don't think you can live without trying.

Dad tried. We used to be.

Then what happened?

A world of bad things.

Is that how you wound up in the desert?

He nodded. A girl got killed when I was a kid. My best friend. He tapped the table, perched his hand on the glass of shine. He wasn't looking but saw Johanna pivot toward him. One day, about a year later, I figured out who did it. So I got on my horse, rode home to find a gun and rode back out. My dad realized what I was doing, who the guy was. He beat me to it.

Oh, Sam.

He pulled his lips into a tight smile. We were gonna run away, go find Red together, Mom and Dad and me. A deputy came before we could get moving. Shot my dad. Samuel shifted in the chair. A pall settled, soaked in him, and his head hung. I saw a chance and took it. Dad was too hurt to go anywhere, so I took the blame for the murders, cut out.

She crossed the room and stood before him. She took his hand from the glass and watched his face. She held his wrist with her other hand and his arms felt pinned to his sides and there was a sensation like a warm shock wherever she touched him. He saw her eyes move to his lips. He felt as though they'd just met. They kissed. They stumbled together, and she was pushing him until his legs hit the bed and they fell into it. Hands in her hair and there was the shock and his hands shook with it, pressing her closer. She kissed his neck, and his eyes filled up with a blue light. Her breasts weighing on his chest. She put her head to his, temple to temple.

Did you come back for me?

Yes.

She was overtop him, and he put his hands on her cheeks, pulling her lips to his. She guided his hand under her dress. Gooseflesh on her legs. The dress lifted smoothly to her hips, and she lifted her arms and shifted aside and threw it to the floor. Her hair covered her shoulders, her chest. He pushed it back and watched her eyes in the frame of gold, and she began to undress him. Samuel reached to pull the covers over and she forced his hand back. She tugged at his jeans, and he worked out of his shirt, and they were both naked. Shadows cast on the wall. He rolled her to her back and slid between her legs. Slight smile on their lips as they kissed. He dropped to his elbows and slipped his arms under her back and kissed her from collar to collar, her stomach, each breast. Like a ritual or ward. Her legs closed on his hips and she pulled him down. She took him in her hand and guided him and he shut his eyes. Her hands were on his hips pushing him back slowly and forward again until she dragged them up his sides and moaned. Speaking his name into his ear. He shivered and arched his back and felt her nails dig. His mind full of her eyes and the feeling of her hands when she first touched him, even now as her legs tightened around him, and he heard a long rushing and he shuddered again, his breath locked, and she squeezed and writhed until the air burst out of him and they were both still.

12

He woke later in the night. Johanna sleeping beside him, his arm draped over her. Something had startled him, but he couldn't find what. He slid out from under her and felt along the floor for his clothes and found his knife on the table. Johanna shifted.

What's the matter?

He held his breath. One engine, two. A mongrel and the others deeper, a sound from his childhood: diesel. Those aren't our engines. I gotta go.

Sam. She got off the bed and grabbed his arm.

He kissed her. Shut this door up tight. He left before she could say anything, was down the stairs and running.

The gunfire came from eastern O Street, the sounds bouncing and repeating. Patches of loose fog drifted from mounds of snow. A mongrel nearly bowled him over crossing 9th and Q, and the driver floored it to the south. From the east a heavy engine thrummed, and Samuel saw a foreign truck abandoned on the sidewalk at 14th. He ran to it, hugging the wall of a museum when he neared. Gunfire to the southeast, coming his way. Santa Muerte hung from the rearview mirror of the truck. He stuck close to the wall and cut down an alley. Three people ran south past the entrance, carrying rifles, the lead shouting in Spanish. A mongrel turned from the north and charged after them, and the group opened fire, the mongrel going full of holes and stopping in the street with the windshield powdered. The Mexicans headed east, and Samuel left the alley in their wake. He ran to the driver's side of the mongrel and slowed at the pulverized face through the open windshield and the blood thick on the man's front. Feeling for his pulse Samuel's fingers sunk almost to the headrest, and he recoiled. A gun lay on the floor, and he opened the door and took it. He checked the magazine and chambered a round, crouching behind the door. The motor was still running. He grabbed the man's foot and lifted it over the pedal before letting go, and the mongrel rolled down the street and up the curb toward a shop. It smashed the display window, and another salvo of gunfire pocked the passenger side. He could see two Mexicans rushing at the car, one with his rifle trained on it. Samuel moved back into the doorway and edged past to see them, gripped the pistol, and fired. One of the gunmen dropped to a knee, and the other sprayed the side of the building and fell. Samuel spun back. The window shattered, bricks chipped. Snow blew like birdshot past him and bullets dispelled the fog. Minutes ago, he'd been in bed, warm, her hair across his pillow. The doorway held him, then he knelt and launched off the steps and into the street, throwing half a magazine toward the car before reaching the other side and running down 14th. He tucked himself below a parking ramp and caught his breath. Shouts in Spanish echoing up M. From the south a truck revved, P&L, and he waited for it to come near before stepping out with his hands raised. The truck slowed and a look passed among the two workers, and the passenger lifted his hand.

Don't go that way. Samuel pointed. They're holed up above O.

Reese sat behind the wheel. All over the damn place.

Samuel leaned in. You know what's going on?

Charlie and Hawkins came in about a minute ahead of 'em, engine on fire. A whole gang's here, said at least three trucks loaded full.

Samuel scanned up the block and back. Two shots from far off, and then ahead of them the abandoned truck lit and bore down on them. Samuel opened fire, and the passenger jumped out and braced a rifle on the hood, and the cartel truck spun broadside on K and turned west. Samuel jumped in the back and pounded on the roof, and they pursued, Samuel falling across the bed and recovering, hands on the cab. The headlights picked up a flash of a man, a Mexican running in front of them down 10th, bleeding from the head and throwing away a handgun. A moment later Heather crossed the lights, loading her sawed-off, aiming, and sparks leapt from both barrels. The man tumbled and rolled end over end. They slowed, and without looking back she waved them off, staring down at the man. The truck ahead turned on 9th and gained ground as the P&L truck made the turn. Something exploded and the truck jolted, stopped flat. The passenger screamed and a gash was opened in the floor that matched one across his leg, blood spilling from it. Samuel leapt from the truck and ran down the street until he reached N, the stores on the left and right shot up. A man leaning out an upstairs window yelled at him and pointed north.

He ran into one of the apartments up ahead!

Samuel kept going. The door beside the seamstress' shop was kicked in, and a cone of fire spouted from it. He fell back, rolled to his feet and ran to the intersection, ducking around the corner. Patted himself down, frantic, no blood on him. He crouched and spun from the corner and fired twice at the doorway before the slide kicked. He tossed the gun away and drew his pistol. Someone screamed before he could turn out again, and he heard thumps down a stairwell. He aimed and let off when a woman came wheeling into the street wearing a white nightgown. She saw Samuel and ran for him before the nightgown ripped, bloodied, and she fell. The gunman leaned out of the second floor window. Samuel fired and scrambled for the woman and something hot struck him high on his shoulder. He dropped her, deadweight, and ran. His vision went starry and he nearly crashed into the doorway before bracing himself against it, clamping his hand over his right shoulder. Meat stuck between his fingers. He breathed and pressed hard on the wound thinking of how to bind it and the thought unspooled. His apartment was two blocks away. Blood soaking down his chest and forearm. A few more seconds, and he'd be able to move and see straight, and he'd push toward the apartment. His mouth went dry. Johanna could hear their fighting if she hadn't left. He stopped, breathed slow and deep and, shaking, took the handkerchief in his back pocket and unfolded it, pulled his jacket off, and draped the cloth over his shoulder. He took one end in his teeth and tied an overhand knot, jerking his face away. His right hand was numb around the pistol. Gunfire from far off.

Qué onda, güero?

Samuel closed his eyes. Nada, güey.

The gunman laughed. Samuel's shirt stuck to his chest. He hadn't tried to lift his arm yet, and he thought he wouldn't be able to. The gunman shot twice into the bricks at his back.

Qué tranquilo esta!

He braced himself against the door, arm limp at his side. The blood went out of his head, and he had to concentrate on standing. He stepped forward and eyed the level of the second story windows, the gunman still hidden. With his left hand he gripped his right and raised his wounded arm, and he strafed, firing on the open window and crossing the street, and he kept on until the gun was empty, and he dropped it and ran for the door, drawing the knife. In the stairwell he could hear water running. He crept upstairs quick and quiet, and when he braced against the wall, he was afraid. Weak light fell in through the window, and the hall to the end was long and narrow, the first apartment off the stairs blocking him from sight. A faucet was overflowing in one of the rooms. He'd hoped to hear breathing or groans or footsteps, but there was only the flow of water, and as he waited he could see it pooling to the stairs, the oblong reflection of the window. He held the knife out into the hallway and angled it until the pitted metal gave a dim picture of the window. Bullets ripped into the wall, and he drew back. The gunman kept firing, and when the gun clicked, Samuel rounded the corner and strode forward, timing the man drawing the magazine. Before he could cock the rifle, Samuel kicked the gun up and opened the man's chest and with a backhanded motion stuck the knife below his sternum. Samuel saw his face, eyes wide, the thin mustache. The man's last breaths rattled, popped. Samuel fell to a seat.

Weak light in the hall when he opened his eyes again. His shoulder throbbed. The gunman lay with the rifle still in his hands. Samuel leaned ahead and yanked it away and slung it down the hall. The knife stuck deep in the dead man's chest, and Samuel stretched to remove it, the flesh closed tight. He looked at the man's face. The boy's face. Younger than Samuel. He stood unsteadily and stepped on the boy's stomach and pulled the knife free. Through the window he could see the woman and her blood on the pavement. He cleaned his knife on the boy's sleeve and sheathed it. He was the one Samuel had hit earlier, a hole in his leg. Standing, Samuel walked to the stairs, hand out for the wall. Water filled most of the hallway and ran down one side of the staircase. A gunshot from midcity. He slowed at the door to the street and clutched the splintered frame for balance. Warmer, the snow melting, water from the hall running to the gutter at his feet. The truck was smoking a block down. He hung there, gripping the frame, going up 8th in his head and seeing The Remedy and the apartment and the window with Johanna in it, alive and waiting. Two more gunshots, the sound sharp. His mind retracted, unran the distance, and he started for The Capitol, toward the fighting. He didn't know how far he could get without resting. Teastained blood spread across the right side of his shirt, mostly dry.

He passed bullet casings, shattered windows. A few people standing together looking at bulletholes, blood, Samuel.

Near The Capitol two bodies lay crumpled and pushed into a gutter, and in front of a hotel the wreck of a truck around a lightpole. A Mexican was halfway through the windshield with the top of his head gone. Samuel swayed on The Capitol staircase, righting and bracing on the door. Detch was pacing down the hallway and he spun around.

Shit, man, you okay?

Samuel glanced down at himself. I'm walkin'.

We've been hunting around for you. Al had a prisoner downstairs, wanted you to talk to him. He looked aside. Al strangled him. They're all down in the basement. Detch held an arm out to usher him down the hall to the stairwell.

I heard they got attacked. Samuel waved his hand away and walked the stairs on his own.

Took 'em right out of whatever town square they were rolling through. Hawkins got away and drove the mongrel through a barn to get Charlie back. Charlie's damn arm's cut off.

Jesus.

Detch let him go down the basement corridor alone. At the first door Samuel heard voices and knocked, and the door opened immediately. Steiner was piled over himself in a corner and two of his guards stood nearby. The strangled Mexican lay flat on the floor with his neck black and his eyes blooded.

Sam. Steiner reared. I'd yell at you, but you look a bit shot. You okay?

I'm gonna need patching.

Soon as Aaron gets back, we'll send him to the nearest town we know has a doc. He gestured across the room for Samuel to sit. The room stank.

We still don't have anyone?

Not so much as a vet. They don't like coming, or we haven't found 'em. I still don't like the idea of rolling faces into a city, abandoned or otherwise. Too dangerous.

So what's going on here? He gestured, pivoted at the hip. Did we get Bradshaw?

Called a truce. Norton went to him yesterday, and they had a talk. We met before sunset and hashed some things out.

Samuel crossed his arms, lifting the right gingerly. Would have liked to have been there.

Steiner ignored him. There's still a few Mexicans holed up in one of the banks on north 16th. Finley's got some boys pinning them down. Matter of time. He looked at his hands. Did you get yours?

Two, I think. Ran into three by the university, chased them to The Haymarket, but they got away, left a guy I winged to slow us down. They got two of ours just that I saw.

They got plenty that I know of. Hit us hard. He cleared his throat. Good news is, we got Bradshaw to give up on tea. He's gonna let it go. We'll still have to scrub it off the streets, but that'll be a lot easier without him greasing the wheels.

Samuel sighed. Is he gonna pay for anything he did?

You expecting a pinky? You got what you wanted. He pointed through the wall. Don't just stand there bleedin'. Go down a room. One of the boys'll fix you up as best we can.

Samuel went out. He waited a moment before going to the stairs, leaning against the walls and winded when he got to the first floor. The hallway was abandoned, and he could see that someone had bled a trail underfoot. He thought to touch it, to see if it was fresh, his. Outside it was bright and cold, and he was faint when he opened the door to his stairwell. When he reached for the railing his shoulder flamed, and he dropped to the floor, eyes wide. The door opened above, and Johanna came flying.

13

He didn't remember getting up. She had put him in the bathtub and was laving water over him and every so often kissing his temple or good shoulder or resting her head against it. A strand of her hair floated on the water, light bent in the tension, chips of color. He felt giddy and warm and the wound was just a knotted ache. Trying to hold her hand, he couldn't lift his, and he almost smiled.

Are you ready?

His head went up. For what?

The shine. I don't know what else to do. It's too big to stitch.

His head swung back. She poured it over and leaned him forward and it felt as if the bullet were passing through him again, but cold and he had to stop himself from sliding into the water. He opened his mouth to keep from grinding his teeth. The bath rank of alcohol, and he thought he could smell the wound, the muscle. Down the side of his chest and stomach the blood clung to him in flakes, dissolving, and the sudden motion lifted ribbons into the water.

Do you have something to bandage this with?

Just get a shirt. Soak it in the moonshine.

Rick will have something downstairs.

He was quiet. Do you want him to know?

I don't care. Not now.

She stood and found a shirt and folded it. She poured the rest of the moonshine on it and wrung it out over his shoulder. He gripped the tub, and she helped him stand and dried him off with a towel. His ghoul stood in the mirror. The wound was round, smooth, red. Looking over his shoulder, he saw the exit, twice as wide and muscle open to the air. He felt bad she had to see it.

Here. She put the damp shirt over his shoulder, smoothed it into place, and wrapped the sleeves under his arm and tied them. Her eyes watching his in the mirror. She cinched the shirt tight. He was cold already and the shirt colder.

In bed she lay on his left with his good arm around her. She'd stripped down before lying beside him, and she was warm and soft and her hair falling across his chest. It was bright outside and the room felt empty. They were quiet for a long time, and he was tired, but there was no sleep. He sifted his fingers through her hair and twisted it, and he could feel her lips curl into a smile. He was drifting into the hallway and the water dripped from the stairs. The memory played with better lighting than the reality.

If we left the city, where would we go? To live. She stretched, covered a yawn.

I thought you wanted to stay in the city?

I do. She held him closer. But I want to stay with you more.

He felt her breath on his skin, warm and cool and warm again. I know a lot of places. But I don't know how safe they are anymore.

Pretend they are.

New Mexico.

Where in New Mexico?

Anywhere. It's all beautiful. He stopped, head elsewhere. We could go to Utah. Do you like the desert?

I don't know.

What do you like?

Someplace that isn't flat.

Okay. He thought. Talking wore at him. How about east? I've never been east.

They slept. When Samuel heard footsteps on the stairs

he tried to sit up, and it was a quick reel from Johanna to the door and daylight. His shoulder throbbed, and he snarled. The footsteps stopped.

You all right in there, Sam?

It was Steiner. Samuel closed his eyes. Yeah. Gimme a minute. Johanna woke, and Samuel had her pull the shirt loose and slip into the bathroom. He put his jeans on and went to the door. Steiner loomed in the hall behind the door. Sorry, I was asleep. Trying to air this thing out. He tilted his head to his shoulder.

Can I get a look at it?

He lifted the shirt. It was layered in pink stains.

Steiner spun him to see his back. The hell was the guy shooting? I can about see daylight through it.

Fluid seeped from the wound, and Samuel wiped it with the shirt and pressed it gingerly down. AK, I think.

Well, Aaron's due back. We'll turn him around for a doc. He glossed the room over and saw the shine glasses on the table. His eyes narrowed. Who's in here with you?

Samuel felt his face pale.

What'd I catch you at? You got Johanna in there?

He said nothing.

I was ribbin' you about being queer, kid. You didn't need to prove me wrong. He stood taller, and backed from the door. I liked you better as a loner. You had this air of authority about you.

Al—

Don't. He put up his hand, sighed. We're on damage control right now. Gonna have a community meeting tomorrow, tell everyone what's going on, let 'em all eat on our dime. Rest up and be there.

All right.

Where's the man you nixed?

Hundred block of 9th, west side. Second floor. You'll see it.

Steiner reached into the room and swung the door almost closed. Don't let Aaron be the fool. He's your friend.

He shut the door. Johanna came out of the bathroom. He met her eyes briefly, and went to the table, then to the window. Steiner's mongrel pulled away.

This was coming, one way or another.

He glanced back at her, the movement stopped before he really saw. I know. He breathed. It tired him. He drifted to the table and sat at it, the drop painful, and he was glad for the pain.

He was unsure when she returned to bed, and when he joined her. He was cold, and wanted to sleep, and it came and was gone. The ceiling gray, strobing dark by some trick of his eyes. He thought of Aaron, unknowing, the city uncanny with dead and damange, that moment of realization. And the other unknowing.

It was afternoon by the time they stumbled into the bathroom. They showered together, and he leaned against her under the water while she cupped her hands and washed his shoulder. He stroked her hair slick and straight down her back. He lay on the bed after, lightheaded, and turned away when she began to dress beside him. He let her pull him to his feet, and when he stooped for his knife on the floor he felt the blood flow to his shoulder, and he stilled, hovering. Johanna watched him, and followed him out. At the bottom of the stairs, he put his hand on the doorknob and looked at her and opened it and they stepped together into the open air. It was warm out and quiet but he fought the feeling of exposure and it sharpened to a fear until he saw inside the empty diner. They went in, and Rick entered from the kitchen with a pad of paper in his hand, and he stopped at the sight of them and smiled.

I heard you got hit, Sam. I'm glad it wasn't serious.

Seems pretty serious to me.

They ordered burgers and sat in a corner booth sharing a side. They held hands under the table, Samuel watching the door. Rick came out shortly with a basket of fries covered in cheese.

Figured you needed replenishing. At the counter he spun around to back through the doors. Burgers'll be right out.

Samuel watched the doors swing closed, and they started on the fries. A mongrel pulled up, and before Samuel could clear himself from the booth, Beth walked inside. She held a hand out to keep Rick from speaking at the kitchen window, and she sat down across from them.

He just got back into town. Steiner wanted you to know. She clutched her hands together on the tabletop. A knuckle popped. That's all he has to say on the matter. I'm here to tell the two of you to leave.

They glanced at each other. Samuel breathed like he would speak and Beth cut him off.

I've had this problem my whole life, where I'm a little harsh. Every so often I remember that, and I try to correct it, and it's always brittle and when it's over I have this little feeling like my socks are rolled up wrong for days. Let's skip that. Leave. My offer for the railroad still stands, but you'll have to take the work elsewhere.

Johanna shook her head slightly. Her hand went cold in his. I know things are bad, and we haven't made them any better with what we're doing, but we're not gonna be chased out of town.

It's not about you two fooling around. It's not about the cartel, or the tea.

What is it about, then?

Beth looked at Samuel, ignoring her. This really is how the world works. I don't know how that bandage hasn't been ripped off you yet, Sam. You can't save this city because you'll cut out the thing that makes it. I imagine it's always been this way, but I know that's how it is now. You're trying to lift the city up over the floodwaters and you don't get the place is an island.

Johanna leaned in. That's a pretty expression and all—

Thank you. It's been rattling around in my head for a day or so.

I've seen corruption. I've seen a city break apart. But there isn't any point in running if there's nowhere to run to.

There's more country out there every day. You'll find someplace.

No. Samuel squeezed Johanna's hand. If we don't make a stand here we never will. People, all of us. I'm not gonna watch it fall apart.

Beth put a hand to her temple, let it drop. Here I'd return you to the ocean metaphor. She slid out of the booth. I tried to help you, Sam. If you make it out of this, remember that. Tell Red that.

He narrowed his eyes, and she turned and left. Johanna stroked her thumb over his and pulled her hand free, turned his face and kissed him.

I'm going to go.

He stood to let her out, head low. She traced her hand across his back.

Don't believe every metaphor you hear. We're gonna keep fighting.

He smiled and watched her leave. When she was gone he sat again, staring at their food. He picked out a glob of fries and ate them and pushed the basket away. Rick came out with the burgers, paused, and leaned against the counter.

Well. He looked at the fries. Can I get you a box?

The sun had just gone behind the buildings across the street. The air in the apartment hung thick with vapor from the shower. He draped the rag over the shower curtain and picked up the bloodsoaked handkerchief that she'd taken off him that morning and set it in the sink to wash. He took off his shirt and the bandaging, undoing the sleeves and letting the shirt drop. He looked at the entry wound and prodded it, pulled back the skin and let it go. It occurred to him that his insides were perfectly black and always had been, that light was foreign to his flesh. Draping the rag over his shoulder, he thought of pulling a curtain or blocking up a window. He finished dressing the wound, and he got the book from the desk and sat on his bed. The light dimmed slowly, and after a while he stopped reading and was only moving his eyes over the same page.

The streetlights were on when he woke, and he turned on his own and lay back in bed. Her scent lifted off the covers and pillow. A car passed below, slowed, and he had to hold his breath and fight down the adrenaline. He read a chapter of the book and drifted off again with his head full of scales, lines of influence and dimension. The stars dispersed. Aaron stood in the doorway.

Hey, bud. Couldn't seem to wake you so I thought I'd just come in.

Hey. Samuel sat up with his good hand.

How you doin'?

Shot.

He looked away, moving further into the room. I only got a minute before they send me out. Have to get a doc for Charlie and you. He paused. I heard you got a couple of them, wouldn't let anyone fix you up.

He stared at his legs, the end of the bed. Glad for the half-truth of his silence. Aaron took a deep breath and his face was set hard.

Goddamn. Just— He lifted a hand and almost laughed. I don't know how to be angry, man. I'm not an angry guy. But Jesus. He turned toward the window.

It gets easier.

Aaron nodded, still staring out the window. He nodded again and the room went cold from the skewing of his eye toward Samuel. He swallowed. Johanna was spooked. I guess she saw one of them. One of the trucks.

We were fighting all over the place.

Yeah. He breathed deep. Can I get you something? Shine?

He shook his head. I'm good.

Can you lift that hand of yours?

Samuel craned his hand up by the elbow, and Aaron strode to him and gripped it and pulled him in for a hug. Before he could do anything, Samuel's eyes blurred thick with tears.

Hey. Hey bud, Jesus. Aaron patted his back.

I'm all right.

Hey. He leaned down to him, holding onto his hand. Let it out if you gotta. I'm here.

Samuel worked his jaw at the air. Long, empty breaths to dry himself out. Aaron let go of his hand and sat on the bed. He stayed there and Samuel kept his eyes wide to the ceiling. Eventually, Aaron patted the bedside.

I gotta get. I'll bring you back a doc, all right?

Yeah. Thanks.

Take her easy. He opened the door and left.

Samuel lay there alone with his eyes burning for an hour until Johanna came in, and she shut off the light without speaking and lay down beside him. He felt the cold between them and couldn't tell who was far away.

14

He dreamt of the city in deeper winter, the lights and bricks sucked of their chroma and the buildings risen from the snow like bloodless fingers. He stood on the overpass and below ran a pack of coyotes, and he was the last person alive. The wind took his breath and cut his face and the burning reached through his dream, and he woke. The rag on his shoulder felt wet. Johanna was hugging his back, and he tried to slide around but he woke her, and in the dark he kissed her and felt no distance. She touched his temple, tracing the forgotten and still-raw scar.

What sort of house will we live in?

Depends. Where are we living?

East. Maybe North Carolina. Virginia.

He smiled. A small house in the hills. Have a little barn that I have to repair because the roof's fallen in.

What'll we do?

Grow corn. Tobacco, maybe. Sell a jar of moonshine here and there.

They hadn't touched each other more than the edges of their arms. She rolled onto her side and put her hand on his chest. Keep going.

We'll have a few animals. Mules to plow the field. Chickens. Goats.

That seems like a lot.

We used to have a whole herd of cattle back home.

Near the light of day, they made love. He carried up eggs and sausage from Sheila, and they ate at the desk together, and she asked when they would see each other again. Neither of them knew. They lay in bed before she dressed. She moved languidly but with conservation, and he wanted to watch her dress over and over again, to watch her walk about a familiar room. She went to the window and peeked over the street and came to the bed and kissed him and turned her mouth to his ear.

I'm in love with you, you know. What are we gonna do about that? She straightened and buttoned her jacket and walked out before he could answer. Play of a smile on her face. When he got to the window she was looking up at him, and he put a hand to the glass.

He spent the rest of the morning listening to the distant sounds of cars and watching when they came near. It seemed like dawn for a long time, the sunlight colored and slanted. When the sun hung overhead, he showered carefully and shaved and washed out the wound with hot water. He let the rag soak before replacing it and fashioned a sling from an old shirt.

The people outside moved as if in wonder, the city hit by a storm or flood. The seamstress stood in the window of her store, staring out. Samuel waved and continued. He took K Street east, scanning for signs of the fight, but most had been cleaned, the wrecks hauled away and the blood hosed off the streets. Bright holes showed out of walls, brick, fresh stone exposed. He was panting by the time he got to The Capitol, a circle of civilians and O Streeters smoking, tobacco and weed, and indoors he leaned against a wall, feeling the sweat on his brow. They'd mopped the floors. There were citizens in the halls milling around, some lined up outside the conference rooms. The few guards and other workers walking by were stonefaced or stoned. Norton ambled down the hall, coming toward him, wiping his nose with a handkerchief.

Charlie's dead. Died about two hours ago. They think it was blood poisoning or something.

Samuel straightened. Are the others okay?

Mostly. One of 'em needs an operation, but other than that, nothing bad. Everyone else is walkin' around or already dead. He rubbed at his face. Spics took out three of our mongrels. One of the trucks. Me and Al been working since four this morning.

Anything for me to do?

Not wounded, I don't think. Rest up. He took a dull gold dollar from his pocket. This'll get you bourbon. Blood, and all that. You got a few rounds coming.

He took the coin. Thanks.

Al's put out a buffet in the conference room. Go get yourself somethin' to eat.

He nodded as he passed him, pocketing the dollar. The crowd grew thicker near the doors, and through them he saw tables laid out with trays of cold cuts and cheese and several crockpots of roast and shredded chicken. There were Light workers in uniform and a few O Streeters and others, civilians. Beth stood in a corner with Maggie, both holding plates. Samuel went up to the first table, and a Light worker dishing his own plate handed it over to Samuel and told him to sit down. People snuck looks his way as he found a seat, and down the table a few citizens were talking, and he heard snatches of the conversation and they sounded righteous and angry. Maggie pulled a seat beside him.

You left before I got to tell you.

He stared between their plates. You're serious about this? Even now?

Yeah. I am. She stretched her arms under the table, squirmed. Look, I know I have a problem. You might not think I'm in my right mind, but I am. And I have reasons for wanting this. Things that would turn you white. She caught someone's eye down the table and leaned over to him, kissed his cheek low, near his neck.

He shivered and pulled away. Don't.

Why not? She smiled, eyes playful. He's not a good

person. He's rotten. If you won't do it, I will. Someday. She stood, her hand on his good shoulder. On Fletcher, outside of town. There's a whole complex, but he only uses the building closest to the entrance. She straightened and took her plate, stacked it in a tub by the door. As she walked out, Steiner stopped her, coming in, and they spoke briefly before she left. They moved to the end of the room and Steiner spotted him and waved him over. Samuel pushed his chair back, leaving his plate. Steiner spoke softly.

I'm sure you got some choice words. I'd appreciate it if you ate 'em for now.

Samuel nodded once. Bradshaw was wearing a porkpie hat and he swept it off his head and shook Samuel's hand.

Sam. I hope we can put everything behind us in light of all this.

He lifted his chin, said nothing.

Bradshaw exhaled, and moved in between them both. He raised an arm to the room. Before he could say anything, Steiner stepped forward, staring Bradshaw down.

I hope you all're enjoying the spread, and you won't bother me a bit if you keep eating while I talk. He paused for a laugh. I want to thank the folks that donated food for us and to thank you for coming. I know this has been a rough couple days. I think it's important that we all try to come together and get to know each other here, now more than ever before. Like as not, starting this project, just having this city, makes enemies for us. I guess that's the world we're in, these days. So I'd like to make as many friends as I can today. If you would, when you leave here, tell your neighbors to come on by and say hello. Now. He put a hand on Samuel's good shoulder. This boy is the hero of The Haymarket. Single-handedly beat back a truckload of those gangsters and got two of 'em before they went packing. And I see a couple good ol' O Streeters in the crowd. Stand up and take a bow.

Beth left out the back. Bradshaw came forward and asked

for a round of applause. When it died off, Steiner let Samuel go, and began to speak about a mass funeral for the deceased. Samuel started out of the hall and went to the north doors, and before he was clear he heard the mongrel, rubber squealing as it turned onto 14th. He let the door shut him inside and started for the west entrance, in time to see Gil and Rogan guide a tall, older man toward the basement. Aaron followed after them, slumped like an empty jacket. Steiner and an O Streeter came from the banquet, and Steiner pointed at Rogan.

Fetch that drunk at The Inn, would you?

Rogan split off, headed back out the door. Gil waited at the mouth of the stairs with the man and Aaron, Samuel lingering, and Steiner ushered them down, into the corridor. He and Gil guided the man to the second door. Aaron and the O Streeter were talking, and Samuel watched Aaron list, crash into the wall, and recover. Steiner came back into the hall, thumbed the O Streeter inside, and unlocked the first door. The chairs and table were still inside from the interrogation. He waved Samuel in.

That operating room's gonna get crowded. You can wait in here. He pushed the door wide, and Samuel entered. Before the door shut Aaron was in the room with him, the bolt him home, and echoed. Aaron paced to the far side, took a seat and then kicked it away.

Oh, Sammy. We were too damn slow. If we'd just gone right off, maybe. If I'd been more convincing. Oh, goddammit.

You wanna tell me what happened?

Aaron looked away like he'd ask someone else to explain. I killed a kid. The doctor's kid. He breathed deep, sharp, head craned to the ceiling. We got there late. About the whole town seemed asleep. Charlie'd been to the place before, so he knew there was a doctor there. But the crowd went wrong on him, back then, so we didn't get any of them. This was back before we had the pitch refined, you know. We used to just show people lightbulbs and batteries like they were cavemen, expect them to fall in line. Aaron halted, glanced down at himself and then at his hand, turning it over. So we knock on a couple doors until someone points us to the doctor's place, knock on his. He answered with a ballbat. Slams the door. Finley tries talking to him, tries to convince him. I try to convince him. He knew who we were.

Samuel watched him. His eyes went around the room, to Samuel's and away. Finally Rogan's had enough, and he pushes Gil out of the way and kicks the door in, puts a gun on the doc. Whole house is up now. Doc's wife, a little girl. And here comes this kid, maybe fourteen, carrying a shotgun. And it'd never happen again in a million years, Sam, but I saw him, saw his eyes and his hand moving, and I knew he was gonna try something. Knew it. Had my gun out before he yelled for his dad to get down. Aaron shook his head, hands up. I shot him. Lifted and fired, lifted and fired— He formed a gun with his hand. Just like that. Like I'd done it a thousand times before.

You were doing your job.

Kid's dad was in the way. Hadn't moved. Not an inch. He couldn't get a shot off no way. Aaron was staring at the same patch of floor as Samuel. I never thought about it, you know? I'd never done it, never shot a gun. But I remembered movies from when I was a kid. It's a lot louder. Then it goes away. Hear the shot, and the kid's just not in the doorway. He's on the floor, can't see him 'cause there's a couch he's behind. Just gone.

Samuel shook his head.

Aaron stared, vacantly. And Charlie died. Killed the kid for nothing. Hell, I killed him for nothing anyway. Now it's just a joke. I. Fuck's sake, Sam.

You were protecting Gil. You had his back. Red was doing the same for me when Graham drew down.

His fingers straightened like he would flick something away. The door opened after a few minutes of silence, and Steiner stood over them. He breathed heavy, once.

Go be with your woman.

Samuel's face heated. Aaron got up.

Maybe we'll leave. Johanna and I. Just get out of here.

Samuel swallowed. Steiner let Aaron pass, and he stood inside the room.

Well, looks like you got yourself a reprieve. For sanity's sake. But maybe if you don't want to be an absolute piece of shit you won't see her again unless you've come clean.

15

He tried the door and waited in the basement hallway, propped against the wall. When the doctor opened the door, his hands were bloody, and the apron he wore was smeared. He had no mask or gloves, and he simply turned away, and Samuel walked inside. The O Streeter with the leg wound rocked on a pair of crutches, getting his feet. His forehead was beaded and his eyes dark, and he went swinging past Samuel. Steiner lurked in the corner, arms crossed. The doctor coughed and pointed to several bottles of moonshine by one of the cots.

Got some liquor if you want it. I've already wasted my anesthetic.

Just cut me open.

The doctor lifted his brow and wheeled away from him. Samuel sat on the clean cot.

Lie down.

Samuel glanced back at Steiner and unbuttoned his shirt. He undid the sling and let it fall. The doctor washed his hands in a basin of shine before lifting the rag on Samuel's shoulder and dropping it to the floor.

How's the one with the busted head?

He'll recover. The doctor prodded at the skin near the wound with his fingers. He took a metal clamp and pushed it into the wound and pressed one side and another. Samuel breathed. The doctor opened the clamp and grasped at the rim of the wound and cut away at something, and Samuel braced, straightened.

It's gonna get worse.

The doctor shifted around and peered in the hole, widened the clamps. Samuel closed his eyes and breathed very
slowly. The doctor started pulling at tissue. He came away
with a bloody string, and he whirled the clamp in a washba-
sin beside the table. He reached for an IV bag and pulled a
plastic stopper and flushed the wound and dug into it again.
Fluid pattered on the floor. When the doctor was an inch or
more deep he clamped and Samuel's vision went white, and it
cleared with the doctor on his back, Steiner leering over him.
He stepped aside, and Samuel tried to sit up to see what was
happening. His limbs shook, and his insides felt loose. The
doctor got to his knees and wiped at his face.

I touched his nerve. I didn't mean to.

Like hell you didn't.

The doctor climbed to his feet. I need to keep going. Believe what you want.

You hurt him like that again, and I'll kill you.

He brushed at himself, holding his hands over the basin
when he relaxed, and raised a hand, as if to block Steiner. Get
out. Or I stop. He smiled, and it fell. My son is dead. You have
nothing on me. You can watch him die from the infection.

Steiner worked his hands, and all Samuel could see was a
blur of flesh expanding and contracting. Sam. Just yell.

Samuel nodded. Steiner went out and slammed the door
closed. The doctor leaned over him and washed the clamp
and scissors with the solution, and he flooded the wound
again.

I wouldn't let you die.

Samuel said nothing for a moment. The doctor watched
the wound, padded at it with gauze. The cotton came away
with an arc of bright blood, like an early moon. Samuel
watched it fall. I'm sorry about your son.

Sure.

He breathed in. I know they didn't mean for it to happen.

Intention's a lovely thing, isn't it? If things only went as intended from Adam and Eve. Can you imagine? Eating fruit all day, looking like a Reuben. But we're in this world. Things go awry. He returned the clamp, cold again.

You're well read, I take it?

Nothing's on TV anymore. The doctor was stonefaced. He pulled the clamp. We can't live on intention. In lieu of true judgment, we have to operate on facts. The doctor wiped his brow with his sleeve. Did you know some Christians think this world is hell? I found myself pondering that, in the car.

No.

It solves a lot of problems. I hadn't given it much thought, but it seems right. To know, to feel, and to understand in your heart that there is a better way for everything to be and to never be able to attain it. Doesn't that sound like hell to you? Roll over. Onto your stomach.

Samuel cradled his arm against his chest and sat up, easing himself down with the left. The doctor flattened him out and cut at the skin again, and Samuel lay with his jaw pressing against the rim of the cot. Pink solution pooled under him on the tile.

I think that's the crux of it. Not the individual hurts of the world. The true pain of hell is supposed to be separation from God. I think I understand that now, in a way I didn't before. It's not just a yearning for Him. It's a yearning for the perfection that brings. The justice. The ease.

You don't find it hypocritical that a just god condemns you to hell at birth?

I'd like to see a better alternative. The doctor yanked.

Creation has no order. He breathed. Sweat beaded, evaporated. We just exist.

You would be an atheist. He pushed on Samuel's shoulder, hands set, began to excise what felt like a whole cut of him, a piece to lay on a scale and weigh. If I were a stronger Christian, I would pray for your soul, but frankly this is as far as my kindness extends.

I don't blame you for that. Samuel shut his eyes tight, breathed slowly. I could believe this world is hell. It fits. But so does an indifferent universe. An indifferent god. Anything else is just—He raised his head, switched sides—a comfort. If facts are all we've got, well.

But we don't live in an indifferent universe.

Samuel exhaled. You imagine God is just biding his time, letting criminals go to be punished later, or to learn a lesson.

The doctor set his tools aside, washed the wound out. Everything has a purpose.

And God is omnipotent. Anything for him is without effort.

Yes. Metal rattled in the basin, and the doctor rinsed his hands.

So for God, doing nothing and doing anything are the same. Tell me how that's not an indifferent god. Tell me how standing by makes him just.

His head cocked. Samuel sat upright, feet an inch off the ground. Saline ran in a syrupy line from his wound down his chest. The doctor passed him a bolt of gauze and turned away. You're showing the first signs of infection. I don't have much in the way of antibiotics, so you'll need to be very careful about keeping the wound clean. No dishrags. Real sterile bandages.

All right.

The doctor took the gauze from him again and began to wrap the wound. You can't puzzle God, you know. You can't catch Him in a bind. He has His own rules and order. You can puzzle me, because I'm human. But He is untouchable.

I hope that thought comforts you.

He finished wrapping the wound, taped the dressing, and handed Samuel his shirt. It does. It comforts me in the same way I can see it comforts you to place all this into a little box of indifference. That makes sense. I can see how you would fear an afterlife. You should. You should fear what's coming.

Samuel stood, shaky as a calf. The doctor went over to the door empty-handed and knocked. Steiner opened it, glanced over the doctor's shoulder at Samuel and let him through.

You patched?

Yeah. He stooped for the roll of gauze and tape, and Steiner held the door for him and Samuel walked out. He climbed the stairs to the hall and found a few people milling, some civilians and a couple O Streeters. The doors hung open, and he passed through them.

He slept. He woke once before the lights came on, and he drifted again just before someone climbed the stairs. Slow footsteps, heavy knock. Samuel got up and flipped the light and opened the door. It was Rogan.

Someone robbed us. All the money's missing from the safe and a hardtop from the garage. Steiner's guessing it was Doubek.

Samuel worked his eyes, still bleary from sleep. Where did she go?

That's what I was gonna ask you.

He shook his head. I told Steiner she'd left her place night before last. He opened a hand to the air and let it fall. If Red were here he might know where she went, but I don't. We haven't been close since she pushed us out of town.

All right. Rogan shrugged, and spun back into the hall. Find Aaron, when you got the energy. Guy's about out of rope.

He nodded, and Rogan started down the stairs. A mongrel shifted below, and he went to the bathroom to put a new dressing on his shoulder. In the mirror the hole was freshly raw and an inch deep. He redressed and taped the wound and lay in bed. Thoughts colluded from the glasses on the desk, full then, and the hours between poor in name and time for all they held. He rose to shut off the lamp, more to see the light of the city than to be in the dark, and stayed by the switch. Then he slipped the knife into the sling, resting against his forearm. There were no clouds and no people out. He walked to Norton's, stopping once to let the stars clear from his eyes. A few engines rumbled from further in the city but the shops and restaurants had blinds drawn, signs turned to 'closed.' Stepping into the bar, he rounded the corner into the quiet, the bartender meeting his eyes and walking away. Samuel saw Aaron in a glow of blond hair under the pool table lights, playing himself. A P&L worker waited nearby, watching. There was no one else inside and the jukebox sat quiet. Samuel stood at the counter, and the bartender came toward him shaking his head.

Everyone's cut off. No booze.

Samuel cocked his head back. Why?

Beth's fault. Aaron slung the cue onto the table and slipped around a chair. Bradshaw requisitioned it all. Gonna sell it off.

Samuel raised his eyebrows and held in a sigh.

I sent Johanna out to try to find some. She said she might have a bottle at her place. I need a drink so fuckin' bad, man.

Let's sit. He guided Aaron to their booth and stopped and felt in his pocket, pulling out the gold dollar. Hey, barkeep. He held the dollar up. Norton said I was owed.

Yeah, all right. The bartender rummaged below the counter. Samuel sidled between two stools, and the bartender raised back with a small bottle, and poured two tumblers of bourbon.

Thanks. He clapped the coin on the bartop and took the glasses, raising one toward Aaron as he came over.

How'd you get that?

Bourbon for blood, I guess. Enjoy. They lifted their glasses and drank, Samuel just a sip. You were saving your crew, bud. All it takes is a moment. If you'd hesitated, who knows what would have happened.

Aaron's eyes fell to the table. He scratched at a waterstain. I still feel like shit.

I'd think less of you if you didn't. He tapped Aaron's glass, and they drank. Samuel left half the bourbon and Aaron drained his.

Where's Johanna? I'm gonna need at least a gallon of shine.

I think that'd kill you.

Well, I promised Norton he could use me as a wooden Indian if I died. Aaron pointed to the door. Stick my hand out so you can shake it when you walk in. I'll be pretty well pickled when I go, ideally.

He shook his head and slid his glass across. You can have mine to start.

Aaron threw it back. Thanks. He set the glass down and looked at the bartender. Hey, you think you could hit us up again?

Dollar's good for a round. Sorry.

Just a little bit. Enough to give me a buzz, man. I killed someone. I should have bourbon coming, too.

The bartender thinned his lips. One shot.

Aaron set the tumblers on the bar. Samuel watched him watch the bartender pour, thin. Aaron craned his head to eye him.

You're the sort of asshole gives a thirsty man vinegar, aren't you?

I'm the sort of asshole that keeps his job. Norton has his eye on this bottle. The bartender set the bourbon below the counter.

Aaron turned back to Samuel. Sam?

Don't do it.

Aaron breathed deep, exhaled, and drank the shot. He set the glass on the bar and flicked it forward hard enough for it to fall over into the sink. The bartender stared him down as Aaron flicked the other over and returned to the booth, eyes wandering, then walked to the jukebox and lit a cigarette.

Johanna came from the entrance, empty-handed. She went over to Aaron, hand tracing a table edge. Samuel looked away. The jukebox started, a loud guitar. Aaron and Johanna sat down together, and Aaron groaned.

Is there any hooch left in this city?

I guess I shouldn't have cracked down so hard. We could go looking if you like.

Some civvies have to have a little. Some restaurant.

Not tonight. Johanna leaned toward him. Nobody's open. It's a ghost town out there.

First thing in the morning, then.

You don't need a drink that bad, babe. You just need some time.

Samuel offered a tight smile and stood. Be right back. He crossed to the stairs and went in the restroom. Washing his hands he saw in the cracked mirror the door opening, and Aaron walked in behind him, and Samuel's back seized as it would at a crash in the night. He patted his hands dry and walked out, returning to the table downstairs, standing beside it. Johanna watched him with an eyebrow quirked, and Samuel closed his eyes and sighed. They waited on Aaron to come back, gripping the railing as he descended. Samuel nodded to him.

I got an idea for some booze. You want to come with, or should I deliver it to you?

Aaron perked. For real?

No guarantees, but yeah. I know one guy who's always a few drinks deep. He might have some stashed away.

Then let's go. He stood by, waiting on Johanna to slip out. She nearly brushed Samuel's hand and gave him a look before they made for the door. Samuel led them down Q, through the empty sidewalks and streets, the last of the snow in dirty, pebbled mountains. Lights were on everywhere, but they saw few people. At 9th they turned south, found The Inn glowing, all the windows bright. An O Streeter slept on the sofa in the lobby, and Samuel shook him awake.

You the guy looking in on Raj?

The guard lurched upright. The drunk? 208, if you want to visit.

Samuel turned to Aaron and Johanna. Wait for me here? I don't want to crowd him.

I'll try not to get the shakes in the meantime. Aaron took a seat on one of the couches, and Johanna leaned on its arm.

Samuel went to the stairs, looked back, and climbed a flight. He found Raj's room near the door and knocked, opened it. The air was rank. Raj lay in bed, his head wrapped and propped up. His eyes emerged from a tangle of hair and thick beard.

Hey, Sammy. I did the stupidest thing the other day.

Samuel forced a smile. What's that?

Tried to break a bunch of bricks with my head. He looked at the ceiling. Apparently you got to use the front, not the back. Have to remember that next time.

They treatin' you okay?

Coulda had me in the stockade, for all I knew. I haven't been out that cold in ages.

Can I get you something? You hungry?

Eh. Raj rocked his head from side to side. My appetite's lost. That door closed? Raj hefted himself upright, wincing, to see. He nodded softly, grimly. They killed everyone at The Jungle. Murdered 'em.

What?

Like it was Wounded Knee or something. I saw the bodies, and someone saw me out there. Before I could get my lily ass away, I was clubbed.

Who did it? Who got you?

I didn't get a good look. I could tell you from a lineup, maybe.

Why kill them?

Maybe they're makin' way for a golf course.

Raj.

He gave a little smile. Couldn't help myself. I only got a few pleasures left to me. He worked his lips over his teeth like he'd suck food from them. Only thing I can think is this story a boy told us all, before I took to livin' in town. He was a tea fiend, said the P&L had thrown him in a prison for it, had him doing work that made him go blind for days at a time. He got away, came to The Jungle where he knew he could score. Raj stopped to breathe. He disappeared one day, but one of the fellas out there when everyone got waxed was a new arrival. He was pretty rough lookin'. Wherever those two were from, I think it's something they don't want us to know about.

Christ. Did he say where this prison was?

Nah. He mentioned a power plant. I dunno if he meant ours.

Nobody's supposed to know where that is. Why would we have a prison in our plant?

Raj gave a shrug, eyes wandering to his. Listen. I'm leavin'. I'm gone as soon as I get my feet. This whole town is rotten—Doubek and Bradshaw and all of 'em. Killin' tramps. We never hurt no one.

Samuel grimaced, took a few paces toward the window. 9th Street went north below them, empty as before. Even inside it seemed quiet. Near the horizon he could make out the swoop of the highway rising, the road he'd take to Fletcher.

So did you come here just to check in on me or did you need to ask me something? I still don't know where Fish is.

I am looking for some similar information. You know anyone making shine on the side, other than him? Buddy of mine is about to get withdrawals since they cut the sale here in town.

I probably do. But you can skip the walk. Take my bottle. He thumbed to the chest of drawers. I always keep a little squirreled. They stowed it for me.

Samuel opened it. Inside were two bottles, one half-gone.

He took the full one and held it in his right hand.

How bad's your wing?

Could be worse.

Raj's lips thinned. Well, buddy, come and see me again before too long.

I will. Thank you. He lifted the shine. Take care.

He nodded, and Samuel turned and walked out. Downstairs he saw Aaron dozing, Johanna at the window. He passed the bottle off to her. Make sure he doesn't drink this all at once.

I will. She nearly frowned. What are you gonna do?

His insides wrung. I'll know by tomorrow. He looked at Aaron and around them, the clerk behind the desk asleep. He tried to smile at her and went out the doors. He cut across the lot by 7th, walking through the rusted construction equipment and breaking into a trot through the open ground until he made it to the creek, ignoring the pain in his shoulder. The Jungle lay ahead, sheltered by the copse of trees. Even without the fire, he saw the tents were down. A strand of barbwire caught one of the windbreak sheets and it was ripped and thin. He stood on the empty camp, grass trod bare long ago and the soil dark. He watched the city, The Capitol, and started north.

16

He walked out of the city on 10th, taking the ramp up, the highway passing over an abandoned neighborhood and leveling ahead of the creek. A mile out he saw tracks in the mud off the shoulder, a mongrel parked under the low, broken branches of a dead spruce. It was already late in the evening, early morning. He went on, faint glow of the city behind him.

He could see one lit window from Fletcher. The pond showed dimly at the entrance. It was a large complex, twenty buildings. He came down the drive and cut over the median dividing the parking lot. Soft, orange light in the window of a second-floor apartment. He found the stairs, waiting at the foot to take off the sling. He spent a full minute crossing the distance between the stairs and the door, the wood making reports of every footfall. The light flickered on the balcony to his left. No shadows, no movement. He drew his knife with his left hand and tried the doorknob. Fingers trembling. It opened. The room long and bare, a kitchen off to the right, a small counter coming out of the wall with a gas lamp atop it. He took the lamp, waist-high, moving toward a short hallway with two closed doors. He held his breath for a sound and tried the door on the right. Light swept over the room, nothing in it but a plain wardrobe, open, clothes hanging. Samuel turned around, crossed the gap to the other door. He waited again and went in. Faint light through the window, and below it Bradshaw sleeping in a twin bed, a sawed-off shotgun on the floor beside a pile of clothes. Samuel set the lamp down, and the shadow of the bed swung up onto the wall. He crouched and drew the gun to himself. Stirring of blankets from the bed. Samuel stood with the gun as Bradshaw pushed against the headboard.

Balls. He blinked. His face contorted against the light or confusion, and then he breathed, relaxed. Well. Can I make a few requests?

Go ahead.

Can I stand up?

Samuel nodded and stepped back.

Bradshaw set his feet on the floor and stood. He was in his underwear.

Get dressed.

Glad to. Who wants to get killed naked? He reached for his pants. How about a drink?

Fine.

Bradshaw smiled, tucking in his shirt. Now we're talking. He pointed to the door, and Samuel moved aside, let him go to it. Samuel lifted the lamp and they went into the main room. Bradshaw glanced over his shoulder. Would've thought you'd be more of an asshole about this. Why not kill me now?

I'm not about to let you cook dinner, but. Samuel shrugged. What happens between now and when I pull this trigger doesn't matter. You may as well go drunk.

He walked to the kitchen. You've never killed someone this way, have you? With time to spare?

I might have.

Bradshaw lifted an eyebrow. Please. Experience was your selling point. You don't have to embellish. He waited on Samuel to speak and reached into a cabinet. There's nothing in here but some peach brandy.

Slowly.

He took out a bottle. No glasses or I'd offer you some.

Peach was always too sweet for me.

Not me. Bradshaw grinned. He took the bottle to the counter and pulled the top. He had a drink, considered it, and had another. He was still smiling. This is an interesting moment.

I suppose. Samuel set the lamp on the floor.

I can see why people always spill their guts before they die. Feels like all you got is words to stop the guy with the gun. Try to reach him as a human.

But you know better.

Yeah. Even so. Something freeing about it. The adrenaline, maybe. Bradshaw pulled from the bottle and wiped his mouth with the back of his hand. What got you out here, finally? Steiner have you follow me?

Maggie told me you were here. And you had The Jungle cleared out.

Maggie. I guess I had that coming.

Why'd you kill them? Why even run tea, when you run a city?

Ran. He lifted a finger from the bottle. You and Al saw to that. He shrugged. It's a simple idea, and it's the least of the puzzle. Vice will exist no matter what. That's just people. He fiddled with the bottlecap, spun it. You may as well control it, make the money yourself. Keep the other bad elements out, keep the whole workings internal.

That's practical, I suppose.

I'm a pragmatist. And you can see how tolerant I've been of you, since you've been ruining my comparatively harmless hobby every chance you get.

Samuel rotated the shotgun, examined it, and saw Bradshaw see. Checking the safety. He smirked.

Bradshaw's face flattened. It wasn't meth that made us do in the bums, Sam. You've been on the wrong trail this whole time. And I'm willing to bet you're here because of that, whether you know it or not. You said it was Maggie that got you up here, but I wouldn't be surprised if this wasn't all set up.

Don't. Don't bargain.

I thought it didn't matter?

It doesn't. It's just pitiful.

You're sure you can do it? Will it be easier if I lunge at you, give you a reason?

I've already got plenty.

You might not believe me, but I bet you're in the wrong house.

He pulled the trigger. Nothing happened. Bradshaw grinned.

I never leave it loaded. Habit from havin' a kid at home. He swung the bottle at Samuel's head. Samuel jabbed the gun forward and it struck Bradshaw in the throat as the bottle knocked against his skull and he went blind. He caught his feet halfway to the ground, and Bradshaw was staggering away, gripping his neck, before he leaned for another swing. The bottle came down on Samuel's back, and a fist crossed his brow and Samuel twisted and swept the knife across Bradshaw's stomach. He hit Samuel in the shoulder before he saw his intestines droop from his shirt, and Samuel cut his throat. Bradshaw took a step back, hit the counter behind him, and rested his hands on it. The bottle dropped unbroken at his feet, and his blood fanned out for two heartbeats, and the spray fell to his chest. He watched, and Samuel watched him. No move to cover the wounds. It seemed some time before Bradshaw slouched, and his eyes met Samuel's, and he let himself down onto the floor. The blood spread slowly across the tile, flooding the grout and moving in peculiar squares. Samuel took the bottle from the floor. He wiped the mouth on his shirt and opened the door to the balcony. The air was cold and clean, and he could smell the water nearby. He drank and breathed deep.

She knocked in the morning while he was dressing and began unbuttoning his shirt from the bottom as he finished the top.

He took her hands and held them still, pushed them from his chest.

What's wrong?

I'm going to get us some coffee. I didn't get any sleep. He backed away and watched her face, questioning, and went down the stairs. A mongrel honked in the intersection, and he jumped, cursing. The car went past, Reese behind the wheel, nodding curtly. Samuel nodded back, and went in The Remedy. Some of the late shift were still there, eating, one sleeping in a corner booth. He ordered a single coffee from Sheila and smiled weakly when she handed it over. He took it upstairs, shutting the door with his boot. Johanna was sitting at the table, and she watched him split the coffee into another glass, and he put it in front of her and sat. She covered the glass in her hands.

I had to kick Aaron out last night. He drank that whole bottle of shine you got him, and he just begged me to hold him. I felt so sick touching him. She spun her cup, spun it back. I can't do it anymore. I know he's fucked up from every-thing, but I just can't fake it. I told him I needed to be alone.

He sighed, rubbed at the scar on his face. I killed Brad-shaw.

Johanna halted, her hand over the cup rim.

He had all the hobos killed. Massacred them.

Oh my god. She backed from the table slightly. Why would he do that? Was he cleaning house? Did they know something?

Raj seemed to think so.

She took up her glass but didn't drink. Maybe we should leave. Work for the railroad, like Beth said. Did you ever hear of the Pinkertons?

We're not done here. I'm not.

You killed the man behind everything. Johanna put the glass down. The black coffee sloped, sloped.

He's not the end of this. They'll just keep going, keep

making, truce or no, and more people will die. Beth knew about it. Half of O Street must have. All the P&L boys.

You can't fight everyone, Sam. You nearly died already. Throwing yourself at them isn't the answer.

That's my job. Cleaning this place. Protecting it. How else am I supposed to?

It's not your job to die doing it. Are you just waiting around for them to kill you?

I'm not waiting.

She rose. She took the glass to the basin by the back window and dumped it out. She came back to the table in a silent hovering gait. I don't want to fold on this, Sam. We haven't so far. But I don't want us to get hurt or killed for a job we can't finish. You can't fix every problem with your knife. And not every problem can be fixed.

He breathed slow, stuck to the chair but wanting to stand. I couldn't live with myself if I left. I can't quit.

You can, if we have to. I'll drag you out of here.

I'd end up like my dad. And I don't want to be like him. You wouldn't want me to be. All screwed up in the head.

You left before.

He gave a slight smile. I'm not perfect.

She scowled at him, took his face in one hand and, pinching it, kissed him. No, you're not.

When she was gone from the street below, he put the knife in the sling and left. It was overcast but warm, wanting to rain. He returned to The Jungle, hunting for sign. The dirt was chaotic with tracks, foot and truck, dump truck, so many he couldn't tell a direction. No marks in the clay by the creek, none in the sand. He walked the banks back and forth on both sides, and after covering The Singles, he gave up and left for The Haymarket. Coming through the alleyway at 7th and P, he found a truck ahead, braking at the sight of him in the rearview. Rogan and Aaron got out. Rogan threw an arm onto the roof of the car and nodded him their way.

We're commandeering you, Butch. He took a cigarette from his pocket and put it between his lips. Heading to Missouri.

What for?

Meet up with this used-to-be biker gang. Say they'll take a shitload of moonshine off our hands.

Who's this coming from?

Steiner.

Samuel hadn't moved. Aaron opened the door wide, bags under his eyes and face a drag. Samuel climbed in and Aaron got in after him and shut the door. Rogan smiled and started the truck and they wheeled to O Street and went east.

Samuel looked over at Aaron. You doing okay? You didn't drink that whole bottle, did you?

Aaron shook his head. I'm fine.

They crossed over train tracks and a creek, passed old billboards with only the framework standing. Passed blocks of strip malls. Two dogs ran across the divided street and Samuel saw the coyote in them. The truck rolled down a soft hill and back up, crossing a bare field and then strip malls again on either side, a gas station, a restaurant. Windows all broken out and signs weathered.

Either of you sing? I got a decent blues voice. Blind Willie Johnson. My daddy taught me. Rogan glanced at them, crossed an arm over his left. I guess he ain't most people's speed.

Samuel said nothing, and Aaron grunted. He put his head aside and closed his eyes.

You know my daddy told me they put Blind Willie Johnson on a rocket. Shot him out into space on a golden record. You believe that? This blind buck picking on his guitar and just moaning. He doesn't even sing. Going through space.

It began to rain. In Samuel's mind some spinning contraption, a box, going through the black. They passed through the end of the strip malls and out of the city. Rogan sped up.

These guys we're gonna go see.

Samuel looked at him. Yeah?

There's talk of linking up with them. Teach them to start a city like we did.

That disconcert you at all? Having a gang run a city?

Rogan switched driving hands. What do you think we are? His chin rose, as if he were examining something. Trust me, gang's just a little version of a government. Or the other way around.

After a while they turned onto a state route and headed south. The grass and weeds were long on the side of the road, and old fences ran miles with nothing penned inside. A small wood grew from the horizon, a village. Signs staked into the shoulders of the road: MEASLES STAY AWAY. A sawhorse for a roadblock. Rogan maneuvered the car around it. Several houses shuttered, a store, a rickety gas station with the metal canopy fallen almost into the street. Someone walked out of a house behind them, arms high and waving.

They drove south long enough that the clouds pushed on behind them, their borders heavy with dragging virga, the sunset painting the sky. Rogan pointed to the glovebox, and Samuel took out an old map and handwritten directions. There were two pistols stacked underneath. Aaron didn't stir.

We should be getting close. Rogan took the directions and read them over, glancing up at the road. Half a bleached banner for fireworks. Minutes later they saw the tops of hotels and signs for an airport. An empty car lot. They came up on an exit, and Rogan turned onto it. Hey, Blondie, wake up.

I'm awake.

Signs for departures and arrivals, painted with worn graffiti. They went below an overpass, and Rogan parked in its shadow. He got out and motioned for Samuel and Aaron to lean forward, and he cranked the bench ahead and pulled a rifle out from behind it. Sam, go up top and give us support.

Rogan stepped back and let Samuel slide out from the

driver's side. He took the rifle and Rogan got back in, Aaron looking ahead still, and they drove on. Samuel examined the rifle, a .30-30, sleeve of ammo on the stock, and led the bolt back to check the chamber. He held it cradled in his right hand and climbed the embankment to the overpass. He crouched behind the guardrail near the onramp and sighted the truck in the scope. It parked, and from a large garage came four men, heavyset, carrying two wood crates between them. Rogan and Aaron got out, and Samuel saw Aaron paw at the gun in his waistband. They stopped with several yards between them and one of the men from the gang came forward. Samuel could see they were talking, the gestures. The lead man in the gang opened his crate with a prybar he took from his belt and backed away. Aaron stepped forward. He pulled out a matte black rifle, spoke to the lead man, and turned in Samuel's direction with the rifle up. He fired a few rounds into the ground, the gun lighting and then the report reaching Samuel. The other gang members started going through the crates in the truck, opening them. Rogan fired a pistol, arm extended. One of the men spewed a mist of moonshine. Samuel scratched at his brow, lifting the rifle off the guardrail and moving to the grass beside him. He laid on his stomach. In a lot beside them, nearer to the airport terminal, there were still cars parked, rusting, windows broken and gas caps hanging. It was nearly dark. In the crosshairs he could imagine deer, his father shuffling beside him, unscrewing a thermos of coffee. Snow, pure snow, before the dust. He could smell the coveralls, smell the clean winter air the fibers kept year-round, the stiffness of the material. A long train-ride away, smells of home he couldn't conjure but would know. Aaron shot the glass out of a streetlamp, and Samuel put him in the scope. There wasn't enough light to see his face, the lack of expression he knew was there.

The men unloaded the truck, and Aaron and Rogan hauled the guns up into the bed. They said their goodbyes, waved, and Samuel started down the ramp and posted a dozen yards from the overpass. Aaron pushed his door open and slid to the middle and Samuel got in, easing the rifle down behind the seat.

Rogan switched on the lights. That went pretty smooth.

Samuel glanced out at the dark sheet of gray past the window. Rogan handed his pistol over, and Samuel put it in the glovebox and waited for Aaron to pull his out, but he didn't. Aaron craned his head onto the back of the benchseat and shut his eyes. Samuel's shoulder was stiff. There was nothing to see beyond the headlights of the truck, and in them an undeviating strip of macadam.

Down the road he woke to the truck pulling off. He lurched forward, grasped about, and remembered where he was. Aaron pointed toward the door.

I gotta take a piss.

Samuel reached across himself to open the door and climbed out. He saw Aaron's hand resting on the back of the pistol, and he froze beside the door. Aaron gripped Samuel's good shoulder as he dropped from the cab. He walked into the dark until he blurred, a shadow against the grass. Rogan slid out and took a metal gas can from the back and filled the tank. A minute passed, and Aaron reformed in the light of the cab before climbing inside again. Samuel and Rogan got in, and they started off. He didn't sleep until the last thirty miles, and he woke as they came into the city. Light cutting from the dark earth and the vacant east end and deeper into the old downtown, a haze giving each beam form, and together an architecture. Still dazed, he thought he might have been dreaming, a rough map of the streets projected into the clouds, orange for The Haymarket, lighter to the east, the white of The Capitol, and The Capitol reaching upward itself. They crossed over into the light, and the demarcation was sudden. The truck pulled to the west entrance of The Capitol, P&L trucks lined up outside, men lingering by the doors. Rogan threw it in park. They slid out and Aaron walked to the rear, going for a crate and motioning Samuel off.

We got this. Go on in.

Samuel looked to Rogan. You sure?

You'll just hurt yourself.

Okay. He lifted his right hand in a vague wave and went up the walk. Inside the west hall a number of P&L workers paced or leaned against the walls by the entryway. Reese was seated on the base of the stairs and Samuel nodded to him. What's going on?

Reese shook his head. Bradshaw never showed up today. Maggie called us all in and got Steiner. We're gonna go out looking for him.

Samuel glanced down the hall toward Steiner's office. Aaron and Rogan came in carrying one of the crates of guns between them, a couple workers lurching off their posts to help. Before the doors could close Harrawood slipped inside. His hand was wrapped in cloth. Samuel ground his jaw. Gil stepped out of one of the doors down the hall and started calling out to people. He lifted his chin at Samuel.

One cluster after another, huh?

17

Johanna was waiting for him in the stairwell with an army duffel, the cloth flat, unfull. There's something going on in The Bottoms.

He closed the door. What do you mean?

I don't know for sure, but there's people behind the fence, and I smelled something awful. Like bodies.

What were you doing down there in the first place?

Things haven't been adding up. I couldn't figure it out until I had some time to myself, and it hit me. She gestured to the door, and he opened it. They went out and started south.

What hit you?

She was silent a moment, walking fast. Nobody in The Remedy, nobody near. There aren't enough kettles in The Still. I saw them when we were fighting Bradshaw's men, and I thought about it then, but I buried it. The amount of corn we bring in for mash? There's no way the kettles hold even half that. You remember harvest time around here. We buy up silage, too. It's a wonder the cattle around don't starve. All that must go somewhere. We're not just putting it in silos. We must be using it.

They were nearly out of the light, passing P&L Central. A lone worker through the door, moving around a desk and throwing on a coat. The inside went dark, and he stepped out behind them, and they faced forward, walking fast, until they skirted The Singles.

You think we're making shine in The Bottoms.

That's my suspicion. I've seen trucks go that way with no good reason. And when we had that fire, while you were gone? The lights flickered. Why the hell would the lights flicker? It's not like we've strung down there.

We must have. It can't be coincidence.

She glanced at him. I wanted to wait on you. It doesn't make any sense for them to keep it all fenced off unless they didn't want us to know about it. And that on its own isn't a good secret.

I got a feeling this is what Bradshaw was hinting at. You got guns in that bag?

Bolt cutters. Figured you couldn't climb with your shoulder hurt.

I'm getting you that heel sash, like I said.

You'd hate to have me as your boss. She grinned, let it slip away. They kept on, jogging in careful step, ducking behind a hedgerow at the sound of a mongrel. Johanna stopped them again when they were within sight of the fence, a sign hung to it with a crude black skull and bones.

It all looks like this, that I've seen. Houses and more houses.

A screen.

They followed the fence west, where it cornered. Samuel pointed to a dilapidated foursquare half a block north. Its siding fell in peels, gutters loose from the eaves.

Graham drew on us in there.

Johanna looked from the property to the fence, back. I didn't realize it was so close to The Bottoms.

They pressed ahead, trailing the fence south. No gate, no lights. Johanna led him around the next turn in the fence and stopped a few hundred yards after. She took the bolt cutters from the bag. A wind blew from the north, clouds rushing above the light of the city, and it struck them, a black and putrid stench that blurred their vision. Samuel put his face into the cloth of his shirt, and Johanna started on the fence. Each clip carried off the houses, garages, and the fence rattled louder with every cut. She pulled the fencewire back, and

Samuel slipped through, and she followed, handing him a flashlight. They crossed a street, riven with grass and weeds. In front of them was a row of untouched houses, home and backyard and home, shield of ordinary. They passed through a sideyard, and Samuel saw there had been a picket fence, the postholes softened with grass.

I think we're close.

Ahead was another block of houses, a yard with crooked trellises weighted with rosebushes. They paused beside a porch, listened, continued. Behind the last block lay a clearing, three acres of open, uneven ground. A fresh patch of dirt at their feet and beside it the bodies lay unburied. They were a bloated tangle of singular gray, from the light or their bloodlessness, clothes torn and stained. At least a dozen people, he thought, more than there had ever been at a time in The Jungle. The zealot with the cardboard sign, the preacher, a young man with a bullethole just below his eye.

Johanna turned on her flashlight, going from face to face, and cut it. The hobos.

More than just them. There's others. He pointed, knelt beside the youngest. His arms were eaten with trackmarks and his feet bare, trackmarks between his toes. Samuel stood, lit the nearby acreage, and covered the light with his hand. It's a graveyard.

Across the clearing was a row of shacks that looked cobbled together from parts of houses. Beyond them the silhouette of a warehouse, a hum from that direction. Samuel cut his flashlight, and they started toward it. From somewhere in the city an engine revved. The shacks were little more than clapboard and tin, the size of an outhouse. They rowed the south side of the street as far as Samuel could see in the dark, flanked the warehouse. Johanna started ahead and he took her hand and held her back.

There's a truck coming. He pointed, and they ducked against the shack wall and watched as headlights appeared

to the west. The truck was canted with weight in the bed,
barrels, and as the truck slowed at the warehouse, the frame
shifted, bounced. It reversed, backed off the street. The warehouse doors swung open, and the droning increased. A man
stepped outside carrying a wooden ramp. Samuel leaned forward as he set it down.

I think I know him. That's Travis.

Who?

Samuel shook his head. He's supposed to be in jail.

I think he might be.

They watched as the driver of the truck got out and slipped
on a paper woodworking mask, peered in the direction of
the shacks, and went to the bed. The driver shouted into the
warehouse, and another man came out. In the light Samuel
could see the sunken cheeks, the thin arms, steaming in the
cold. The second man reached for the bed, missed, reached
again and ran his hand down the side, positioning himself.
They began to unload the barrels, rolling them down the
ramp and into the warehouse. Travis had a black eye, the
cheek misshapen like a halved apple. When the barrels had
all been rolled inside, the driver closed up the warehouse
doors and started the truck. Samuel and Johanna hid at the
rear of the shack until it cut by, and they stood on the street
watching the brakelights at the fence, a gate, and then the
truck drove off. They headed for the warehouse and Samuel
opened one of the doors, nearly losing his grip on the handle
in the blast of hot air that rushed past them. Inside was a
battery of four generators, bigger than a truck, with barrels
lined along the walls and coils of wire spiraling to the ceiling.
Travis siphoned the fuel from a barrel with a plastic tube
and watched it run into the generator, then straightened and
turned to them at the door, squinted. He wore a ratty shirt
soaked through with sweat, and he was pale and despite how
thin, he seemed overflowing with blood, every vein in his
arms standing. Samuel let the door shut.

Christ.

She nodded, turned, and started to walk west, deeper in. Samuel followed.

They kept to the shacks, close enough to duck away from the road, though no one came. There were nearly thirty shacks in all, down the single street, and several blocks down from the first, they came to another warehouse, the same size and shape. Samuel pried open the door to the nearest shack and waved the flashlight across it. A small table inside, no chair. A marine smell to the air. Set against the wall was a cot, and a woman slept, thin and ignorant of the cold. He had the light directly on her face, and she didn't move. He knocked on the wall beside him with the light. The woman rolled over, sat up slowly. Her head cocked to the door, and Samuel put the light to her again and she stared through him.

Is it morning?

He backed from the doorway, cut the flashlight. It took a moment for his head to clear, and Johanna caught up to him. They wandered further. Two more warehouses, one burned black and the doors open. Someone had painted three cross-es on the wall, through the ash. Dragmarks at the entrance, and just inside the walls, Samuel lit rows of glassware, a bale of Mormon tea. He turned to Johanna, and she shook her head. They left the burned warehouse, and nearing what he thought was the center of the fencing, they found an old, squat church. A man smoked a short cigarette out front. The doors behind him were chained and locked. The man perked.

They didn't get you, did they, Reverend?

Samuel looked at Johanna. The man waited, drew the cherry toward his fingers, trembling. His eyes were split, ambling.

You ain't the reverend, are you?

No. Samuel breathed in. What happened to you?

You walk like him, is all. I thought maybe they'd arrested him, too.

He took a step forward. Mister, are you blind?

Mostly. Did they just bring you in? Usually they don't let the new ones wander around. They putting you to work with the generators or sticking you in here?

What's in there? Johanna began to walk to the side of the church.

The stills.

They met eyes. Johanna lit the church roof. You make methanol.

Wood alcohol, jake. Yeah. He cocked his head. If you're new, you'd better get back home. I'm just an old codger to them, but they keep watch over the able-bodied. They'll beat the ever-livin' daylights out of you.

We've got bolt cutters. If you follow us, we can lead you out.

You broke in? He laughed. I got the jakeleg. I'd just slow you down. Get on out of here before someone clubs you. Go on. He shook his hand in a kind of scoop.

We'll be back. Johanna thumbed to the north, and they started away, out of the open ground and toward the false neighborhood lining the interior. When they were nearer to cover they slowed, and Johanna gripped Samuel's arm.

What do we do? Do we blow up the generators?

That wouldn't help anyone.

We have to stop this. We can't just let 8th Street make people blind. It's the methanol that does that. It'll blind you, kill you. It's poison.

We'll find a way.

This is what got you and Red kicked out. It wasn't losing one of his men Bradshaw cared about. It was how close you got to the truth.

It's through and through. Samuel quit walking, then backed them to the wall of a house. It's through and through. I gave that guy at the warehouse over to Steiner to be jailed.

He had his hands on the house, back to it, fingers splayed

like he would grip the wall. Thinking loosely, some upper part of his mind running the lines of conspiracy.

Sam, come on. She took his hand, and led him past the last row of houses, to the fence. She cut through it and they slipped under the cut, and continued north. The lights of the city now seemed paler, colder. Quiet. They were in sight of the cook's dismantled lab when they saw the search party come out of the house next door, begin to enter the store. Samuel made Maggie, Detch, two other Still workers. The four of them were motionless until Samuel and Johanna took the curb. Gil emerged from the house, glassed them with his flashlight.

What are you all doing?

Looking for Bradshaw. Aren't you?

Got him in that bag, huh?

Johanna lifted it from her shoulder, brought it forward. Yeah. He's a lot smaller in person. She set the bag back, looked at Maggie. Sorry.

I don't care. She shook her head. I'm just out to see the body.

Samuel glanced away. The rest of them shuffled anxiously. Detch lifted his chin.

What do you think we're gonna do, Sam? Without him.

I never knew that he did all that much. Beth talked him up, and he talked himself up. We got a lot more problems than one missing despot. And he ain't gonna be out here, anyways. Samuel spread an arm to the intersection. I doubt he ever went down the alphabet farther than G.

Why'd you come up from the south, then? Gil moved toward them, stepped off the curb.

Futility is a hobby of mine.

I'm serious.

Johanna turned to Samuel, and he nodded. She opened the bag and showed them the bolt cutters. We were past the fence. They've got people locked up in there, going blind from jake poisoning, running generators. There is no power plant, no one we pay with the money being brought in. They've got batteries of generators in these warehouses run on methanol, and it's killing the people working them.

What? That's bullshit. Right? One of the workers looked to the other, to Detch.

It wouldn't be the first time Bradshaw used a drug to keep someone in line. Maggie backed from the group, glanced toward the city. I'm done looking. Someone get me if you ever find him. She headed north. Johanna started after her.

Don't go spilling this to just anyone. Samuel watched the four men, each staring at him. You're liable to get killed for knowing. They've been doing their best to hide this. Killed the hobos at The Jungle to keep it hidden. He started to follow Johanna, and Detch reached to stop him.

What are you gonna do about this?

What are we gonna do, Detch? He shrugged away from him, and trotted off. Maggie and Johanna had only gone a block. Johanna saw him coming, kept talking.

They all knew. All three of them, if not Norton, too.

He never knows anything. He never cared enough to.

Can you find some way to tell the city about this? They've got a right to know.

No better than you could. Best I can do is a bullhorn, if you found one. Start putting up posters for another movie.

Samuel paced with them. They were nearing The Capitol, and the street now was well-lit. The small parts of noise that made the city grew louder. The cars, the buzz of lamps. At the President Apartments, Maggie split from them, and they stopped to watch her go to the door.

You're not staying in The Singles?

She shook her head. If I can't take a night away from help, I'm lost. And neither Detch or Heather give me a moment alone. Besides—She looked across the mall to The Capitol—this way I can keep an eye out.

She was gone, and Johanna and Samuel stood quiet until Johanna faced the way they'd come. I should go.

Samuel nodded. They'll have me on some errand again, tomorrow. I won't see you.

I'll try to think of how to solve all this.

He smiled. Maybe just stay safe.

She smirked. I can do both. She spun him into the dark past the apartment entrance and kissed him, and walked away.

Before dawn he went into the bathroom shirtless and tried to lift his arm. The wound puckered and he dropped under himself as if he would dodge the pain. He showered and dressed and watched by the window until he saw Sheila open The Remedy, and he went down for his breakfast. Rogan came through the door while he was finishing a biscuit.

Time for another trip, Sam.

He pushed his plate ahead. Where to?

Far. Past the Black Hills.

Samuel scooped a last bite of biscuits and gravy, swallowed. Sheila took his plate and mug.

Did you all hear about Mr. Bradshaw? They say the Mexicans got him.

Rogan glanced at Samuel. With a time machine?

She put a hand on her hip. No, smartass. They hid so they could get our leaders.

You're wasted on breakfast, sweetheart. We need you in our thinktank. Rogan took a dollar from his pocket and laid it on the counter. Quicker we get.

Samuel nodded and followed him outside. A truck was parked out front, running, Aaron inside. It was loaded down with crates of shine, and as Rogan went around the bed, he pointed toward the cab.

Went ape at Norton's yesterday. Tried to fight the bartender.

He grimaced and opened the passenger door. You doin'

all right?

Aaron slid across the bench seat. I'm fine.

Rogan got in and they headed west. They drove for hours before turning north, and on until it was well into the afternoon. They had to drive around a fallen overpass, nearly miring the truck in a field. The plains spotted with trees and slowly multiplied to groves and woods. Beyond, the land dipped and rose in front of them, and in the slow valley was a town laid out on streets of broken pavement and ice. Horses hitched in front of the few larger buildings sidled at the approach of the truck, and men watched from doorways, stopped in place down the plank sidewalks. Samuel got out, and Aaron after him.

Did we just go back in time?

I suspect this is the future. Samuel shut the door. They both stretched, and their breath steamed in front of them.

Rogan shut off the truck, and they gathered around the hood. Who wants guard duty?

Aaron raised his hand. I'll take it.

Rogan started for town and Samuel followed. They wore pistols in their belts from the run to Missouri and Samuel carried the knife in his sling. The largest building in town was a two-story hotel, old and square, and they walked toward it. Rogan nudged him.

You ever been in a hurricane?

I was about in a tornado once.

Oh yeah? What was that like?

Scary. Sky turned colors. I saw the storm coming from a ways off, really pretty, and once it got close, everything went dark. They mounted the plank walks and their boots sounded like hammers. They stopped before the hotel doors. Cracked green paint and wavy glass.

I've been in a couple. Used to live on the coast. It's like you combine a big storm with another big storm, and it sits on your house for all day. Plus the storm surge, since I was by the ocean. You know what that is? It's the sea carried up—He held a hand level to his chest—because of the low pressure. Comes in like a flood from a river. I had this neighbor, older fella, fat. You know what he did, when this one hurricane came?

Samuel shook his head. They were on opposite sides of the doorway, and he watched Rogan's hands, his shoulders. He was smiling just slightly, and his eyes were easy.

Tied himself to a tree. Right to the trunk, thinking he wouldn't get carried away. But he forgot all about the storm surge, see, and his ass drowned standing up in six foot of water. Found him when the hurricane ended, rope in his hands. Couldn't undo the knot.

Samuel waited for more, and nothing came. Rogan's smile deepened, and he opened the door. Samuel followed him. A man in an apron mopped at a corner of the long, old-fashioned barroom. Tables throughout, a small sideroom on the right. A few coal oil lamps hung above them. The man gripped the handle of the mop and propped himself up with it, watching them come in.

You'll have to go down the way.

What is it? Rogan cocked his head.

The man pointed through the wall. There's a place will serve blacks down the street. We don't serve them here.

Rogan grinned. Need to get you some signs, mister.

We don't get many negroes in this town.

I believe that.

Let me take care of this, Tom. Samuel came forward, and Rogan put his arm out to stop him.

Ain't the first, won't be the last.

The man set his mop against the wall. Samuel noted his hand going for his apron pocket. You fellas wouldn't be from the city, would you? Bradshaw's men?

Rogan let his arm down. We are.

He nodded slowly, not looking at them. Should we get to

it? I know you had a long drive.

I'll pull her around. Rogan cocked his head toward the bar. You wanna wait here?

Sure. Samuel took a seat. Rogan walked out, while the owner slipped behind the counter.

Could I get you some refreshment? We got our own booze, dope, meth. You guys call it tea, right? That's some pretty good marketing. We just call a spade a spade.

Samuel kept his face blank. No.

I got to warn you, you don't have too much longer before it's heroin takes over for your tea. We've started growing, up here. Acres of poppies. Gorgeous when they bloom.

Mud squelched from outside. Samuel made no move, and the owner left him, opening a door at the back. A crossbreeze blew through the bar. He heard them unloading the crates, and Samuel got up to watch. Walking out the back, he saw the owner hand Aaron a small metal case and an envelope. Rogan smiled politely at the man from over the bed, said something Samuel couldn't make out. The owner reeled back, turned, a weak grin stuck to his face.

Well, I appreciate you coming. Tell Lester I said hello.

Rogan lifted a hand. He got in the truck, and Samuel slid in beside Aaron. Rogan put the truck in gear, and they turned around, headed home.

What did you say to him, back there?

Rogan patted the wheel. Just killed him with kindness.

Down the road Aaron reached below the seat and took out a bottle of shine. Rogan glanced at him and shook his head slightly. Aaron uncapped it and drank. He held it out for Samuel and Rogan snatched it.

How many?

Just a few. Can't expect to cut liquor off like that without consequences.

Rogan drank and handed it to Samuel.

I asked him to. Samuel held the bottle by the neck, tilted

it up for a small pull. My shoulder's been killing me.

They drove on. Aaron didn't look his way until they stopped the truck in the evening to stretch. As he jumped to the road, he looked at Samuel, hesitating.

Thanks. He walked to the shoulder and across the ditch. Rogan got out and started refueling the truck from a can in the back. Samuel got out and arched his back, twisted at the waist.

What were you talking about, with the hurricane and all?

Rogan smiled. That? Oh, I was just rambling. Thinking about things that once you start you can't stop.

He straightened, put his forearm on the bedrail. I would have thought you'd try to put a bullet in me, if you knew.

That hurts.

You struck me as a company man.

I'm nobody's man. Rogan righted the can and replaced it in the bed. I'm with the company because no one person's gonna rebuild humanity. If you've got designs on a revolt or something, I'd remind you America used to be a democracy. Words over bullets.

Samuel glanced at the road, the way they'd come. He heard Aaron in the grass behind him.

But seriously, don't go tying yourself to a tree in a hurricane. That's just dumb.

18

They let Samuel off at his apartment. When he got out of the truck, Aaron took a bottle of moonshine from under the seat and handed it out. Samuel lifted it in thanks and watched them drive off. The cool weather followed them from the north. It was cloudless and a little damp, and he felt the condensation on the door of The Remedy. The lights were on, but no one was inside, and when he entered he heard a quiet thud, and Rick came out of the back rubbing sleep from his eyes.

Sorry, Sam. Been dead all day. I thought about shutting her down early.

Don't blame you. Could I get a little bite?

Sure. He poured Samuel a coffee and handed it across before starting to the kitchen. How was the trip today? He ducked inside.

Disconcerting.

No response from the kitchen. The door opened, and Johanna stood there wearing the black coat. She came over and took a seat next to Samuel.

Come to Norton's?

He checked the kitchen before he touched her side with the back of his right hand. Why is it even open?

She shrugged. Rick came out of the kitchen and stopped in the doorway. Can I get you anything, Jo?

She shook her head, and he disappeared again. Johanna set her arm on the counter. We need to keep acting normal.

He put his hand beside hers. We should tell him.

She sighed. I wasn't even talking about that. She reached

for his coffee and drank. You didn't see him last night. He was a wreck. I don't think we could stay.

He took a deep breath and held it to check himself. I know. Samuel took his mug from beside her and finished it, then picked up his bottle of shine. He stole a bunch of high proof today.

She rested her head on his shoulder. I want you so bad. I want out of this mess.

Samuel covered her hand, gripped it and let go. Rick backed through the kitchen doors with the plate, and Samuel ate his fries, left with the burger, and stowed the shine in the apartment stairwell. On the street they played at nonchalance, at friendship. A few blocks down Q, Johanna leaned into him, and moments later a Light worker rounded a corner and nearly collided with them. He pivoted on his heel, and walked backward to eye them, and Samuel chilled, panicked, thought what he himself would do and stared back at the worker. Half a block later he was replaying it, the overaggression, the startled instant of collision, and had he given them away with a look?

When they reached the alley they both felt the pressure for a kiss, and Samuel kept his distance, almost embarrassed. You go ahead. I'll be in.

She pursed her lips, and went down the entryway. He waited, toed a black streak of gum in the alley, watched the road. No one came. He went in. Norton gave a weak wave from behind the bar, and he found Aaron and Johanna at their booth, a bottle of moonshine down to half on the table.

Aaron pushed it Samuel's way.

Still on the first, don't worry.

Samuel took the bottle and drank, wiped his mouth with the back of his hand. Aaron went for the bottle as soon as it was down, then handed it over to Johanna.

That town's a drug den, Sam. Built on dope, run by dealers.

Bud. Samuel grimaced.

Aaron looked down, and Samuel met eyes with Johanna. He began to speak but closed his mouth as Detch ran in and took a seat at a booth, out of breath. Moments later two Light workers rushed in. A tumbler hurtled from the booth and hit one of the workers in the head, bounced, and shattered on the floor with the worker following. Detch grinned and hefted another glass in his hands, dropping it, and the other worker rushed ahead. Samuel stood as Detch backed almost into him. Norton reached below the counter.

The Light worker sneered. You ain't spookin' anyone, Parrish. I know that's your cutting arm.

You sure?

The worker came ahead. He leaned forward, and Samuel lifted his hand to the sling and the worker lurched away, arms up to block. Samuel held the knife with his thumb and middle finger. The worker dropped his hands and his eyes narrowed, but he backed off.

Watch yourself. We'll be after you soon. The worker took hold of his partner, and they left.

Norton was still next to the shotgun. I'm writing you up for the glass, Detch.

Yeah, yeah. He waved him off and let out a loud sigh. Thanks for the save. Boys were hunting me all the way from Vine.

Samuel turned to him. What for?

Said they needed some booze. We got it all locked up at the warehouse, you know, and they drive up saying Steiner wants two crates of shine, won't say why. He paused and glanced to the door. I closed shop, and they got all tough. I think they're just jonesin' from the lack of speed.

Samuel turned to Norton. Hear that?

Norton lifted his hands. I backed out from the whole mess. I run The Still and this here bar and that's it. No leadership position for me.

Detch took a seat at the bar. That's real noble of you.

Aaron pushed the bottle forward to Samuel. He nudged Johanna, and she stood, and he went to the stairs. Johanna leaned across the table.

I want to kiss you.

Samuel's face heated. That shine hit you hard.

Maybe. I'm tired. She propped her head in her hand. And it was a bit of a turn on, watching you back him down with nothing but swagger.

He smirked, reaching for the bottle. Under the light he saw the handprints, Aaron's, the smears of oil and the clear whorl, tentarch, of forefinger, middle, ring. He was slow lifting the bottle, and he drank. Johanna took it after him, hands touching.

I thought we could sneak back in tonight. Free as many as we can, bring some with us to tell the story. Tell whoever will listen.

He barely heard her. The bottle returned to the table, and the prints were well-lit, the mouth of the bottle printed as well, marked with their lips, their breath. We were careless about it. We let Travis see us, if he could recognize us. We'll end up shot.

What if we told everyone? Literally everyone? Between you and Gil, you could get most of the city in a day on collections.

He stared at the bottle, still. He felt alone, surrounded, covered over in memory. The bar grew dark, the table bright. I guess we could. Get them all talking. Steiner would have to acknowledge it.

They could hear the toilet flush upstairs, and both of them looked to the door. I'll slip out early, say I'm tired. I don't want to be away from you tonight—

No. Samuel breathed in. He stared at her. We tell him. Now.

Sam. She was white, that quickly. Now?

He stood. Cold wind flooded the entrance, and Harrawood came in. The bathroom door opened. Harrawood spoke to Norton, and Norton took out the bottle of bourbon from below the bar and poured him a drink. Harrawood carried it over to the jukebox, ignoring Samuel. Aaron started down the stairs.

Sam. Do you mean it?

He held out his hand to stop her. No. Wait. He cleared his throat. Hey, Detch?

What's up? He spun around on the stool.

Would you give Johanna an escort home?

I'm fine. What's this about?

Something's happened. He glanced to Aaron, rounding the bar, bouncing off a table. His pulse was high in his throat. Aaron joined Samuel, head bobbing to Johanna.

You drunk already? I can take you home.

You couldn't find your dick to piss out a fire, dear.

It couldn't of gone far. I just had it.

Detch cut in. We'll escort each other, Jo.

She looked from Aaron to Samuel, trying to keep the question small. I'll see you boys later. She smiled at Detch and took his arm, and they left.

Aaron thumbed after them. What was all that?

I got a bad feeling. Samuel eyed Harrawood briefly. I saw something last night that I wasn't meant to see.

What?

You ever hear any rumors about how Al and Lester keep the lights on?

I heard about that killswitch he used on you guys, and supposedly he's got one for the whole town. Dunno if that's true or not.

But nothing about how we get our power? Maybe something about The Bottoms?

He shook his head. We got that plant hooked up up north, right? Or wherever its secret location is?

That ain't it. I wish it was. Samuel leaned in over the table. There's a whole mess of bodies down in The Bottoms, past the fence. And a bunch of people stone blind from jake they brew inside to run generators. I always believed the charter hype about the plant, myself. But the lights are kept on by prisoners, and they keep the generators running on poison. I don't think it's safe out there. I think this is what got Red ran out so fast. We stumbled on a party held by its guards.

You're serious? He looked toward the door, then Harrawood. Some of his color had run off. You're not just looking for another reason to come at Bradshaw?

He's gone, Aaron.

How do you know for sure?

Samuel stared at him.

Aaron was still as he could be, drunk, and he pushed back against the booth. You—

If you knew the things he'd done. If you saw them.

Aaron rolled to his feet. I'm gonna. He nearly fell back into the booth, and as he turned, he covered his mouth. I'm 'bout to throw up.

Well, shit. Samuel took Aaron's arm, dragging him to the stairs, and halfway he vomited bile and shine and hung from Samuel, jerking like a flag.

Goddammit, Sam, will you get him to the can?

Samuel shot a look at Norton and hauled Aaron across the floor and up the stairs. He kicked open the door to the bathroom and set him over the toilet. Aaron groaned and rolled his head on the rim. Samuel patted him on the back and left him to get water. He waited at the bar for Norton to fill a glass.

Harrawood raised his chin. He doin' all right?

He'll pull through. Samuel turned away.

Hey. Listen to me for a minute. He tossed his head at Norton, and Norton walked to the far end of the bar. Our personal shit aside, if you just leave all this be, nothing has to happen. Nobody else gets hurt. Just accept that some mistakes got made on the way to greatness, that we're all human, and you and me and everyone else can go back to work. Movies on Saturday night and coffee houses and all the other things you and I never got to have. All the things these people lost.

I know they didn't sell you on that.

Harrawood had been stern, flat, but his mouth began to crook into a frown while his eyes warmed, and he laughed. No. No, they sold me on three hots and all the heads I can break. That was my bill of goods. He played with his tumbler. In all this time, twenty people. Twenty people dead and the twenty or so more we got down there, either crooks or bums, and we get a city in return. Seems like a fair price. They get to stay drunk, get fed. We get civilization. Hardly a price at all.

Who told you?

I saw the cut in the fence. Ain't nobody but you would work so hard to ruin a good thing.

Samuel turned away, starting for the restroom.

Steiner called a meeting for tomorrow morning. State of the Union sort of thing. We can talk everything over then.

He went upstairs. Aaron had vomited again, now resting against the stall with his jacket for a pillow. Samuel set the glass beside him and shook Aaron awake. He made him drink half the glass and poured him more from the sink. Aaron took it, and Samuel helped him to his feet.

I'm better. Get me outta here.

Samuel guided him down the stairs. Harrawood was seated with two O Streeters, and they all turned to face the pair as they came out. No one moved and then Aaron lurched forward.

Leave him the fuck alone.

Vince held his glass to his lips. A space where his finger should have been. You mean Sam? We're here for you. Steiner'd like a word, if you're done throwing up.

Aaron straightened. What for?

Samuel put a hand on his back and pushed him to the door. Come on. They can try and take you. He wheeled Aaron out, and the three at the bar watched them go. I got you. He put his arm under Aaron's shoulder and bolstered him. They were turning the corner when he heard them push out their stools, and when Samuel and Aaron got out the door, Rogan and two more O Streeters waited at the end of the alley with a mongrel.

Shit.

Aaron ducked from under Samuel's arm. Is this about the shine?

One of the O Streeters shrugged. Harrawood and the other two came out behind them.

Aaron put his hands up. All right. Let's just get this over with. He turned to Samuel. Don't worry about it. I'll see you tomorrow. He took a few steps forward, and one of the O Streeters opened the mongrel door. He got in and looked out at Samuel. Have some prairie oysters at the ready.

Samuel stuck his hand out, half-waving. Rogan got in the car, and the others followed suit, Harrawood moving beside Samuel. The mongrel drove off, and they watched it go.

I guess it'd be convenient for you if he disappeared.

Samuel closed his eyes. He turned to Harrawood. When all this falls apart, I want you to be the first person I see. I hope you're waiting outside my door.

19

She woke him rolling over in bed, and he rested a hand on her shoulder, and she sat up. A blue light in the windows.

I think I want to leave.

Samuel frowned. Okay.

The city. I want us to leave the city.

He raised up on his elbows, rubbing his temple, the scar. If we're going to leave, we have to try and set some things right. I couldn't leave not trying.

She stared into the blanket between her knees. It's not worth it, whatever you think we're doing.

You thought it was, last night.

She didn't move.

All these people came here looking for a future.

And you tried. We all tried. And now it's time to go. We can leave here and look back one day, and it will be so small. I promise you. It'll be such a small time in our lives. It'll seem like a mistake two kids made. A happy one, because we met, and got out and built this whole life.

He watched the light through the windows, the tops of The Haymarket buildings. The people here ought to know what's happening. If I can't tear the city down, maybe they can. He pulled himself from the sheets and went to the window. If I do that much, maybe I can leave. And be all right with it.

She dressed in the glass. They kissed and again at the door, and she held onto his hand until he withdrew it. When she was gone he showered and shaved and cleaned his wound, smaller. He got the gun from his bag. The air outside was dry and fast, and it pulled the clouds over The Haymarket. Detch was coming up 8th, his face swollen on the left side, his cheek dark purple.

What's going on, man?

Samuel breathed in. Not sure. What happened to you?

Tuned me up when I showed at Vine this morning. It feels like the war's starting all over again.

It's only gonna get worse. He started walking past. Take care of yourself.

Hey. Is it true? You cut off a dealer's hands?

Samuel cocked his head. No. I only ever docked two fingers in my life. One by accident.

Word is you cut off Tover's hands.

Samuel shook his head. He breathed and looked toward The Capitol. He went east, cutting into an alley on Q at the sound of engines, running it across P and again into another alley. A mongrel blew down the street headed west with a truck following it. Samuel waited before exiting the alley, watching them go. A Light worker on foot eyed him hard, panning his head as he passed. He cut down 14th to K and crossed The Capitol lawn. A few O Street guards lined the walls, and he went to the senate chamber. Steiner loomed over the table at the back, Maggie at his right and Harrawood his left. Rogan stood halfway down the room, Aaron beside him, haggard and dark-eyed, and Gil was at the table. A couple O Streeters and P&L workers stood, as well.

Used to be a lot more people meeting. I don't know how I feel about that. Steiner paused and waved Samuel in. Come on, Sam. Take a seat. This is just to keep us all up-to-date, put some ideas on the table. Things we all know already, mostly.

Samuel stayed near the back, hands on a chair.

Well, for starters, Lester hasn't been seen for a few days. That's unprecedented. His normal haunts have been checked, old houses, new houses. I'm not the type of guy to assume everything's okay and he's just marooned on the shitter somewhere. I also don't care to speculate whether he's dead or run off with the Queen or got kidnapped or what have you. Monsters ate him. I can't help it, so I don't care. As of today, until he's found alive, I'm putting Maggie in charge of the Light side of the business. She knows the work better than anyone. Maybe better than Bradshaw, himself. That part's not up for debate. What is, is whether or not you all are open to the idea of bringing in some outside muscle to beef up our security. Aaron, Rogan? The Missouri boys you met up with. You think they'd work here in town?

Aaron shrugged. We've had worse.

Rogan dropped his leg from the wall. They seemed fine to me. I can't say much for the content of their character, but they did look like they knew what they were doin'.

Sam? What'd you think? We all gotta live with 'em, but you're who they'll be working with.

Hard telling from the far end of a scope. You know these people?

I know Phillips, their leader, and his boy. All their real teeth got pulled years ago, but they know their guns and they have some, too. That's a big leg up. We'd integrate them with heels and O Street. Fix up their bikes to run on our rocket fuel, and they'll be happy. Good for us to have transport with mileage like that, too.

Nods about the room. Samuel was hardly breathing.

Can I get some ayes, then? Show of hands? All for.

They all raised their hands, Samuel his left, the right close to the knife.

Good. Now, things have been shaky as hell this past week, I know. I'm hoping that's all behind us. This is the first step in getting secure. We get secure, and we can start working like a regular city again. Start getting back out there, bringing folk in. Turning on more lights. Maggie says she's gonna get to work fixing up some luxuries for folks. Right?

She nodded, solemn. Radios, TVs, phones. It won't take

too much work.

Hear that? We'll get that university library cleaned up and get a rental store going. Steiner smiled. I'm excited. I know that seems callous. But this is the next step. We can't let tragedies dissuade us. He paused, lifted a hand. That's all I got.

Everyone but Samuel began to filter out. Steiner watched him, and Rogan and Harrawood lagged at the door. When Aaron was about to exit, he stopped, and Rogan tilted his head and put a hand on his shoulder, pushing him on. Steiner hadn't moved except to take a heavy breath and let it out.

Wasn't sure you'd show.

Engines, from outside. A mongrel spun its tires. Samuel was very quiet, listening to the men behind him. Nothing came to mind to say, to do.

Let's go upstairs. You and I will talk. Steiner rounded the table, and Samuel pivoted on his heel, watching him go to the door. He stopped there, Harrawood holding it open, and Steiner waited until Samuel followed. He heard Harrawood's and Rogan's footsteps before the door shut, and the four of them went to the stairs. Steiner held up with his arm on the banister.

You two hang back. Go have a pop.

Al. Harrawood had his hand resting over his hip, atop a gun under his shirt.

Go on. He flicked his eyes to the entrance, and waited until Rogan and Harrawood walked out. When they were outside, he started climbing the stairs, Samuel a few behind, and they went to his room. He left the door hanging wide for Samuel and went around the chairs and table to sit at the couch, a decanter of shine and a glass sitting out. Samuel didn't move from the door.

You aren't here to turn yourself in. You'd be shiftier if that were true. So you came to kill me. And you want some kind of explanation first.

Why would I turn myself in?

So it is the latter. Okay.

I'm here for you to come clean.

Steiner laughed and took up his glass. Sam, you got a lot more blood on your hands than I do. He drank, smiling around the rim.

Bullshit. The massacre at The Jungle? The Bottoms?

He sturgeoned, glass almost to his mouth. The Jungle was an honest mistake. Some kids went beyond orders to contain an issue. They were supposed to round them up and give them jobs. The Bottoms, obviously, is the issue they were trying to contain. He pointed with a finger off the glass. Shut that door.

Samuel passed the threshold, swinging the door closed.

It was always meant to be temporary. The whole arrangement. Someday I'd figure out how to work the generators so they weren't so dangerous, or Bradshaw or Maggie would, one of us. We'd get rich enough to not use methanol. But until then, it just made sense to put workers down there nobody'd miss. Even better if they're people we needed to keep an eye on.

You talk like it's some work camp. You've blinded these people. Fried them. It's criminal. And you know it, or you wouldn't keep it a secret.

No one is proud of a prison. It started off a secret because we didn't know how people would react. You can't hire for a job like that, you know. I couldn't pay high enough. Everyone else in the city stringing wire and you leaving work every day a little more blind and shaky. He shrugged, raised his glass, drank. Eventually, we knew spilling that secret might ruin us. Would ruin us. So I need to present you with your options.

How can you be so calm about this?

You don't sit with something on your mind for as long as I have and it doesn't become normal. Kinda like how you can sleep at night after killing people. Tover, for instance.

I didn't kill Tover.

Well, you should have. He deserved it and you're the prime suspect anyway. He refilled his glass from the decanter. He sipped, pulled. I wish we could have kept you around. I do. But people like you just can't wrap your heads around how things work. You've got that hardscrabble integrity. If it ain't difficult, it must be bad. If I ain't sweating. You couldn't see that that's what a city's about. It's cooperation, whether all parties know or not. You act like a whole, think that way. I used to be like you. I know how it is.

Now you're that train baron you talked about.

Steiner laughed. Yeah. Essentially.

I have this habit of killing men like you. Even before I slit Bradshaw's throat.

He raised his eyebrows. Son, was that supposed to shock me? Offing Lester was my plan all along. For personal reasons, as much as anything. He'd of become a dictator eventually.

Samuel set his hand on the knife. Steiner pulled a gun from the couch cushion and held it loosely.

Ease up with that for a minute. I'm not done ruining your day. He motioned with the gun for Samuel to sit. He was staring at Steiner but navigating the furniture in his head. Around the chair, over the table.

I killed him for nothing.

Oh, no. Not for nothing. You didn't kill him for the reasons you thought, is all. You killed him for mine. That he was a piece of shit is a happy coincidence for us and the world.

Raj, and The Jungle?

My orders as much as his. But fighting him on the meth was legitimate. I want you to know that. I always had your back on that score.

Why'd you go to war if you were working with him? Why let me do all that?

Simple answer is we weren't. We were always a bad day

away from killing each other, like most people thought. You maybe didn't put together he was trying to squirrel his operation away behind the fence. The day you came to me with evidence against him, people on the inside told me about finding makings.

So we fought him to keep me from finding out.

Just in part. I was after a lot of birds with that stone. You, the tea, knocking Lester down a peg.

Samuel was stoic, eyes low. Did Maggie know?

Maggie got what she wanted. Whether she realized it or not. She got the dad she deserves.

He took his hand from the knife. Steiner rose and reached into his pocket, the gun still ready. He came out with a key and lofted it to Samuel.

Skeleton key. Pick a car. He reached into his pocket again and held up a wad of bills. He set them down on the table and stepped back, sidestepped, giving Samuel berth, though he didn't move. There something else you need cleared up? He turned his head slightly. Take the money. Find Johanna, and get out of here. You'll be dead by morning if you don't go.

Samuel swallowed, worked at his jaw. He went past the chair and picked up the money.

This whole place could'a been yours, someday. I would have passed you the crown. You could've come clean with everything. Made a speech. Dedicated a statue.

You told me we need to set an example. Be civil, or people will act like savages.

Yeah, well, that was a lie. There are a lot of secrets that go into making a world, Sam. You never saw any firsthand, young as you are. The way people lived, the way you knew things as a kid—that's living off the things people did in the dark. Your father's father's deeds, on back. Most of the people out there now get to be good because of the awful things I do. I carry that weight. Without assholes like me, the rest would be slitting a throat apiece around the campfire instead of holding down an honest job with a roof over their heads. He lifted, considered the gun in his hand. The public line is that, yeah, we have to set a good example. But the truth is that the secrets we keep, they keep us.

It's not a secret anymore.

It will be, again. It won't take long to retell the story. People choose to believe the better things. They don't like living in my world. Your world. And they shouldn't have to.

They're guilty, too. Whether they know it or not. They should know why they get what's coming.

This isn't Babylon, Sam. He set the gun down, clacking on the glass table, and took up the shine.

It's falling, all the same.

Not if I can hold it up. Steiner put an arm along the head of the couch, reclining.

Samuel backed a step, another, until he was clear of the furniture and beside the door. He opened it, breathed in, and left. Out of the room, the door closed and echoed, the hallway and stairs telescoped, swayed. He gripped the railing. Footsteps echoing. No one waited for him below. Coming out of The Capitol he felt dizzied again, the air so open and empty and it seemed captured that way, and then a mongrel drove past, a woman walked by on 14th. He took the skeleton key from his pocket and started running down the mall, all the way to 8th, to The Boneyard. The main garage was closed, and he kicked in the first door he came to. It swung into a long room with two wrecked mongrels in the middle. Oil and ethanol thick in the air.

A mechanic squirmed out from under the closest car and sat up. What're you doing in here?

Samuel walked past him, down a hall until it emptied out into the main garage. The old dump truck sat within. There was a button for the garage door, and he punched it and climbed into the cab, keys already in the ignition. The truck started, buckling from side to side, and he hit the gas.

It rolled out slowly and turned hard. Tires rubbed against the curb and then over it, dropping a parking sign before he went east at K. On 9th he opened it up and the truck rumbled, scraped, and went no faster. There was no one behind him in the mirrors and nothing in front all the way to Highway 2. A P&L truck drove past him at 16th, and the driver stared after him, but Samuel only waved. Coming into The Bottoms, he headed south again, and when the fence came into view, he put an arm over his face and drove through it. The fence stuck on the grill, snapping the posts, and it disappeared under the truck. He drove past the rows of abandoned houses and headed east, south. A generator warehouse, an O Street guard running at the sight of him. Prisoners came out of their homes squinting and shading their eyes. Nearing the graveyard he slowed, shifting in his seat to look around. There was no way to get behind the shacks. He got out and trotted to the nearest door and pulled it open, clean off its hinges. Inside a man stood still, head turned odd, blind.

Who the hell?

Samuel reached for him and pulled him outside. I need you to come with me. He shoved the man to the passenger side and helped him up, placing him in the seat.

Where are we going?

Sit tight. Samuel returned to the driver seat, hit the gas, and ran the shack down. At the far corner of the field, three prisoners were burying the bodies. Samuel slowed, parking the truck half-on a paved drive beside a backyard garage. He took the key and got out.

Quit digging.

The prisoners stopped. He ran over to them and grabbed the shovel from the nearest man and pitched it, landing headfirst into the dirt. The bodies were in one shallow grave, the hole a quarter filled. Samuel dropped into it and started tugging at an arm in the mass of limbs. He gagged.

What's he doing?

Samuel freed the body attached to the arm, a man unknown to him. He held the hand cold and loose and clambered out of the grave, hauling the body behind him. The prisoners dispersed, and he met eyes with one, a woman. Brief recognition there.

I could use some help.

What are you doing? The woman came nearer.

Loading these bodies in the truck. I'm taking them. And whoever wants to come with me.

Where?

We're getting out of here. Telling the people in this city what they've done to you.

He dragged the body to the truck and lifted it up, rolling it into the back, then ran and dropped into the hole again. The woman watched, and the others joined her at the rim, and Samuel stooped to heave the next body up. The gap in his shoulder puckered, seemed to shift down the length of the wound. He shook it off, lifted. The body was bloated, gasses belched inside. She had been shot in the head. A stench greener and more putrid arose, and he swallowed bile. The prisoners took the body and carried it over to the truck. Among the dead was Tover, handless, color still in his skin. Samuel's back ached, and one of the prisoners slid down to help, lifting the handless body up. They kept on to the last, and Samuel sagged against the wall. The prisoner with him pointed to his shoulder, blood streaking down his shirt. Samuel frowned, and climbed out of the hole. The bodies were piled in the truck, awkward, awful. He turned to address the prisoners.

The fence is down on the north end. You can walk right out. I'll carry you, if you like, but make up your mind now.

The three looked at each other, and the woman started for the passenger side. I'm going. You all can rot here.

Samuel nodded to the truck. There's still room if you don't mind company.

One of the men shook his head. The other was scanning around himself like it was a trap.

To the north. Go now before they get guards up there. He made for the truck and climbed in. It was cramped with the three of them inside, rank. The blind man next to him faced straight ahead. Samuel put the truck in gear, and the woman buckled her seatbelt. He backed around, leaving ruts in the grass, and put it in gear. They drove over the flattened shack. Two P&L trucks blocked the street to the west, two men standing beside them. Samuel floored the accelerator.

Get down. He reached his arm across the passengers' shoulders and pushed them. When the first gun lifted, he slunk low in his seat and the windshield starred. They smashed into one of the trucks and slowed, nearly stopped. He spun the wheel, shots pocking the door. The windshield fell in on them in one long slate. The passenger door opened and the woman screamed and kicked the head that appeared. The P&L man fell back, and she slung the windshield after him and they broke through the trucks and gained speed. Bullets rang off the bed. The woman swung the door closed.

Holy shit. The blind man patted himself, his chest, his face. What's going on? Who are you?

He's a heel. The woman leaned forward to see him.

They drove out of The Bottoms. The sun shone through gaps in the clouds. The truck rattled as they pulled onto 9th Street, riding the center line.

When we stop, you need to run. Find someone who doesn't work for the company, or just get out of town.

Don't you worry. I'm jumping on the first train with an open car.

Can you make sure he gets away? Will you be all right?

I guess we'll see. She paused, looked out the window toward The Singles. The man was bobbing slightly with the motion of the truck.

What am I gonna do?

Samuel checked the mirrors. We'll get you taken care of.

They rolled on The Haymarket, and Samuel laid hard on the horn. People walked in and out of the restaurants and stores and there were a few P&L vehicles parked on the streets. Everyone near jolted at the sound and watched them go by. Faces appeared in windows. He turned onto O, still pressing the horn, and threw the truck into park. He yanked the lever for the bed, saw the back lift. A woman screamed. Soft thud of the bodies, serial, as if they were meant to fall.

Samuel shifted to face to his passengers. Good luck.

The woman looked at him, then opened the door and reached for the blind man's hand, and they got out. Samuel dropped to the ground on the driver side, and a man came up to him, wife on his arm.

What the hell is this?

Samuel ignored him, then climbed onto the wheel of the truck. These are the people who died keeping your lights on. He raised an arm. People watched, from doorways, from windows. This is your city. This is what 8th Street Power & Light does to people. You cross them, and they imprison you in The Bottoms, blind you working in their power plant. They run it on poison, and it blinds people, kills them. He pointed across the road at the woman and blind man, walking together westward.

The husband stared at the bodies. The woman beside him spun away. Samuel brushed by, and before he made it to Q he heard hard engines, and one of them was the limousine, pulling to a stop in front of him. It shone sleek black. Aaron and Rogan got out, and Aaron smiled.

Hey, bud.

Samuel reeled. Did you make out okay?

Got promoted. All that cloak-and-dagger shit was a goof. I've been ushered into the higher ranks.

What's that mean?

It means I know everything. Let's celebrate. He opened

one of the rear doors. Johanna was already seated inside. She looked at the floor.

Samuel hesitated. Their bags at her feet. Aaron. Listen. Right behind me are the people they killed out in The Jungle. I hauled two prisoners out.

Come on. He seemed not to hear, smiled. I got all that shine to drink. Can't do it by myself. Aaron clapped him on the back and led him forward. He ducked finally, and Aaron motioned for him to sit beside Johanna before getting in himself. The driver door opened and shut. Aaron ducked to the front and pulled a bottle of shine and uncapped it. He knocked on the dividing glass, and Rogan started the engine, and they were off, heading east on O Street. Aaron poured three glasses and handed two forward. He rolled the glass between his hands.

So you two are fucking.

It felt like Aaron had reached across the car and gripped Samuel's breastbone in his hand. Johanna turned rigid beside him.

I'm taking that as a yes. Not that I needed one. He drank from his glass. He was stonefaced but calm, his hand relaxed. How long? Since you got back? Longer?

Samuel glanced at her. She had become very small and still, her arm closest to him tucked in her lap.

Drink up, guys. I poured it, you drink it. He raised his chin. That's poetic, yeah?

They said nothing. Samuel looked at the door, the handle. Aaron tapped on the glass, and the divider drew down and he leaned over, handing the bottle forward and whispering to Rogan. He took the bottle back, and the divider rose again and Aaron straightened.

Rogan said he wanted to beat your ass, Sam. I told him it weren't necessary. That and you'd probably split him from the asshole up, wouldn't you?

Samuel felt the blood pound in his eyes. The weight in

his chest became a hot pressure through the air, and he could feel himself sinking. He shook his head.

No? Really? Think you couldn't beat him, or is it because you think you deserve it?

I deserve it.

You're telling me if he came at you right now, you wouldn't let the blood out of him? I don't believe you. I think a whole trainload could come for you, and you'd leave 'em piled at the door.

He shook his head again, slightly.

You don't think so? He bent close. That's not who you are? You're not the guy who pulls his knife every chance he gets? How about the guy that fucks his friend's girl soon as his back is turned? You that guy? 'Cause from where I'm sitting, that's all you are. I got nothing else to go on. I got you bragging about Bradshaw, and I got bodies and a guy with no hands and a girl right here won't even look me in the eye. But that's not you. He lifted his hands. I don't know what got loose in you, Sam. I don't know if this is what you always were. He shrugged. It occurred to me you were trying to confess, that night. That night Johanna came to see you, and I was there? Explaining to me you do this because of your atoms. It was all inevitable. He reached across for Johanna's glass and pointed at Samuel's. Drink your goddamn drink.

Samuel drank. He breathed and drained it.

Thattaboy. Aaron poured it full and poured himself another. He fell quiet, the car jostling. He set his elbows on his knees and templed his hands. I loved her, Sam. She might not have loved me back, and that's fine. But I loved her. I was crazy about her. Would give her the world. Woulda married her someday if she'd have let me.

I'm right here. Johanna smacked the window beside her. Say it to me.

Aaron jerked across the car and Samuel was up with his hand on the knife. They froze.

See? What do you think, was I a second away? A little more shine, bit less irony? He pitched his hand back and forth in the air. If I hadn't called you a cold-blooded killer, do you think you'd have cut my head off just then? He returned to his seat, and lifted Johanna's glass.

Samuel sat back. Aaron poured her glass full, handed it over, and she drank. They were quiet for a long while, and Aaron deflated, stared at the floor.

I want to be pissed about those prisoners. I do. Tom and I talked it through half the night. But mostly I can't see past you and her in bed together. I think of us out drinking, and I think we're havin' a blast, and in your head you're just screwing her and thinking of how great it is to be Samuel Parrish. The guy who gets to judge everyone else. Who no one ever thinks is doing anything but being too good for this city. But you weren't. You aren't.

They had driven out past the city limits. The limo came to a stop beside an exit and sat there for nearly a minute. No one moved. Rogan put it in park and opened his door. Samuel glanced to Johanna, hand pushing his jacket out of the way of the knife. The door beside Aaron opened, flat light pouring in, and Aaron winced. Rogan helped to pull him out, and when he appeared in the limo again he had a pistol aimed at Johanna's chest.

You first, Sam. Get out. He was unwavering, his arm and hand and the gun motionless.

All right. Samuel raised his hands, put one on the doorhandle, and pushed it open. He looked at Johanna again and slid out onto the pavement. Aaron was leaning against the hood of the limo, gun tapping his thigh, not looking at Samuel. The other door opened and shut, and Rogan grouped them together and motioned them down the road several paces with his free hand.

It's on you now. He spoke with his head turned.

They saw Aaron, still looking at nothing, or the ditch,

the fallow land. The wind picked up, and their clothes blew about. A wave rolled across the field of dry grass beside them. Time passed, a minute or fifteen or more, and Rogan let the gun drop. He put it away and stood beside Aaron and spoke with his back to them. He opened the passenger door at the front of the limo and got Aaron inside, rounded the front and ducked out of sight. A door opened and shut, something dropped onto the road. Another door opened and shut. The brakelights went up and the limo started rolling, took the exit ramp and crossed over the highway, wound back and started west, passed them, on and away until it was out of sight and only a quiet lowing when the wind broke. Their bags sat in the road. Johanna had a gun in her hand.

Where'd you get that?

I took it off the boy I busted at The Still.

He smiled. Wish I'd known.

She said nothing, smiled briefly, and they were quiet.

They cut along the country road, headed north, until they reached a train crossing a few miles outside of the city. It was late afternoon, and the wind had swung around from the south and it was almost warm. They sat at the crossing, backs to the sign. The Capitol stood tall, a few buildings decking it, and the rest of the city was under the horizon. Thin stover surrounding them, trees in the opposite distance, a farmhouse. He changed into a clean shirt. The train was a long while coming, late into the afternoon. They snagged the handle on one of the cars, and when he looked back, the city already seemed far away. Johanna knocked on the door of the passenger car until a uniformed man came over, and Samuel pressed a handful of bills to the glass. The tickettaker slid the door wide and let them in, slipped the money into his pocket, and said nothing. The car was nearly empty, and most of the passengers pretended not to see.

20

The car shook, and he awoke. It was dark. The train slowed, coming into a city. From the moonlight he could see the bluish sides of warehouses, row on row of apartments and stores, churches. A road above them. Johanna shifted, and he watched her, eyes tightening from her own dream. The window turned dark, and after a minute the train pulled into the station. Some passengers stood to disembark and Samuel bent for their bags.

We've got a long way to go. Johanna raked her hands through her hair. We can stay.

He sat down. She kissed his cheek. The few passengers leaving stood at the door, and an attendant came through and held up his hands.

There's been a spill on the tracks ahead, everyone. I'm afraid there will be a long delay. Ice water is being offered in the dining car.

Johanna looked at him. Are we in a hurry?

He lifted the bags. Never again.

The station platform was crowded, lit with lanterns. The way inside the station was blocked off, and they were diverted up stairs alongside it. He thought he heard a river. When they walked out to the street, they saw the whole block lit by gas. Muted light, small periphery. A smell of oilsmoke all through the air. The buildings were newer than he'd seen before, and most of the windows dark. He didn't know what time it was. They walked straight away from the station, staring down the intersections and listening to the quiet. A few passengers wandered nearby, and they could hear another train arriving.

The moon had dropped below the skyline, and it cast darkness where the buildings stood. Several blocks down there was a building with the front window lit, a hotel, and with smiles still stuck on they went inside. The lights were electric. A clerk came from a back room and took his position behind a desk fixed between the front wall and a staircase, and he smiled tiredly. Samuel stepped forward, dropping the bags and reaching into his pocket for money. The clerk quoted him a price, and Samuel set a bill down. The clerk hesitated and Samuel raised an eyebrow.

Something wrong?

No, we just don't see old notes too often. You came in on the train?

Samuel rested an elbow on the counter. That's right.

The clerk nodded to himself and took a key from a shelf and handed it over. They climbed the stairs, and Johanna unlocked the door. It was a small room, and the bed took up most of the floor. A faded painting hung over the headboard, a beach and small houses.

Johanna sat and ran her hands over the bedspread. Did you ever watch movies when you were a kid?

Not really.

I did, all the time. She sprawled onto the bed. The room was lit with lamps, and in the dim light she looked knowing and proud and happy. He settled onto the bed and dragged himself even with her. We made it. She rolled over onto her stomach and stretched to kiss him.

Sometime in the early morning, he woke beside her under the covers, naked except for his dressing. A little daylight spilled from behind the curtains. The pistol was in the nightstand drawer and his knife beside the lamp. He dressed in clean clothes and his jacket and buckled the knife on and went downstairs. The pattern of the wallpaper spun, black flowers against the buttery white. The clerk at the front counter looked up and came forward when Samuel rested against it.

What can I do for you?

Samuel thumbed to the door. Any place around here to get breakfast?

We serve breakfast, sir. He pointed to his left, down the corridor to a dining room. And we can bring it to your room, if you'd like. The clerk found a menu below the counter. Here.

Samuel looked it over, placed an order, and paid. In the room he found Johanna dressing hurriedly by the bed.

God, I thought you left.

Why would you think that? I was ordering us breakfast.

She shook her head, shirt rumpled. She pulled at it. I don't know. I guess I'm waiting on something to go wrong.

He frowned, quiet. Within minutes someone knocked at the door. A man wheeled a cart in and took off two cups of coffee and plates of eggs and sausage and hashbrowns. They laid the plates between them on the bed and ate in silence. When they finished, Samuel set the plates on the desk, and Johanna opened the curtain and peered out to the street below.

She gasped. Sam. Look.

He went over to the window and followed her gaze. At the end of the street, they could see half of an enormous tower, the cloudcover that had moved in overnight cutting the top flat.

Do you want to go see it?

We could. He smiled. He put an arm around her waist and held her close to kiss her hair. Let's clean up and take a walk.

They bathed together by candlelight. With the bathroom door shut, it might have been the middle of the night, an evening lingering in their memory, winding down. Having eaten well and laughed across a dinner table and taken in a show, walked the streets of this new city with no concerns. Others watching and jealous. She lay back against his chest, and they stayed in the water until it cooled, and they refilled the tub and lay still until both of them were nearly asleep again. Samuel kissed her shoulder and kept his lips close. She hummed. She sang. He felt her breathe through the song, and his hands went to her sides, her breasts, feeling her stomach tense. Her voice cymbalous. She turned her head when she stopped, resting against his. He circled his arms around her waist.

Where do you want to go next?

Anywhere. Nowhere. How long could we stay?

A little while. A couple weeks if we don't buy train tickets.

How did you get the money, anyway?

A going-away present from Al.

Mm. She hummed. Let's not say their names. Her hands traveled up his thighs. We'll spend another day here. Then see where the train takes us.

The water cooled, and they finished, shivering. Johanna climbed out of the bathtub and wrapped herself in a towel. Samuel stepped out of the tub, prodding at his shoulder, splaying it with his fingers. I'm gonna clean this out real quick.

Okay. I'll ask someone where we should go?

No.

What?

Stay. He smiled, and she kissed him again and left the bathroom. The light shone from outside and the room fell dark again. He slid a candle closer and washed out the wound before he poured shine over it. He doubled a pad of gauze and dried it and rolled the last around his shoulder. Johanna left the room and for a moment he felt faint. Stars blew in his eyes, and he leaned over the sink until they faded. He dressed again with the knife and he took the pistol from the night-stand and tucked it into the back of his jeans. Johanna was talking to someone down the hall, and he opened the door to meet them. She wore a light red dress, the petals of a flower bursting like a firework on her hip and she'd put up her hair, still wet, revealing her neck and pressed to her head was a gun and holding the gun was Harrawood.

I'm sorry. Johanna gripped at his arm, around her throat. He was just there when I came downstairs.

It's all right. Samuel paced away from the door, side-stepped, coming toward them.

I'm so sorry. I should have had my gun.

It's okay.

Throw that knife out, Parrish. Harrawood nodded to the carpet between them. Take it out slow.

Don't, Sam.

It's okay. It's okay. He had his left hand up like he would calm them all. He didn't remember raising it.

The knife.

Samuel crouched slightly. Johanna yanked on Harra-wood's arm, and Samuel saw the scratches there and the growing welt under his eye. Samuel pulled the side of his jacket away with his left hand. He took the knife from his belt slowly, limp in his fingers. They were less than twenty feet apart.

Now drop it.

His hands were numb. His heart beat so fast. He held his arm out and let the knife go and Harrawood shot her and threw her aside. Samuel drew the gun before she hit the floor, and he fired tracking up from Harrawood's leg to his chest and the side of his skull opened. The gunsmoke rolled thick. He rushed to her. Her eyes were wide, and she shook a little. Blood ran down her temple and from her ear. He pulled her up and sank against the wall with her and he held her to him holding her close holding her and pressing their cheeks to-gether. The clerk climbed the stairs, just his head visible, and he asked if everything was all right.

He spent days ascetic, a daruma. Fever dreams of flowers, Johanna's dress and the one she wore at her temple. The wallpaper. Dreams of days in which they saw grass, and summer, color beyond the palette of design. Cities built in green and gold, in brown earth. Dreams of control, wakeful, in which he would not force himself to turn and see her. Hands touching hands on the trunk of a tree. Could he jump higher as a child? When the man came to take him, he was very cold in his limbs, and the man helped him to the street, and Samuel laughed at his own height, navel-high, his eyes swallowed and peeking out through a hole in his shirt. His mind there, in his belly, his head left to fend for itself.

They washed him and redressed his wound, washed his clothes. Fed him broth. Coming up into this fugue each morning after the bliss of a sleepful death. He was combative, found they'd tied him to a cot. They had painted the room with the black damask in a forced cure, or they had tattooed it to his eyelids.

His mind returned some time later, in its proper place behind his eyes. The man who'd brought him from the basement led him to a locker room, shower stalls. In the foggy mirrors, he found a self. Eyes kohled. His clothes were set on a bench and a safety razor was laid by. He shaved, considered the artery pulsing at his windpipe. Backing from the mirror, he saw the distance to Johanna, gunsmoke in steam. The caretaker was waiting outside the bathroom and he guided Samuel to the building entrance, and he saw his first daylight. The gun and knife returned to him. Outside the sky was a thin gray and it was warm and the oilsmoke hung in a layer just over their heads. Manure in piles throughout the streets, and the city so clean otherwise, the glass and steel. The tower, a bridge.

It's been raining for a while now. This is the first break we've had in days. He looked at Samuel, skin around his eyes aged but the eyes themselves untouched. He waited for

Samuel to speak. They kept walking. There are a lot of people like you. Maybe most people are now. I envy the children, sometimes. This is all they know.

They stopped at a restaurant, and the caretaker held the door for him. He waited a moment, and went in. A man pointed them to a table near the front, and they took their seats. The caretaker unfolded his napkin, flapped it, settled it on his lap. Their waiter brought menus, and Samuel let his lie.

I understand you're in pain. We should speak about it. I lost my partner years ago. I know how hard that can be.

To what?

Cancer. He had a very treatable form of cancer, but the technology was no longer there to help him. The caretaker drank. I'm told it was less painful than had he gone through chemotherapy. That's a treatment of tumors by poison.

I know what it is. I'm sorry.

And I'm sorry for your loss. He breathed in. Is there anything I can do for you?

Put me on a train. Samuel looked to the door. The waiter returned, and the caretaker ordered for them both. Samuel handed up his menu, and the waiter left.

I struggle every day. With living. With faith. All of it. From getting out of bed in the morning to taking a dump to working with people like you. Sometimes the enormity of it, that sheer, that huge landscape of living, it overwhelms me. But if I wait long enough, some little thing comes along and brightens my day, or I'm simply distracted. It takes work, being that sad. You have to focus on it. A flea or two keeps the dog from thinking about being a dog.

Samuel turned his head, a smile breaking. He closed his eyes.

Sam. The caretaker leaned in close. I don't want to hurry your pain. But the things you said the other day—

What things?

The caretaker winced. It's no surprise you forgot. You

talked about where you're from, what happened to you. There's nothing calling you back.

Samuel pushed back his chair. Thanks for the meal. He got up from the table and headed for the door. The caretaker called after him, followed out into the street.

Sam, wait. Wait. You're here for a reason.

He turned to see, slowed. What reason is that? Jesus?

The caretaker caught up with him, paced the sidewalk alongside him. Maybe. Don't you think you should find out? He pulled a small green booklet from a pocket, a Bible. Here. You need God, Sam. That's not a sign of weakness.

Samuel took the book as if it might be something else, held it closer to his face. The whole world needs God. But he's not there. He handed it back. And if he is, the world is just how he likes it. He pushed away from the man, hand out to the wall to brace himself through the veil coming over his eyes. The caretaker followed him a few paces and stopped. Samuel's vision cleared.

21

The lights did not come on the evening he was within sight of the city. No engines over the sound of the rain. He entered by 27th Street, and for a long time there was nothing, only the streets empty as they'd been. The rain eased while he rested under a store awning sometime before dawn. Howls from the southwest. By the time he reached The Haymarket, the sun was coming up and the sky clearing. With the sun came a breeze and on it the smell. The light fell down the streets through the buildings a heavy gold, and it shone on the bodies hung from the lampposts all along 9th. They were decapitated, larval, wrapped in sheets, and bound hand-to-foot. The sheets had been ripped and the thighs of some were cords of open muscle. Dripping with rainwater. In the park he saw whole trees leafed black with vultures. Where O Street lifted to the west, the human heads hung like gourds from the guardrails, and the ropes creaked and swayed.

He went east on K, toward The Capitol. A body lay folded around a lightpole, and bullet casings had rolled to the gutter in a brass river. Down the street sat a truck with its windshield shot white. He checked his gun and went to the west entrance of The Capitol. The statue of Lincoln was knocked down, and a body hung over the stone backing. Behind it was Reese, his stomach on his lap. Samuel opened the west doors with his back and rolled along one side. The light from the doorway fell on a warren of dead. Bodies slumped and piled at corners, men shot kneeling, their foreheads against walls and wheels of blood spread from their skulls. The front desk was blown to pieces. Some of the dead were Mexican, and with them he found grenades and automatic rifles. He let the gun rest at his side. The room was thick with the smell of blood and gunsmoke. A Light worker on the steps with an armless trunk. Down the hall he saw bodies in front of doorways and it was the same on the second floor. All the doors were kicked in with far walls and windows shot through. No one in Steiner's room. He crossed to the stairwell and descended. The basements empty, doors open. Bootprints in blood thickening down the corridor. The last door had rends in the metal and there were two bodies inside. Steiner and a bodyguard, blood fresher than pooled around the others. He stayed, rooted, then went back to the lobby. Aaron stood on the staircase, face twisted into a grin and eyes narrow. He walked through the bodies and out the doors. Samuel followed behind him, watched him go by Reese and the fallen statue without a duck or nod, until Aaron descended the stairs to the street and turned around. The grin had faded, but his eyes were the same. He held a pistol.

I thought about you making it. I sort of figured you would. He spread his arms. How'd it happen?

Samuel closed his eyes. We were standing like this. He had a gun to her head.

Just like this?

A little closer.

Aaron took a few steps forward, and Samuel nodded. Aaron mused. His face gripped and then it relaxed. He scratched his cheek. Well? Try me. It's fitting, isn't it? Let's see you work.

Samuel was still. Gun at his side. Calm, and when Aaron's arm jerked, he let his gun fall and leapt forward and Aaron fired, too high, and Samuel held the knife in his hand and the distance was crossed and Aaron fired again and Samuel laid his finger over the back of the knife and sank it into Aaron's belly to his fingertip. He saw his eyes, wide white and benign. Samuel drew the knife out and stepped back, taking Aaron's gun and casting it into the bushes beside them. Aaron let out a gasp. He pressed his hands against the wound and saw the blood spreading through his shirt and over his fingers. He tested his footing. He looked down at himself.

It doesn't hurt.

He panned his head about, away and back, at the bushes and at the knife. He listed but caught himself before Samuel could reach him. He started walking west, and Samuel followed. They turned up 13th, and Samuel watched him double over with the first wave of pain. He righted, gripped a parking sign, and went on. They passed a mongrel with a tight bracket of bulletholes below the doorhandle, the driver slumped to the console. Blood on the ground, Aaron's. They passed O, and Aaron jerked his head like a deer, startled, and continued until they came to Norton's. The bar lay in night, and he tumbled through the tables and chairs. Samuel made his way behind the bar for matches. He found a lamp and lit it and he lit another and carried it over to the booth where Aaron lay reclined. He set it on the table and slipped behind the bar for a bottle of moonshine and a tumbler. The flames reflected off the mirror, the hanging glasses. Samuel cast pillars of shadow as he crossed them. When he came back to the table, Aaron fumbled upright, gripping his belly as though Samuel had just entered.

What did you do to me?

Stabbed you. He opened the bottle and poured himself a shot. Aaron snatched at the moonshine and drank. Samuel watched him, and when Aaron tightened, he took the bottle and set it back down, dark blood printing on the glass. That burning you feel is the shine leaking out of you. I'd go easy. Drier you are the better.

Aaron closed his eyes. They were quiet a while and then he winced, groaned. Samuel looked over to the bar and saw two glasses, chairs pushed away. He turned to Aaron.

You want to wait it out?

What?

I said, 'Do you want to wait it out.'

You're not gonna kill me?

You're killed. It's just gonna take a while. Samuel drained half the glass and wiped his mouth with the back of his hand.

I don't want to die. Aaron lifted a hand and looked at it, fresh blood and dry. Can I have a little more?

It'll hurt. Samuel pushed the bottle across the table. Aaron took it up and drank and he leaned back clutching the bottle to him. Samuel watched him close his eyes, take in a deep breath to speak, and he held it and let it go. Then he took in another.

I wanted to forgive you. He blinked slowly. Because how else would I be the better man? He breathed in again and winced.

You already were.

Everything fell apart so fast. I spiraled, after that kid. He lifted the bottle and took a quick drink. I was so angry.

Stop it.

He looked at Samuel, hurt anew.

We knew what we took from each other. Don't be pitiful.

Aaron's eyes cast down. At his hands, the bottle.

This is how things happened. You played your part, and I played mine.

You stabbed me.

You had it coming.

And you don't?

I do. It's on its way.

He curled, hissing, and relaxed. For a bit there I thought I was turning into you. We'd end up fighting together, back to back, you know? Fend off the Mexicans. The drama before we took over, before we started on that dream I had of us. And that would be the work. The thing we did to earn it. I— He trailed off. After you said you killed Bradshaw, then everything with Johanna. You weren't who I wanted to be.

He rolled his head away. But I took a grenade from one of the Mexicans. Waited two days in that hall. Two days for Steiner to come out. And I did it.

Why?

His hand in it all. Letting me give the order. All of it.

Maybe you did turn into me. Samuel pushed his glass across the table. That's why I came back.

Aaron wouldn't look at him, but lifted the bottle and poured from it, trembling.

Samuel took the glass and drank. He told me he planned everything. From the infighting with the Light boys to me killing Bradshaw. Set himself up to take power and then let me take the fall.

Well. You're welcome.

Samuel raised his glass. He felt the night outside weighing in through the windows, felt the death in the city and the stillness.

Would you talk, please?

Samuel took a drink. What do you want me to say?

I don't know. He rocked his head aside. You just gonna watch me die?

It seems wrong to leave.

Aaron smiled softly, and his eyes went up. Did I ever know you at all?

As well as anybody.

You still believe in your physics after everything that's happened?

I don't think it matters. It doesn't matter what makes us do the things we do. Whether it's God or atoms, it's all just a comfort. People want some way to explain the things they see, the things they do.

We want off the hook.

Maybe, yeah.

I would have forgiven you.

I think I knew that. The idea of asking for it was too much.

The thing is, Sam. He looked at the bottle in his hands. You wouldn't have had to ask.

Samuel pinched his mouth tight. He drank.

What are you— He seized up. What are you gonna do after?

I don't know.

He set the bottle on the table. How long will it take?

Samuel stared at a figure, a face in the grain of the table. A day, maybe two.

You couldn't have made it any quicker?

He smiled slightly. Aaron let out a breath like a laugh, and they quieted.

If it gets to be too much just say so.

Aaron shook his head. The door whined, a blow of fresh air. No one came around the corner, and Samuel glanced at Aaron before walking to the entrance.

We're closed. He went to the door and opened it into the night. A man shuffled away, jaked. Samuel shut the door and sat. Aaron had shifted, propped himself on an elbow and looked at his stomach.

I was hurt, when you left. No goodbye or anything. No note. I know you had to take off quick and all, but it stung. Made me feel like all that time didn't matter to you.

I'm sorry. I didn't think—

I know. You're not that kind of guy. I am. And that's okay. He sighed, cut the breath off with a twinge. It didn't matter when you got back. It was all erased. We could start at that dream I had. He laughed, nearly a cough. Samuel pushed the bottle toward him, and he ignored it. I had this other day-dream, you know. Baseball. We got that stadium just north of The Haymarket, all overgrown right now, but. If we got a league together, wouldn't that be somethin'? Just us playin', at first. Me pitching. But eventually, come to find out, there's better players among the civvies, and people come from all around to play, and it's us in the stands. Popcorn, hot dogs.

Waving pennants.

There was no way.

I don't think you ever quite got it. What a city means. Living on a farm, being like you are, I think it suits a loner. Maybe you were starting to get it. The community—even someone you don't like, they're still with you. You got a bond. You all came together to live in one spot. You're all contributing. He breathed deep, shut his eyes. There used to be a dozen kids on my block. We used to play in the street. Play baseball. Wasn't any cars to avoid. Had about a bat between us, all taped up and wonky. You get a game together and, even back then, people knew. They knew it was special, knew there weren't gonna be many more, not where we were. It was nice to have that to look forward to. Dad out there in the bleachers, watching me. Everything okay for a couple hours.

The night went on, and they were mostly silent. They drank the remainder of the moonshine. Aaron began to slump down into the seat, and Samuel watched him breathe. He stood to stretch. Aaron woke, jolted and groaned and curled onto his side.

I'm here. Samuel put his hand on the table.

He eyed him from under the wood, chin tucked to his chest. Am I supposed to have a fever? I'm cold.

Probably. Samuel slipped off his jacket and draped it over him. He took a chair from a nearby table and carried it across the floor to the booth and sat in it, propping his legs on the bench. Aaron closed his eyes tight, and Samuel saw him tense and grip at his jeans. Blood collected in the grooves of the seat. Every so often a drip. The lamps dimmed. Sometime in the early morning, Samuel woke to howls, and clawing out of sleep he thought it was Aaron, but they came from far off. He stood slowly, listening for Aaron's breath, and stepped outside. It was cool and a fog ran through the streets and coyotes barked and yipped to the west. He went back in. It was very dark then, and he found his way to the booth following

Aaron's breathing. He neared, painting Aaron there, curled fetal, his breath shallow and rapid and Samuel smelled the sickness on him.

Aaron.

He didn't move.

Samuel touched his leg. Aaron. He drew the knife.

Don't. Just let me live it. Aaron shifted, rolled over. That's what you'd do, isn't it?

He slid the knife back. Yeah.

Kind of a copout to go early.

There is no early. You go when you want to.

How about fifty years from now.

Samuel laughed. He turned away. Maybe if you'd done your job and got us a damn doctor.

Just leave, Sam.

I don't want you to be alone.

Aaron said nothing for a while. I still feel like you should die. It seems right. Maybe that's bitter of me.

No.

You get to live.

You get to sleep. Samuel lifted his glass, not a drop. He tilted the bottle. He left the table, slowed at the bar, and waited. Aaron made no sound, and Samuel walked to the door. He lingered again in the threshold before going out.

The sun was just rising over the tops of the buildings and the fog began to warm. He started west. Before he reached 9th, a figure came out of the haze, and Samuel crouched and saw it was Detch, gun in hand. They both eased.

Christ, Sam, you scared me. Detch rotated the gun, as if it were strange to hold. Would'a thought I'd seen a ghost anyway, with all the shit we've been through. He tucked the pistol into his jeans. When did you get back?

Yesterday.

Detch thumbed over his shoulder. I was out looking for stragglers. I guess you count. Come on, we'll head back. Detch turned, staring through the fog. I heard you died.

I imagine they said all kinds of things about me.

The fog lifted above the O Street overpass. Detch's head very still, looking forward. The ropes above them creaking in the breeze. Descending to 8th, they could see several hundred yards ahead. A train sat on the tracks, two blinds exploded, and farther down, the engine smoking thinly, blackened. Pieces of tin, screws, sheets of metal were strewn across the ground, growing larger as they went. The roof of The Still had been blown off, the doors gone from their hinges. The kettles inside looked like broken metal eggs. They continued, passed the open Boneyard gates and the doors all up and empty. Coming on The Singles, people sat on the porches of the shotgun shacks, civilians and old tenants. A man standing in the road looking at the city, his eyes vacant. Heather sat on the curb, eying Samuel as they neared. Toward the end of the block he thought he saw Raj, and the figure lifted a hand. Detch led him into a yard down the street, and they went up the tiny porch and through the door. The windows were open and the shades back, and when Detch called out, Maggie and Rogan appeared holding cups of coffee. Rogan's head was wrapped in a bloodstained cloth.

Sam? Maggie set her cup by and hugged him.

His arms pinned at his side and his body awash in a familiar panic. Yeah.

I thought you were dead.

He breathed in, pulling free of her embrace. No. I got away.

Rogan met his eye. And Johanna?

Vince Harrawood found us.

He grimaced and stared into his coffee.

Detch took a seat on the edge of a couch and jutted his chin at Samuel. So that part's true?

Samuel nodded. It was.

Listen. Maggie reached for his arm. We're gonna try to

regroup. Between us we know how to run everything in the city, and the motorcycle club will be here any day. We'll get back on our feet. Start over. Start fresh.

Samuel smiled and looked away. There is no starting over.

She dropped her hand. I'd want you to lead us.

He began to shake, smirking, eyes to the ceiling.

We'll do it how you wanted. Rogan set his cup down. Run the generators clean. Give a proper burial to everyone in The Bottoms and free the rest, help rehab them. Cut the tea, cut the jake. We'll make the most of this. We've got to.

Samuel tried to calm himself. He leveled off and looked at Rogan and Maggie, spun on his heel and went out the door.

Detch caught up to him, stopping on the porch. Sam? Are you gonna help us?

He turned at the curb. I killed Aaron.

What?

Maggie and Rogan appeared behind Detch in the doorway. Detch reached for his gun, and Rogan took it, held it off.

You of all people. How could you?

He stared at them. She's dead.

She was his girl!

Hypocrisy is a luxury. A minor sin.

Then stay. Maggie passed them both, put her hand on the porch railing. We're all hypocrites. We all have regrets.

Samuel glanced at the city and back. What'd they do with the prisoners, the bodies? Did the people do anything? Did anyone say anything?

Maggie quieted. They cleaned them up, hosed down the street. Steiner apologized. He said you'd gone crazy.

Samuel smiled, face tight. He started walking.

Where are you going?

He kept on. The fog had lifted higher and dissipated, threads through the tops of the buildings. Coming up on 9th Street, he felt the wind change and could smell the metal spilled on the street. The bodies swayed on their lamp-posts. Crows and vultures like clockwork figures lifted their heads and bobbed meat down their throats. Doors all down the street were open wide, the seamstress' shop windows smashed. He stood in the intersection for a moment and went into the nearest apartment building. Up the stairs. Each door kicked in along the hall, wood cracked. He pushed into one and searched the kitchen, rifling through cabinets, drawers, on to the next apartment and the next, rooms mostly blood-less, little struggle. In the third apartment, he found a bottle of 8th Street High Proof, and he tucked the bottle under his arm. Samuel left the building, blue showing above him. He headed for Norton's.

ACKNOWLEDGEMENTS

The author would like to thank, first and foremost, Leah Angstman, who has almost single-handedly turned me into a legitimate author, and done so much for me besides. I wouldn't have gotten anywhere without Rob and Jeff, of course. For the regular cast: Mom and Dad, Terry, CJ, and the rest of my family, thank you. Thanks to Todd Wood for giving me a job whenever I blow into town. Thanks, Leonid, for being the unkind eye. Thanks to everyone at Donkey Coffee for tolerating my eight-hour stays; I should have been paying rent. Thanks to Sabrina for not making me, and Jake, too. Thank you to Old Sugar Distillery for sponsoring *Above All Men's* book tour, and thanks to all the folks out there who let me read at their store, or with them, or put me up for a night. Thank you again to Pine Crest Bed and Breakfast; I'm probably never more at ease than at your table, scratching Boson's head.

Eric Shonkwiler is the author of *Above All Men*, a novel, and *Moon Up, Past Full*, a collection of novellas and stories. His writing has appeared in *Los Angeles Review of Books, The Lit Pub*, and *The Millions*. Born and raised in Ohio, he received his MFA from University of California-Riverside, and has lived and worked in every contiguous U.S. time zone.

39934254R00146

Made in the USA
Middletown, DE
29 January 2017